S.P.A.C.E

S.P.A.C.E

Spacial Populations and Cosmic Enigmas

JAMES MOCLAIR

authorHOUSE®

AuthorHouse™ UK Ltd.
1663 Liberty Drive
Bloomington, IN 47403 USA
www.authorhouse.co.uk
Phone: 0800.197.4150

Published by AuthorHouse   05/22/2013

ISBN: 978-1-4817-9363-6 (sc)
ISBN: 978-1-4817-9364-3 (hc)
ISBN: 978-1-4817-9365-0 (e)

CONTENTS

CHAPTER 1

Trilo-raptors

The immensity of space is hard to comprehend, it is speculated that space has no limits. Therefore one could never travel to the end of space because no matter how long you travelled, you could not reach an end that does not exist.

A singular universe was once all that could be envisaged; now multi universes with numerous complex theories are discussed and debated amongst the universal scholars. One thing that is a constant in all known and unknown universes is life and death walk hand in hand. Stars are born and stars die; as they die they consume the planets, moons, all other solid object and gases that occupied that system. If life had formed on any of the planets or moons that to would be extinguished. This is the way.

This cycle of life and death has been embraced by the life forms that for a brief period in universal time have flourished on certain planets and moons that orbited the once radiant stars. As one star dies, more are created and the life cycle starts over again.

Over the millennia of evolution on each planet or moon, living organisms and various complex life forms have evolved, changed and adapted to survive. Some have evolved and gained immense intelligence. This evolved intellect has expanded so greatly that it has allowed these life forms explore not just their home planet but also the vastness of space itself.

The motive for exploration of space varies immensely; some species wish to seek out new life forms, while other wish to gain knowledge of the intricacies of the universe, others do this out of desperation as they themselves have depleted all the natural resources in their local solar system. But for the triloraptor race it is just for the desire to kill, feed and kill again! This was the triloraptor way, the universe is a feeding and killing ground, one that is so vast they can never run out of prey and one that was always being replenished. This is the way.

The triloraptors are an extremely old race from a planet and system long consumed by the star that once gave them life. That star and planet are now long forgotten, to the triloraptors thoughts of the past are irrelevant, after all it was just a planet, they had seen so many and most just consisted of rock, dust particles, ice and poisonous gas clouds. The ones they looked forward to finding were the ones with an abundance of life. The one they were just about to descend on was perfect.

Day one.

The sun was just rising over Brobryne marsh lands, it had done this millions of times but today was the first day of the third quarter and that meant the cold harsh winter was on its way. Over the summer months the immense marsh lands had provided a rich source of food for all the birds' species that had gathered there but, today marked the end of this. Each species, some totalling thousands, would over the course of the day vacate this haven and start it's migration south to the warmer and milder regions. These migrations have been going on for thousands and thousands of years. This was the way.

From space, this migration was being observed and the final preparations were taking place, air temperature, wind speed and weather fronts were being monitored carefully.

Five thousand of miles to the east of the marsh lands lay the vast flat grassy plains where hundreds of thousands of beasts grazed. They had travelled hundreds of miles, faced all kind of perils and hardships but now they could feast on the lush plains. The herds felt at peace and for a time they could settle down, graze and the dominant males would mate. This was the way.

The grazing beasts knew nothing of space, they knew when sunrise and sunset was, they knew about the changing of the season's and generally a full belly and plenty of drinking water was what all they desired. But the triloraptors knew all about them and within a very short period of time both would meet but, only one would survive!

Water covers over seventy percent of the planet's surface. West of the grass lands is the Ardian Ocean, this is one of five oceans and six seas on this planet. Numerous rivers and fresh water lakes that scar the planet's surface discharge surplus water into the oceans and seas.

Each Ocean, sea, lake and river has a huge diversity of aquatic life and each one like all large water masses, had its own uniqueness. The Marlian Sea has an extremely high salt and mineral content, while the Ardian Ocean is a tropical ocean with warm waters. The five lakes of mardina are over 1.8532 kilometres (1 nautical mile) deep; only certain species inhabit this abyss as the tremendous water pressures would crush most aquatic life forms.

The aquatic life forms of the oceans, seas, lakes and rivers on this planet have numerous aquatic predators. Some sea creatures are over twenty metres in length and weigh several tonnes; with jaws five metres wide and razor sharp teeth, these ferocious aquatics can devour any other aquatic in seconds. At the other end of the scale is the ferocious three centimetre long pian fish that inhabits the shallow waters of many of the river estuaries. They hunt in shoals of thousands and with their razor sharp teeth they can strip a one metre fish to its bones in under a minute! None of this is of any consequence to the triloraptors, where life exits, triloraptors bring death. That is the way.

Close to the planets equator is a land mass that was once, thousands of years ago a hive of volcanic activity. The massive volcano's, some are over 44 thousand metres high, are now dormant. The valleys below are lush in vegetation and have forests of large hardwood trees, while the slopes of each volcano are covered all types of evergreen shrubs and flora. From the basins of the volcano's, down into the lowlands and forest areas there is an abundance of insect and small animal life forms. To catalogue them all would take years.

To an outsider this is a small piece of heaven. To the triloraptors, even this place of scenic beauty is just another killing field and what they had in store for this area was for them, just the icing on a very large cake!

Back on the Brobryne marsh lands the first few birds took to the air ready to start their migration, almost immediately, as if by instinct other's followed, within minutes the skies were full of the migrating flocks. It was at this exact point of time that the triloraptors put their first attack into place.

From space the signal was given and at tremendous speed the first trilo-attack craft entered the planet's atmosphere. As it broke through the planets stratosphere, it immediately slowed down to just less than 1,200 kilometres per hour. In dry air at 20 °C (68 °F), the speed of sound is 343 meters per second (1,125 ft/s). This equates to 1,236 kilometres per hour (768 mph), or about one kilometre in three seconds and about one mile in five seconds. It had done this so it would not break the sound barrier and spook the migrating flocks.

The trilo-attack craft, one of many poised to attack, would, by even the hardiest of space travellers be considered to be enormous. Its overall length equals 1.6093 kilometres, it width an impressive 2682 metres. What is even more impressive is the crafts hexagon exterior, 1.6093 kilometres of featureless gleaming obsidian-black metallic compound. With its sharp pointed nose cone, it resembles a giant black crystal.

At 1.6093 kilometres (one mile) above the planet's surface and 6.4372 kilometres (four miles) south of the Brobryne marsh lands the craft came to a halt. The metallic compound on two sides of the craft surface dissolved into liquid state and then five hundred oblong hatches appeared on both sides of attacks crafts body. From each hatch, in perfect co-ordination, a triloraptor took to the air.

Hundreds of years ago, the female triloraptors were much taller that the males. Universally this is true of most of the raptor species. This however, was not acceptable to the vanity of the triloraptor males! Once triloraptor genetic engineering had been mastered, the DNA structure of all males was modified and enhanced. They now stood at well over two metres tall with a wingspan of over four metres. The males and females were now equal in height. With one thousand of them in the air it was both a beautiful and terrifying sight.

In perfect flight formation and keeping a high altitude, the triloraptors headed north to intercept the oncoming migrating flocks.

As a hunting species, triloraptors are able to see far more detail than most other living creatures. The central region of the triloraptors retina is called the fovea. It is adapted to seeing detail. Most species have one fovea, the triloraptors have three fovea. One of these is dedicated to forward vision the other is dedicated to lateral vision (i.e. sideways) the third is dedicated to upward vision. The three fovea form a small pit in the triloraptors retina and act like a telephoto lens. At just over 1.6093 kilometres (one mile) away the triloraptors could with their extraordinary good eye sight not just see the oncoming flocks but every single bird!

From the triloraptors altitude the attack plan was, with the aid of speed to drop from a great height (stooping) and then strike the prey with their feet. This would either kill the prey outright or the triloraptor would pursue the injured bird to the ground where it would dispatch its prey by gripping it with its talons and exerting so much pressure that its prey would be crushed to death. As triloraptors are carnivores, they would then devour the prey entirely, regurgitating (casting) the indigestible matter in pellet form, once or twice a day.

The lead birds of the migrating flocks were the first to see the oncoming, one thousand strong airborne triloraptors. They instinctively panicked and broke away from the flock, others impulsively followed but, it was in vain. One thousand died in the first few moments, others were also quickly killed. What the flock would never appreciate is the triloraptors they had encountered were only juveniles! This was just an exercise to them in the development of honing their killing skills!

Still totalling several thousands, the largest portion of fleeing birds changed direction and headed back to the Brobryne marsh lands. This is exactly what the triloraptors had planned. Triloraptors have superb weapon technology and the first to be deployed was by the triloraptors standards an antique, but this antique worked superbly. It was an invisible four sided, oblong walled laser grid. Two walls at the outset spanned 16.0930 kilometres (ten miles) long and 4.8279 kilometres (three miles) high. The sides of the wall two were 1.6093 kilometres (one mile) long and 4.8279 kilometres (three miles) high. The grid was a maze of lasers that could be programmed to expand the size of gaps in the maze or to do the opposite. The setting for today's operation was 1 cm; nothing flying in the air today would get through this.

As the flocks flew over closer to the marsh land the grid was activated. The bird flew head long into the invisible barrier. Within seconds the invisible barrier became visible with minute dissected body parts and blood, the air filled with the aroma of cooked meat!

Out of panic the flocks changed direction and flew west and for a few short minutes, they thought they had escaped, until they ran head long into the 1.6093 kilometres (mile long) south facing invisible wall! Again the invisible barrier light up with the colour of blood and body parts, thousands more died. The survivors now turned north and out of fear and desperation flew even faster. What they didn't know was the grid size had now been reduced; it was only 1.6093 kilometres (one mile) square! Within moments the fleeing flocks again hit the invisible wall of death, more died but, then the laser wall was deactivated. To the flocks of birds nothing had changed, they could not comprehend what had been happening; they just flew in all directions in a frenzied state. To the thousand strong airborne juvenile triloraptors, it was time to attack again!

By the time the sun was ready to set on the Brobryne marsh lands, all of the thousands of birds that had started their migration that morning were now dead. The marsh lands for hundreds of years to come would remain barren of its feathered wildlife. That was the triloraptors way.

On the same day, five thousand miles west of the Brobryne marsh lands, dawn broke on the grassy plains. Pesticide control was the first line of attack for the triloraptors. The plains at time of the year were not just attractive to all the kinds of grazing beasts; it also attracted millions and millions of flies. At times the air was so heavy with flies that the beasts we're not be able to breathe without inhaling them into their mouths and nostrils. The triloraptors would also encounter the same problem.

Sunrise was the ideal time to deal with this small problem, with the sunrise came a heavy mist and this would intensify what was about to happen. The second trilo-craft had positioned itself at an altitude of 8465 metres (half a mile) above the grassy plains; it then fired a ten second blast of ionizing radiation that had been modified to electrically charge all the air molecules. The blast covered a radius of 160.9300 kilometres (100 miles); within seconds the air within this radius crackled with the electrical charge, it had just enough power to exterminate every airborne fly and insect! The moisture from the mist also helped to ground the charge killing any flies, insects or lava that were close to ground. The grazing beasts also felt the electrical shock, it spooked the herds and caused an inconsequential stampede but, the injuries to them were minor compared with what was planned!

As soon as the trilo-craft had delivered its lethal blast of ionizing radiation, the triloraptors craft flew to the edge of one of the largest grazing herds, turned parallel so its nose cone was pointing skywards and then started too descended silently and slowly. At one hundred metres, it came to a halt and the lower sides of its body seem to liquefy and from its body, four giant obsidian-black metallic stabilises extended from is hexagon body. Once they were fully extended the trilo-craft continued its decent and then it landed gently.

After being startled and slightly singed from the blast of electrified ionizing radiation, the grazing herds had settled back to what consumed most of their lives, feeding. They seemed oblivious to the craft that had just landed and stood 1.6093 kilometres high and 2682 metres wide. They were equally oblivious when two sides of the craft appeared to dissolve and on both sides five hundred oblong hatches appeared. From each hatch a four metre wide platform emerged and standing on it was an adult triloraptor.

In front of each platform hovered a one metre obsidian-black metallic hexagon. The edges were not visible as it spun at 5000rpm and at its centre it measured one centimetre thick. From its centre, it tapered off until its edges formed a blade that was sharper than any surgical scalpel. This weapon is known as trilo-tron, t.r.o.n standing for; transitional robotic organic neutraliser.

Each triloraptor had a discrete translucent visor fitted around its eyes; the visor was the command centre for the hovering hexagon weapon, numerous other weapons and devises on board the craft. It was connected to the triloraptors synaptic brain connections, neurological receptors and the crafts central brain. In essence through the visor, each triloraptor was interconnected to each other and all were interconnected to the attack crafts brain. Each attack craft's brain then formed a network with the mother ship being the main brain of the network.

Looking through the visor, the triloraptors could see various symbols; the symbols were activated by thought waves. Each major symbol had several sub menus. The symbol shape that was activated was that of a single hexagon weapon, this brought the option of guidance control into its sub menu, with this activated the triloraptor could control the hexagons weapon flight in any direction, its speed and the overall flight range. It also brought up a menu bar at the bottom of the visor that allowed its controller to change the shape of the disc instantly.

Each triloraptor scanned the outer region of the herd; it then singled out its prey. This was logged and recorded on the triloraptors visor display. Now, no other triloraptor could attack this beast. When all one thousand triloraptors were all ready, this only took seconds, a small symbol in the corner of each triloraptors visors turned red. This was the single to begin the attack. One thousand triloraptors simultaneously launched its spinning hexagon weapon toward its chosen prey.

The triloraptors were masters at killing with these weapons, the trilo-trons blades were so sharp and hard that no bone on the average grazing beast's two and a half metre long body would stop it its deadly path. Each of the one thousand chosen prey died instantly as the bladed weapon sliced them completely in two! The attack was so silent and fast, with the exception of a few close beasts the main herds had not noticed this slaughter and continued grazing.

This was just target practice, now it was over; one thousand triloraptors took to the air. The visor symbol had now changed from a single hexagon weapon to a hexagon and triloraptor symbol. The trilo-tron weapon was re-united with its controller and now each would fly and kill in perfect harmony. Each triloraptor would now hunt its prey randomly and adapt the trilo-tron weapons shape to suit the kill.

Several different species of beast used these lush pastures to graze; it would be difficult to ascertain at a glimpse which of these fine beasts had the largest herds as all had several thousands. Some species were only one metre tall, weighed no more than thirty kilograms (66.15 pounds) and had long straight horns. At the other end of the scale the largest beast stood two and a half metre's tall, weighed almost 1,015.87 kilograms (one ton) and the males had massive tusks that could be over a metre long. To the one thousand airborne triloraptors these variations in size and weight would determine exactly how it would kill that particular species.

As the triloraptors flew close to the herds, panic erupted and the beasts scattered in all directions. This is exactly what the triloraptors had anticipated; with its prey running it would be a more creative kill.

A triloraptor had chosen its first running kill, a small straight horn. The small beast tried its hardest to evade the flying triloraptor but the triloraptor was too skilful, it swooped down, grabbed the beast by its straight horns with its feet and lifted it into the air with ease. At approximately thirty metre's high the triloraptor released the beast.

At the same time in the triloraptors visor, the triloraptor changed the trilo-trons weapon's shape to a javelin, instantly the weapon changed shape and now was a two metre long razor sharp javelin. At the command of its controller, the javelin hit the falling beast's chest and then went straight though it, killing it instantly. The javelin then did a gravity defying turn and at tremendous speed struck and passed through the dead beast body once more. By the time the small beast's dead body hit the floor the triloraptor and its weapon were already in pursuit of its next victim.

Its next victim was, one of the main male tusked beasts in a now stampeding herd of the 1.015.87 kilograms (1 ton) species. The triloraptor swooped down just in front of the beast causing it to swerve left; the beast did not see the two metre long, one metre wide and half metre high obsidian-black metallic solid brick in its path, another shape from the trilo-trons vast arsenal. The beast's front legs collided with solid brick causing it to lose balance, the beast stumbled and fell. With one beast down the other stampeding beasts ran into the fallen beast, they too lost their balance and crashed to the ground and died as they were then crushed to death by the stampeding herd. Thirty beasts were killed and hundreds were injured before the stampeding herd of thousands could change its direction. This was a good kill for the triloraptor and a ploy that had been adopted by numerous other triloraptors. By the end of the day, the total killed and severely injured by this simple but effective tactic would be in the thousands! However, they were the lucky ones.

It was now time for the next stage of the attack. From the triloraptors parked trilo-craft, the remaining triloraptors had been busy carefully scanning the grass lands terrain. A signal was sent to the one thousand airborne triloraptors to drive the herds to the north edge of the plains. As the herds headed north, a proton energy beam, brighter than any white light seen was fired from the craft. With ease, it tore a rift half a kilometre wide, half kilometre deep and one kilometre long into the grass lands. This was done four kilometres due south of the herds. The beam was so concentrated in proton energy that the soil, rock and other raw materials that came into contact with it immediately melted into magma and then crystallised, as it cooled the rifts walls and floor was as smooth as glass. As the beam was turned off, the order was then given to drive the frantic herds due south.

The ground thundered as the one ton beasts and other beasts totalling thousands charged south. To keep the panic at a feverous pitch, the airborne triloraptors continued skilfully killing many of them with their multi-functional weapon.

As the beasts charged forward the ground just seemed to swallow the leading beasts, the herds kept heading south and more and more just disappeared! Looking across the vast plains, everything looked as it had for hundreds of years, what the charging beasts didn't know is the triloraptors craft was projecting a holographic image over the terrain and hiding the massive rift was cut into the land. The illusion was picture perfect, even the tall grass swayed under the gentle breeze. Beast after beast fell into the rift; the ones at the bottom were killed by the half kilometre deep fall, the rest died as beast fell on beast, crushing and suffocating each other to death.

Once the majority of beasts had fallen into the lethal trap, the holographic image was turn off, any stragglers would be hunted and killed by the airborne triloraptors. By sunset every beast had been killed. Some species would never recover from this mass slaughter and over a period of time become extinct; this was not a concern for triloraptors. They had killed and that was the way.

From space another triloraptor craft entered into the planet's atmosphere, its shape was different to the attack crafts, it was a massive featureless obsidian-black metallic dome. The diameter of this craft was an impressive one kilometre and half a kilometre high. It size did not restrict its speed, once in the planets lower atmosphere it flew at just under the speed of sound and positioned itself ten metres above the now visible rift.

The trilo-craft hovered motionless for a few moments and then two portions of the underside of the craft began to liquefy, within seconds, two sixty metre round openings appeared, one at one end of the craft and the other at the opposite end. This trilo-craft had one purpose; it was a food processing plant and was operated and controlled by highly sophisticated androids. From one opening, a tractor beam locked onto the bodies of the dead beasts and transported them to the processing plant. The bodies were skinned, de-horned, de-gutted, de-boned and its high protein meat cryogenically frozen and stored in the vast on board cryogenic storage facilities. This food would help feed the triloraptors for a number of months. The waste, skin, horns, guts and bones were ejected through the other opening and fell back into the rift. The whole process took just two hours and then the trilo-craft headed back to the mother craft.

Triloraptors have a strong sense of order, that's what makes them so good at killing. On the same day as the Brobryne marsh lands and the vast flat grassy plains attack, exactly at sunrise in eleven different parts of the planet, eleven trilo attack crafts descended from their planetary orbit each took up a position over one of the five oceans and six seas on this planet. Ten would carry out identical attacks; the eleventh carrying one thousand juvenile triloraptors would allow the youngsters to develop their killing skills.

Calm seas were the forecast for the day as the trilo-craft touched down on the Adrian Ocean. Its hexagon shape made it a perfect flotation vessel; from its water line it stood 1682 metres above sea level. To counteract roll caused by waves or wind, the trilo-craft extended laterally below the water line four enormous gyroscopically controlled fins, two at the front and two at the rear of the trilo-craft.

With the trilo-craft stabilized, its occupants were ready to disembark. On the south side of the trilo-craft, the upper side of the hexagon started to dissolve and a deck formed along the entire length of the trilo-craft body. One thousand juveniles appeared from hatches that had opened. Each had a command control visor on and hovering by its side a trilo-tron weapon shaped like a lance.

Every good fisherman knows that to attract the fish to you, you must bait the area. This was done the day before when a trilo-drone craft deposited half a metric tonne of irresistible bait into the trilo-crafts landing area. Now this part of the sea was full of fish hopeful of their next feed.

Trilo-Android's placed large vats of fish bait on the deck of the trilo-craft. Before each Triloraptor took off, it picked up some fish bait with its feet and then swooped down to the seas surface, when it was ten metres away; it released its bait and then circled the area. The bait was made so it floated on the surface, within minutes the seas surface boiled with fish of all sizes chasing the floating bait.

Triloraptors are by nature excellent fish hunters, in fact on land, sea and in the air they have always excelled in their hunting abilities. The airborne triloraptor moved its head from side to side to calculate the its prey position in the water and to compensate for refraction, it then fired its trilo-tron weapon shaped like a lance, the lance went straight though the one metre long fish killing it instantly. In this one day, one triloraptor would kill in excess of one thousand fish using this method. That's over one million fish killed by the juvenile triloraptors but, not one eaten!

The cycles of life and death are the same in all oceans and seas, dead fish are the food of those who need to feed to stay alive. The one million dead fish in the Adrian Ocean attracted more marine life forms into the area, all desperate to feed. As they feed on the killed prey of the triloraptors, they became aggressive and started attacking and killing each other. Within hours the Adrian Ocean became an underwater battle zone, the largest sea predators were now being attacked by smaller individual fish, shoals turned on each other, the sea bed crustaceans fought and died, the oceans molluscs, echinoderms and sponges also died. The more syndromes became the battle order, the more they ate, the more aggressive they became, the more they killed and the more they died.

Within thirty rotations of this planet around its star, all marine life in the Adrian Ocean was now dead. As a trilo-bonus, death was also inflicted on thousands of oceanic birds and other creatures who had feed on the dead fish and then went into a killing frenzy.

It was a great kill for the juvenile trilo-raptors; they had planned and executed the whole event with an outcome that would make their peers proud of them. The plan was simple; they laced the second batch of the fish bait with a self replicating bio engineered hallucinogenic drug. Even the mighty sea creatures that were over twenty metres in length and weighed several tonnes; with jaws five metres wide and razor sharp teeth could not fight this powerful unseen enemy, the drug. The drug only died when all living things that ate it died!

Sunrise around the globe of this planet had been broken down into time zones by a series of longitude and latitude lines, that way the Triloraptors could calculate exactly when all trilo-crafts could attack simultaneously. As the sun rose over the other four oceans and six seas on this planet the trilo-crafts were already in position.

Each of the ten trilo-crafts measured exactly the same size, 1.6093 kilometres in length and 2682 metres wide. As with all the trilo-craft the crafts hexagon exterior is made of a featureless gleaming obsidian-black metallic compound. The difference with these crafts is they are unmanned mega trilo-trons.

The programming for the ten mega trilo-trons was identical. Each one positioned itself where the sea bed was just 1.60963 kilometres deep. At an altitude of 2.121926 kilometres, they all manoeuvred themselves so that the nose cone of the craft was pointing downward and then slowly entered the sea. They all came to a halt when the nose cone touched the sea bed.

Every mega trilo-trons body then seemed to liquefy and slowly a new shape emerged, a 1.6093 kilometres in length and 2682 metres wide cork screw, all were tapered with its point at the bottom. The trilo-tron cork screws started to spin, slowly at first; to maximise on atmospheric conditions the ones in the southern hemisphere would spin clockwise and the one in the northern hemisphere would spin counter clockwise.

The colour of the crafts gradually started to change from black to grey to yellow to amber to red and then to a brilliant white as their whole bodies heated itself. As the sea water swirled around the glowing spinning cork screw, it instantly boiled sending plumes of boiling water vapour high into the skies.

The trilo-tron cork screws then picked up their rotational speed to 1000rpm, at this speed the sea water started swirling so fast it created a giant whirlpool that ripped up the sea bed; rocks, silt and sand were now part of this enormous whirlpool, any living thing now caught in this vortex was either shredded or roasted. The speed then increased to 2000rpm, at this speed, cool air from the upper atmosphere was now being pulled downward, this air mixed with the boiling vapours thrown upwards. Instantly vast clouds formed and they started to spin in rotation with each vortex, the forces were so great that mammoth cyclones formed with wind speeds in excess of 600 km/h!

In the known universes, cyclones have been studied on different planets. Data from these studies has been exchanged and where life exists on any planet a universal cyclonic category scale that starts at one (mild) and goes to five (severe) has been accepted. A category five has winds with gusts of more than 280 km/h; this would cause almost total destruction, the trilo-raptors creation is off any scale!

As the cyclones and whirlpools began to reap havoc around the planet, each trilo-tron cork screw started to cool down; they all began to change colour back to obsidian-black. Slowly each one up anchored itself and gradually increased acceleration through the eye of the cyclone, at an altitude of 2.121926 kilometres each craft levelled out, changed back into its hexagon shape and soared back into space. The trilo-raptors now left the trilo-phoons as they were called because of their uniqueness, to roam freely.

A categorised cyclones life can vary, at sea it can last several weeks, as it hits land the life span drops to about a week. The trilo-phoons were in a league of their own, they would last for months! At sea the devastation was catastrophic; all marine life suffered with loss of life totalling hundreds of millions. Coral reefs that took thousands of years to form were instantly destroyed. The trilo-phoons close to the planets Poles tore through the ancient ice fields and glaciers, throwing tonnes of ice particles into the upper atmosphere. This in turn caused the planet's atmosphere to cool, subsequently this created snow and freezing ice storms across many parts of the planet and, that started a mini ice age.

As each cyclone hit land, the devastation continued. Whole land masses were reshaped as each trilo-phoon carved its way through the landscape. Millions of land and shore line creatures died. The ferocious three centimetres long pian fish didn't stand a chance. As the 600 km/h cyclone hit river estuaries, they were scooped up along water and silt on the river beds and thrown into extinction.

Day two.

The trilo-raptor race had come a long way in its evolutionary path; they once just preyed on one victim to survive, over the eons of time survival was no longer an issue but killing is. It was the way. From the depths of space, the trilo-raptors watched the trilo-phoons wreck devastation and the death tolls continued to rise past a staggering several billions, their appetites to kill were being satisfied but, there was still plenty of room for the dessert.

The cyclonic storms had not yet hit inland as dawn broke over the calm surfaces of the five fresh water lakes of Mardina. The lakes lie along continental rift zones and are created by the crust's subsidence as two plates are pulled apart. These lakes are the oldest and deepest in this world. At 1.8532 kilometres (1 nautical mile) deep, some lakes have a surface area of 616 square kilometres (228 sq. miles). The lakes primary inlet is the rah mardina river and falls, its primary outlet is Moquest river that then flows for 185.32 kilometres (one hundred miles) and then deposits its water in the sea.

It seemed that evolution had turned a blind eye to the aquatic species that inhabit these 1.8532 kilometres deep abysses; they were the same as they were thousands of years ago. Because sunlight does not reach these depths, the aquatics are bioluminescent with extremely large eyes adapted to the dark, they also have long feelers to help them locate prey or attract mates.

Due to the poor level of photosynthetic light reaching these depths, organic matter is not an option as a food source What they do have in abundance is hydrothermal vents that run along the continental rift zones. The hydrothermal vents form the base of the food chain, supporting diverse organisms, including giant tube worms, clams, limpets and fresh water shrimp. With so much nutritious food available, the deep water aquatics have thrived and shoal numbers were in there thousands, that's what made them a target for the next attack.

The featureless obsidian-black metallic domed craft had been programmed to enter the planet's atmosphere at sunrise and then position itself ten metres above the lakes surface. Its primary mission was to replenish the fresh water supplies. Inside the craft was a highly sophisticated water purification plant. Through openings in the underside of the craft, water was drawn upwards, super-heated to kill of any bacteria, frozen and stored in vast refrigeration units ready for future usage.

The crafts secondary objective was as it left to plant a dual pressure bomb in each lake. As each pressure bomb started to sink into the water it divided itself into two, the first part stopped at a depth of 61 metres (200 ft) the second descended to at a depth of 150 metre's (500 ft).

As the trilo-craft left the planet's atmosphere a signal was sent and all bombs submerged at 61 metres detonated simultaneously, the rest were programmed to go off five-trilo minutes later. Each pressure bomb was the equivalent to a 40 kiloton warhead. The ones at 61 metres caused shallow water explosions; these sent a shock wave upwards and created a spray domes at the water's surface which became more columnar as they rose. The domes shock wave immediately drew thousands of tonnes water into it and sent water plumes 3.600 metre's into the air. The water vaporised and turned into clouds that rained torrents of water back over the area, this caused instability in the high slopes that surrounded the lake and that would eventually lead to landslides.

The shallow water explosions also sent a series of surface waves outwards from its centre. The first wave was about 29 metres (95 feet) high and travelled at 600-800 kilometres per hour, others waves, just as destructive followed. The waves hit the shorelines and then carried on inland for several kilometres; they were so powerful that nothing could stand in their way. As they crashed into the highlands that surrounded the lakes, the already weakened slopes gave way and that lead to major landslides. Death and destruction what was planned and achieved.

The pressure bombs set at 150 meters detonated five-trilo minutes after the first causing massive deep water explosions. Their initial shock waves travelled downward, the concentrated energy hit the continental rift zones plates at several points with so much force that the plates collapsed. The result was catastrophic, the shock waves energy continued downward until it was meet with molten lava now been force upward through the shattered plate lines, this in turn caused several massive shock waves that spread out in all directions. As shock after shock wave smashed into each other the damage to the plate lines expanded outward for several thousand kilometres, triggering an earth quake so massive, it was off any scale ever formulated.

All life in this aquatic time bubble had now died; the lakes beds filled with lava, mud and rubble from the landslides and over time became dry beds. The rah mardina river and falls that once feed the lakes eventually recovered and rerouted itself but the primary outlet river, the river Moquest just dried up and died. This marked up another victory for the Trilo-raptors.

CHAPTER 2

The Icing On The Cake

It was a beautiful clear morning; the sun had just risen as one of the two hovering trilo-attack crafts dropped off the one thousand trilo-raptors. They flew freely around the massive volcano's enjoying the pockets of warm air that were producing updrafts. From there elevated heights and with their superior eye sight they could see their prey in the lush valleys below. The hunt was on, they swooped down, dispatching their prey as violently as they could and then feasted on its carcass.

Today was a very special day for these one thousand trilo-raptors, it was death-day. All one thousand triloraptors had reached the age of one hundred and twenty trilo-years old. A trilo-year was still based on their mother planets seasonal orbital cycle around its star. In triloraptor society it had been accepted several hundred ago that for a main stream triloraptor its life span would be one hundred and twenty years. In that time the genetically enhanced triloraptor had lived an extremely healthy life. Being genetically enhanced, they could live for almost twice that but, they had killed, feed and breed and with new generations been borne, it was now time to die.

Triloraptors have no fear of death; it was part of their culture. As a species, they had no sentimental feelings, they feed to live, breed the keep the species alive and when they were gone, nobody would mourn for them. The only thing they are fanatical about is, killing.

At noon, the sun was high in the sky over the volcanoes; it was now time for the second hovering trilo-craft to open its hatches. From each hatch, a four metre wide platform emerged and standing on it was a triloraptor, all had a menacing trilo-tron hovering just below them.

Each triloraptor was clad from head to toe in an obsidian-black metallic trilo-combat uniform. The uniform was made from trilo-r.i.t.s, r.i.t.s stand for; robomatic inter transdimensional substance, the same metallic substance that the trilo-crafts and trilo-trons are made of. At just two kilograms in weight and perfectly designed to form a second body over triloraptors head, body, legs and wings, the triloraptors can fly much quicker, strike much harder and their bodies can withstand heavy impact from weapon attacks. In fact the trilo-combat uniform enhanced the triloraptor skills by one hundred fold.

In unison one thousand trilo-raptors swooped down towards there designated prey. For the one hundred and twenty years-olds, it was the first time in their lives that they were the prey. They were completely unarmed; they all knew their deaths were going to be gloriously painful. However true to a triloraptor, it would fight until it was dead. That was the way.

All triloraptors took to the air but, it was a one sided battle. The combat clad triloraptors used their superior speed to out manoeuvre the triloraptors and once they were in range they sliced thought the airborne triloraptor wings with razor sharp armoured wings. This sent the triloraptors tumbling to the ground with the hunters in eager pursuit. Within milliseconds of the injured triloraptors hitting the ground, the hunters were on them, thrusting their armour piercing talons into the backs the triloraptor high into the air and then skilfully slicing one of the raptors legs off with the trilo-tron. Again the raptors fell to earth but before they hit the ground its hunters leaped upward and grabbed their torsos with their powerful feet. They then hauled the triloraptors high into the sky and then go; as they fell they used the falling body as target practice to carve more parts off their bodies.

Death had not yet come to all one thousand triloraptors, terribly injured they again crashed to the ground but their hunters were waiting for them. The hunters loomed over their prey, surveying there injuries and then using their armoured hooked beak they tore out the dying triloraptors eyes. The agony was not over yet, there was still more to come!

A fine rain started to fall over the volcanic area, soon the rain turn into a torrential down poor, within minutes everything was drenched. Each of the triloraptors clad obsidian-black metallic trilo-combat uniforms switched on their external uniform temperature control and set the temperature at 3683 K (3410 °C, 6170 °F). As the suits reached 3683 K (3410 °C, 6170 °F) the whole area erupted into a massive fire ball. The one thousand downed triloraptors caught fire and then burnt to death.

The two hovering trilo-crafts had spayed the area with an incerder-liquid that would burn so hot it would burn and melt everything it touched; the triloraptors suits were the incerder-liquids triggers. The incerder-liquid was harmless until it was heated to 3683 K (3410 °C, 6170 °F) at this temperature it crystallised and then ignited; each crystallised droplet would then burn for five trilo-minutes.

The triloraptors inside their suits were safe for the time been but as the incerder-liquid started to burn white hot and melt the volcanic rock, it was time to leave.

The volcano's had capped and restrained the planets pressurised molten lava for thousands of years but as the exterior of the volcano's started to melt, the lava burst free, sending molten rock and rubble thousands of metres into the sky. Streams of the lava also spilled freely from its shattered slopes and flooded the valleys below. The whole area was now destroyed and all life that was, was not anymore!

Each trilo-craft left the planet's atmosphere and then linked up in space with its mother ship. On board the mother ship battle plans were already been drawn up for the next planet to attack, it was time to move on but not once they look back at the destruction they had caused. That was the way.

CHAPTER 3

The Interplanetary Universal Congress Meeting

An emergency meeting of all congress members had been called, the agenda, triloraptors. All meetings were held at the virtual congressional halls on the Uni-net. The uni-net has no planetary titleholder, it was recognised that this service is a basic inter-planetary right; each planet must by the law provide this service to all its inhabitants. Now the uni-net is used by trillions and trillions of sentient beings around the universe as a daily form of interplanetary and galactic communication for news, exchanges of information, business and cultural, social and recreational purposes.

In the past congressional meetings were held where the members would have to travel to the terrestrial venue, because of the vastness of space, this could take years! It became even more complex when they arrived, each species would have to have its own environmental chamber and numerous translators for the all the different forms of communication. Now life had been simplified, each member had a virtual link to the uni-net via there synaptic brain connections and neurological receptors. All they had to do was mentally accept the invitation, go through the uni-net security protocols and instantly they were there in the virtual congressional halls.

The uni-net had solved the language communications problems with its instant translation program, so now; all members could communicate directly with each other. Although inter planetary specie prejudices were frowned upon, sadly it still took place. To overcome this, the congress had also universally agreed that each member would appear virtually as a coloured orb. The congress member could choose its colour from the colour spectrum but for identification, no one member could have the same colour.

With all four thousand five hundred planetary members present the Chair elect called the meeting to order.

"Fellow interplanetary universal congressional members welcome, it's good to see you again. I hope everyone is well."

Triloraptors," yelled the Jade green orb, "There a menace to the universe, they have to be stopped."

"My friend" said the Chair elect; "I must protest at the way you use in your words, we must respect the universal law on the way."

"Respect" retorted the jade green orb, "What respect do they have for all the lives they have taken and the damage they do to each planet."

"Neilo" The chairman said using the green orbs name. "We are all here to discuss the actions of the triloraptor race but we cannot ignore the laws set by this council over one thousand years ago that all specie is allowed to follow its own natural way.

Neilo chose to pulsate his jade green colour in a show of anger, he then replied.

"Chair elect, we all know 'the way' is our accepted law, further, we all know it's the triloraptors way to hunt and kill and we all know that as long as they do not kill intelligent life forms there ways are accepted but, I put this to all members here. Is it acceptable that the triloraptor have wantonly again destroyed a planet surface and eco-system and is it acceptable that planet will not be able to support numerous life forms for several decades to come."

The chair elect scanned the room and all orbs pulsated in angry unison and each said "no"

"Chair elect," said the fluorescent yellow orb, "we have discussed this race now several times, sanctions against them are impossible, and they are nomadic. They really don't need us; even if we revoked their membership of this Interplanetary Universal Congress, it would not make the slightest difference to them."

Neilo replied, "I agree, we need to take this to the next level." and then his orb vanished.

All members looked at the vacant space, the yellow orb asked,

"What has happened? Is there a fault with Neilo's uni-net connection?"

"I don't think so" replied the Chair elect. "If the assembly will bear with me for a few moments, I will have the technicians check this out." His orb blinked out.

It seemed to take for ages before the Chair elect orb returned but, the assembly was called to order and in a tone no one had heard before, the Chair elect was sobbing.

"My dear friends," he said weeping. "I have some terrible news for you, Neilo and all of his species are gone." He wept uncontrollably; he then blurted "His planet, Olotinium has been destroyed!"

"Triloraptors," were the calls from some members of the interplanetary-universal congressional members.

"Chair elect," the fluorescent yellow orb said. "This is indeed a grave situation and you are clearly distressed, as we all by this terrible news.

I would also like to caution the members on speculation and vote that this meeting be adjourned until we find out more facts. I would also suggest that all members' advice there planetary Security Council's to go on full alert."

All agreed and the meeting was duly adjourned.

The Chair Elect signed out of the uni-net and looked at his personal virtual viewer, the news had already broken. Virtual images were already been transmitted of the debris fields that was once a vibrant planet. The destruction of the planet Olotinium had also brought chaos into the planets solar system; with no planetary gravitational force, its two moons had collided and they too had so been destroyed. The nine other planets in this system were also in gravitational disarray. News reports estimated the death tolls at over 165 billion!

"How can this be." he uttered, and then his emotions got the better of him and he burst into tears.

He was from a race known as the solgas, a four legged mammals that are vegetable and shrub feeders, highly intellectual and extremely emotional. As the news spread across his planet, each of his species broke down and cried. That was their way.

For the Chair elect there was no let up, over the next few rotations of his planet he would have to attend numerous virtual meeting on the uni-net for clarification on the situation. Regrettably, he or anyone else had no answers. And with that, speculation grew about the triloraptors involvement. To help quash the speculation, it was agreed to call an immediate uni-net meeting of the Interplanetary Universal Congress and invite the triloraptor ambassador. Invites were sent and accepted by all, including the triloraptors who responded in record time.

All Interplanetary Universal Congress members assembled in the virtual congressional hall, the only member missing was the triloraptor ambassador. The Chair elect opened the meeting.

"Fellow interplanetary universal congressional members welcome, it's good to see you again. I would like to thank you for attending this meeting at such short no . . . ."

Before he could finish his words, the triloraptor ambassador appeared, the room gasped. Instead of appearing as an orb, the ambassador stood in full combat uniform with a trilo-tron hovering in front of him!

Before anyone could speak, the triloraptor ambassador said,

"Interplanetary Universal Congress members, I am here to give you all a warning! Any hostilities towards the triloraptor race will be dealt with the gravest of consequences. Already, several of you have deployed massive armed forces along your borders. We recognise that this is your right. But, your intentions are not honourable. The triloraptors have followed the law of the way, you must do the same!

And with that, he disappeared.

The virtual congressional hall went into an uproar, the chair elect decided it was best to let everyone vent off a little steam and then called the meeting back to order.

"Respected members of this congress" he said. While this assembly has been in open discussion, an analysis of the triloraptors ambassadors address has just come through. On the question of the triloraptors involvements in the annihilation of Neilos planet Olotinium and race, no conclusion can be ascertained. We must therefore investigate this matter further."

It was clear the Chair elects words fell on hallow ground as all orbs pulsated in anger. The fluorescent yellow orb said.

"Investigate what? With all our technology we have not been able to find out what has happened, what else can we do?"

The midnight blue orb said;

"We can protect ourselves, it is quite clear the triloraptors are playing the word game with us. I and my race say it's time for action. I move we the respected members of this congress unite and go to war against the triloraptors."

For the first time as Chair Elect his ruby orb pulsated in anger, he said almost shouting,

"Have you all lost your minds? We have no evidence that the triloraptors are involved! How can you possibly consider going to war! All you have is hate and anger."

A hushed silence fell over the assembly, the Chair elect then said;

"I declare this meeting closed, we can meet again soon, when we have more information."

As he signed off, he found his four legs were shaking and his mouth was completely dry. He took a drink of water and thought, 'who will be the first to go to war against the triloraptors and who will be the first to die'. He decided, that was for another day, the sun had set and he was tired, he walked out of his virtual room and headed towards his sleeping area. It was then that the assassin's struck. A razor sharp blade cut upwards, slicing clean through his breast bone and not stopping until it came out of the top of his head, the cut had sliced the front part of his body in half! As he fell dead onto the floor, the assassin's rolled his body onto its back and then using the blades with surgical precision; they cut the body up and left so that it looked inside out! The assassin's had not yet finished, the chair elects six wives and large family who all lived in the same complex, each were then butchered in the same way!

It wasn't until the following morning that the butchered bodies were discovered. This had been the first murders to happen on the solgas planet. Solgas's were a peaceful, loving race. Even a raised voice was upsetting to them, they couldn't help it, it was there nature and they would burst into tears and then apologise profoundly. So for something as horrid as this to happen on their planet, they all went into shock and a national week of mourning was immediately implemented.

As crime was non-existent on this planet, the solgas's had no expertise in investigating a murder, so a team of investigators were called in from the I.U.C (Interplanetary Universal Congress). The investigators were androids that were programmed in all aspects of inter-planetary crime, inter-planetary forensic science and inter-planetary forensic pathology.

The Chair elects murder fanned the flames of anger from members of Interplanetary Universal Congress but, all agreed to hold back on any actions until the I.C.U investigation team had been able to compile a preliminary report. In the meantime, in a virtual emergency meeting, the congress members agreed that the vice chair should take on the role as the new chair elect. It had been a move that would send a strong single to the triloraptors; the new chair elect was in earlier meetings the first to call to go to war! The new chair elects first suggestion was that they should all increase their own internal security. This was accepted unanimously.

Written communications from one planetary race to another were difficult because of language translations. The uni-net had solved this with its word mail program that automatically translated the words into the language of the receiver.

"Madam Chair elect" said the word mail program, "you have a word mail from the I.U.C investigations team leader."

"Open" she said.

"Madam Chair elect, our preliminary investigations have found that we can establish the exact time of death of the previous chair elect. He died precisely at 10-43pm; we have established this because it was at this time virtual link to the uni-net was disengaged. Cause of death to him and his family, a sharp implement its origin unknown. Other than that, we have no other leads. Madam Chair elect, our team has carried out a thorough investigation but we have not been able to find one atom of forensic evidence. I have attached a file with all the relevant investigative data and autopsy reports. Copies of these have also been sent to all members of the I.U.C."

The word message ended.

"No forensic evidence" said Sombula as she rubbed her two elbowed antennae together. "How can this be?"

Sombula, now chair elect is one of several empresses of a species of formicidae, a type of highly intelligent ant. There specie can be traced back almost twenty million years and they have been one of the most successful specie for intergalactic exploration in the known universes. Over the years they had successfully colonised many hundreds of planets, they had also seen at first hand the destruction caused when the triloraptors left a potential colonisable planet, and that is why they despised them.

Sombula switched on her uni-net link and called a meeting of the members of Interplanetary Universal Congress. The members had been waiting for this call and the meeting was convened immediately.

"Members of this Interplanetary Universal Congress, no doubt you have seen the I.U.C investigations team leader preliminary report. The report is inconclusive in its findings; whoever has done this is extremely clever, you would have thought that with our advanced technology this would have been cut and dry. There is only one species I know who could kill an entire family and leave no evidence, triloraptors. I therefore have two proposals to put to you, we do nothing until more of us die or we unite and go to war."

The fluorescent yellow orb, who was now the vice chair said;

"Chair elect, before we consider your proposal, perhaps it would be wise to seek advice on the legalities of this war. What we do not want is for this to back fire on us at a later date. While this is being looked at by the congresses legal advisers, we could do a virtual feasibility exercise of war itself. We, the Interplanetary Universal Congress have never fought a collective war and as part of the exercise we could get our forces commanders to draw up contingency plans for a hypothetical united attack. Our war capabilities and technology is somewhat dated in comparison to the triloraptors, they have trilo-r.i.t.s, (robomatic inter transdimensional substance) we need time to find ways to defeat this technology."

"That, vice chair sounds like good advice, what say the congress members on this" asked the chair elect. And then everything went black!

"Is everyone still connected" asked the chair elect. "Yes" hailed numerous voices.

With that the virtual congressional hall light up but now its walls were a mass of molten fire, with no apparent door or exits. Next, the ceiling caught fire as it did it began to rain balls of molten fire down onto the now panicking congress members. They all dropped to the floor but then the floor burst into flames! In panic each member tried to disengage there uni-net link but nothing happened!

Now, in blind panic the orbs flew around the blazing room trying desperately to get out.

"Stop" yelled the vice chair, "it seems as if someone has hacked into the uni-net and broke through our security protocols. What you see here are virtual fire walls, stop panicking, this is a virtual reality and therefore we cannot be physically harmed."

It was then that he noticed that the whole hall was slowly getting smaller!

"Look" said the vice chair, "there only doing this to make us panic, stay calm, I am sure the technicians will sort this out soon."

"I think you have forgotten something." said the vivid orange orb. "We are linked to the uni-net not only through our synaptic brain pathways; our neurological receptors are also linked". Gasps could be heard over the roar of the flames!

"Are you saying we can burn?" asked the Chair elect.

"Our physical bodies won't burn, but we could all go into a catatonic shock and that could kill us." replied the vivid orange orb.

A voice could be heard from the other side of the fire wall.

"Who's there?" the chair elect yelled above the commotion.

At that, the triloraptor ambassador attired in his trilo-combat uniform and his trilo-tron at his side walked thought the wall of fire and into the ever shrinking congressional hall.

"No talking," he said, his trilo-tron formed into the shape of a cylinder and he said, "exit quickly."

The trilo-tron then positioned itself in the fire wall to form a safe exit. All four thousand, five hundred members without hesitation filed through the cylindrical exit and out into safety of the virtual congressional foyer. The triloraptor ambassador also exited but, he casually walked throught the wall of flames.

The triloraptor ambassador addressed the traumatized assembled group.

"Members of this Interplanetary Universal Congress, by now you will have ascertained that your secure uni-net link has been hacked into. Perhaps what you have not realised is that the information needed for this was taken from the Solgas's chair elect uni-net synaptic brain link data chip. I would also speculate that certain sensitive security data stored on the chip has also been compromised. The uni-net programmers and technicians need to reprogram each of your synaptic brain links and the virtual congressional programme immediately. Until this is done, I would advise everyone not to use the uni-net!"

And with that he disappeared.

"Chair elect, I don't know about the rest of you, but this awful experience almost scared me to death. Do you think the triloraptors have just saved our lives?" asked the vivid orange orb.

"Or" replied the vice chair. "Do you think they are playing triloraptor games with more delaying tactics?"

"At this point of time, I don't know what to think" replied the Chair elect. "I do know that this program has been corrupted and it would be wise to disengage our links until it is repaired and new security protocols are enforced."

Each member disengaged there link and dropped dead immediately! The disengagement had triggered a hidden disintegration sub programme in there synaptic brain and neurological receptor links causing their brains to completely vaporise!

What they or anyone else from the Interplanetary Universal Congress hadn't realised was, the triloraptor ambassador had also disengage his uni-net link, and had also died instantly!

Within moments of this happening a voice message was broadcast over the whole uni-net. The voice was gruff and had an evil undertone to it.

"Ruler's, Sovereign's and Governments of this universe and every being in this universe, you will surrender unconditionally immediately!

Armed forces will disband immediately; all planetary defences will be disabled.

There will be no planetary or individual negotiations!

Rulers, Sovereign's and Governments, you can unconditionally surrender immediately by pressing the surrender button at the bottom of this voice message. Instructions will be then sent to you, they must be obeyed!

Resistance will be met with death and destruction.

Demonstrations of what could happen have already been shown with the complete destruction of one planet and all its inhabitants."

The voice said in a roar,

"No individual is safe! That has been demonstrated with the assassination of the Solgas's Chair elect and his family.

As a further demonstration, all four thousand five hundred representatives of the inter-planetary universal congress have just been killed. They were killed by the same device that you have inserted into your heads, the uni-net link!

Your uni-link has now been modified, it functions as normal but it also has a disintegration sub programme installed. The sub programme can be activated immediately and will then kill you instantly. Should anyone try to tamper with this device, security protocols are also installed that activate the disintegration programme immediately.

To demonstrate that you have no option but to surrender, in the next few moments you will hear a bell. As the bell tolls, 10,000 beings on each planet will die."

Everything went quiet for a few moments and then, DOOONG! With that, millions lives had had been taken, they dropped dead instantly, all had their brains vaporised. In every language possible the number 'millions dead' now flashed red on everyone's virtual viewer.

"The next time you here the bell toll, 20,000 beings on each planet will die. The longer you leave it to surrender, the more will be killed.

This link will remain open until the surrender is complete."

And then there was silence.

CHAPTER 4

A Big Change Is Coming!

On board the triloraptors mother ship, a forensic autopsy was completed on the ambassador's body. The forensic science and pathology report stated his death was due to his brain vaporising due to the modified uni-net device. The reports concurred and also stated that the technology for this was not known but the device would now be passed onto the unconventional scientific department for further analyses. A conclusion to the reports read; as no other triloraptor has the uni-net device fitted, the threat to the triloraptors species seemed insignificant. In the rest of the universe, it was a different story.

Each planet was using every resource possible to find out whom, why and what can be done to stop this, but there delay was costly.

From out of the silence of the uni-net link, the second bell tolled, DOOONG! Instantly several million beings just dropped dead! Again In every language possible the warning 'millions more have just died 'now flashed red on everyone's virtual viewer.

A voice thundered over the uni-net,

> "You are trying my patience! Surrender now or when the next bell tolls, a planet will be destroyed". In addition to this, each Ruler, Sovereign and Government Leader on each planet will also die!"

With the threat of death to the Rulers, Sovereigns and Government Leaders, the unconditional surrender came immediately!

Everyone waited in apprehensive silence for the voice to return, then after what seemed like an eternity, it spoke in a dictating manner.

"I am the overlord of this universe. Every life form is now a slave to me.

You will live to serve me. You will die to serve me. This is now the way!

Your orders for now are as follows;

1. "Any slaves who have not had the uni-net implanted will do so immediately. If anyone refuses, they must be executed immediately. Executions will be carried out in communal areas and there bodied left for all to see. It will be up to each planetary Ruler, Sovereign and Government to enforce this".

2. All new borne will have a uni-net device fitted immediately, failure to so will result in the death of the new borne and its family. It will be up to each planetary Ruler, Sovereign and Government to enforce this".

3. "Armed guards will be placed around the perimeter of all uni-net installations and buildings. Any unauthorised individuals or groups close to this perimeter will be executed immediately. It will be up to each planetary Ruler, Sovereign and Government to enforce this".

4. "All of uni-net workforces will be housed on site at uni-nets installations and buildings, they will also be given armed guards, should anyone approach these individuals, be it family or friends, they will be executed immediately. It will be up to each planetary Ruler, Sovereign and Government to enforce this".

5. "The use of the uni-net by individuals for inter-planetary communications, social, cultural and recreation usage is banned immediately. Anyone attempting to use for these purposes will be executed immediately".

6. "Research institutes, scientific institutes, interplanetary research institutes will cease all research projects

immediately. New instructions will be sent out to these institutes. Failure to obey will result in instant death. All of the scientific workforces will housed on site at institutes buildings, they will also be given armed guards, should anyone approach these individuals, be it family or friends, they will be executed immediately. It will be up to each planetary Ruler, Sovereign and Government to enforce this".

7. "Recreational and inter-planetary travel will cease immediately. Only approved travel will only be allowed. Anyone travelling without approval will be executed immediately. Each planetary Ruler, Sovereign and Government to enforce this".

8. "No community meetings will be allowed. Any such meeting will result in death".

9. "You will be required to attend future virtual uni-net meeting. You will be informed of these. If you do not attend, you will die".

10. "Until further notice, planetary food rations will be imposed. This will be lifted once I see these instructions carried out satisfactorily."

And then there was silence.

Within moments of the end of the voice transmission, each Planetary Ruler, Sovereign and Government Leader was then summand immediately to a virtual uni-net meeting at the inter-planetary congressional hall. They had all been advised not to come as a coloured orb; they were to attend as themselves. They were further advised that failure to attend would result in instant death, so they obediently attended.

Each made a grand entrance and to impress the overlord, they were dressed in all there fineries. The first shock they had was how the congress hall had changed, where it once looked stately, it now looked drab with black walls, black ceiling and black floor. The second shock came when a loud voice boomed,

"Disrobe immediately or you will die."

The Overlords voice roared louder.

"How dare you come to me looking like that? You are slaves."

Each Planetary Ruler, Sovereign and Government Leader obediently disrobed.

The Overlords voice once again boomed;

"You have been summoned here to clarify your status. When I talk, you will not talk. You will just obey everything I say without question!

For the time being, on your own planets you are going to be allowed to continue as its Ruler, Sovereign or Government Leader. If you displease me in any way you will die and be replaced by another.

I expect all rules, I have thus far stated to be carried out immediately. You know the consequences of failure!

Now, I have new instructions for you.

It has come to my attention that the nomadic species known as the triloraptors are not linked into the uni-net. This is not tolerable; my orders to you are; get your battle fleets together and go to war against this species. You will not stop until they are crushed and every one of them killed. The only thing you cannot do is harm their mother ship.

A virtual battle command centre has been set up in this building. I will expect to see all of your forces commanders their when this meeting ends. You will not discuss this amongst yourselves or with your forces commanders.

I also have an interest in a planet known as terra. On this planet, a species known as Homo sapiens (humans) are developing mentally, there are of a use to me. You will go to this planet and claim it on my behalf. Each human will then have a uni-net device fitted."

The Overlords voice boomed even louder,

"Now go."

Each Planetary Ruler, Sovereign and Government Leader could not wait to get out; they had never been spoken to in that manner, they were made to suffer the humiliation of having to disrobe, they were the elite! They would not forget this day.

They were also survivalists, each immediately turned off the virtual link and submissively contacted there forces commanders with instructions that they were to attend a war council at the new virtual battle command centre immediately. The commanders were also told that if they wanted to live, stand to attention and say nothing unless directly spoken to.

Each commander's uni-net virtual link took them to the virtual congressional halls foyer. Two thousand four hundred of them lined up in silence. A voice told them curtly,

"Enter now"

As each commander entered they were impressed by its size, it was an enormous domed hall. They were also impressed with the high degree of technology. From floor to ceiling in the centre of hall, the known universe was mapped out in detail by an enormous virtual display. Around the edges of command centre similar virtual displays were exhibiting armaments, some they recognised as their own and others they had not seen before. As they looked up, every type of battle star ship known to them was flying in perfect formation clock wise around the domes ceiling.

Without warning a loud explosion went off in the centre of the hall, its shock wave was so powerful it sent them crashing into each other. They were all dazed and in shock. As the commanders tried to regain their composure they realised the hall was empty, everything had disappeared.

"Commanders" The Overlords voice called, "you are weak. Sounds of explosions should not intimidate you. You have had life way to easy but, I assure you this will change!

Your loyalties to your Planetary Rulers, Sovereigns and Government Leaders are now over. You will now be loyal to me, overlord of this universe. To ensure this loyalty, your families have been taken."

Gasps could be heard.

"Silence" the Overlords voice demanded, and then continued,

"They will be treated well and returned to you when you complete your first two missions.

Commanders, you are going to war and you will win. Failure is not a liveable option for you, or your families!

The war I speak of is against the triloraptors, your fleets will converge on the edge of Olotiniums solar system. Then you will hunt down the triloraptors, capture their mother ship, and totally destroy them."

"Overlord," said one of the commanders, "May I speak?"

There was a short pause; the commanders looked at each other in dreaded anticipation and thought the fool, he's dead.

The Overlords voice returned and said,

"Continue,"

"I don't know what strategy you plan for this war but, I have a suggestion that will get you your desired results."

"Continue," the Overlord voice said.

"As one of our laws, we have always respected 'the way' of each species. The triloraptors way is to kill, hunt and feed. They have advanced technology that could easily destroy us in a direct confrontation. But they have a weakness. There are nomadic and have to stock up there food and water supplies. We could use our superior numbers to form blockades that would stop them from killing, hunting and feeding and replenishing their vital supplies. We could then lure them to a planet where in desperation, they would have to abandon their mother ship to kill and feed. At that point of time we could move in for the kill, destroying them and then capturing the poorly guarded mother ship."

"Estimated casualties," the Overlords voice said.

The commander replied,

"Insignificant, the mission is all that counts."

"Excellent" the voice said, and then inquired, "What is your name and from what planet do you come from?"

"I am Coppilia, from the planet Quzzzuzzz, one of the serpent species."

After a long pause the Overlords voice spoke,

"Coppilia of Quzzzuzzz, I have decided that you will head this mission. You will be my attacks fleet admiral, all commanders will follow you.

"Thank you overlord, it is an honour to serve you"

"It is indeed" said the voice. "Now, I also have another task for you. You will organise a few battle ships to go to a planet known as Terra. Your forces will then enslave its Homo sapiens (humans) inhabitants. All Homo sapiens must be then be linked up to the uni-net; I want casualties to be low. Be warned, they are a primitive, extremely hostile and have nuclear capabilities."

"Overlord," said another commander, "may I speak?"

"Continue but, you had better have something constructive to say." replied the Overlords voice.

"I have" The commander chose his words carefully. "In view of your orders for minimal casualties, would you consider a first contact approach? We could make contact with the governments of this planet."

"Silence," the Overlords voice shrieked. And then continued,

"Do you think I am a fool? These Homo sapiens are paranoid over what they class as aliens from space but, they have had good reason. Certain members of the illustrious Interplanetary Universal Congress have over a long period of time been adducting them for scientific experiments! There governments know of this, they have several of your crashed space crafts and trying to back engineer its technology. They will never trust a soft approach.

You will go there, kill a few millions, that is an acceptable number, and then enslave them.

Now, no one will leave here until you work out the final details of both missions. When you are finished, I will expect a full and detailed plan of every phase of both missions. We will then go over this detail by detail."

As the Overlord turned off his uni-net link he thought, 'All this time and planning, now everything is coming into place. I have conquered a universe, enslaved most of its inhabitants'. He laughed to himself and said out loud.

"That was the easy part. What lies ahead is my true conquest."

CHAPTER 5

Command Centre

Back at the virtual battle command centre, Admiral Coppilia and the planetary commanders had worked for over one planets rotation on the final details. After running numerous battle simulations of each stage of their plan to form blockades, they had agreed to use fifty thousand interplanetary congressional battle star ships. They would slowly drive the desperate triloraptors to a planet known as Notus. Notus had everything that the triloraptors needed, plenty of life to kill, food and water. What they would not know is; a massive land army of over one billion elite soldiers would also be waiting for them, the army would be equipped with the latest armaments. Using the combined air and land forces, they would destroy the triloraptors and capture the mother ship. The plan was complete; computer predictions were now giving them a 95% victory.

The capture of Terra had caused lots of arguments but an agreement had been struck on what seemed an ingenious plan. Ten battle star ships would be used; each battle ship would have ten thousand troops and numerous teams of experts to carry out the disarmament of the Homo sapiens nuclear weapons, numerous missiles and installation of the uni-net system and its individual devices.

All battle ships would enter the planets solar system and take up strategic positions on the dark side of the planets moon. That way they could avoid detection from the planets space and ground observatories. They would fire a volley of thousands of guided missiles that would look like a massive meteor storm into the planet's atmosphere. To make this more believable to the Homo sapiens, some missiles would just burn up as they entered the planet's atmosphere, and others would crash into what would seem like random sites, however the majority would strike the larger cities and military installations.

The crashed meteorites/missiles would immediately release a highly developed form of Propofol gas into the atmosphere that would render all air breathing inhabitants immediately unconscious and suppress there central nervous system. Once the Propofol gas was inhaled, it was designed to last for several rotations of the planet, but for the invading forces safety, it would also disperse in just a few of the planets hours. That would then give the troop's time to set up planetary command bases and the uni-net team's time to start their work.

It was calculated that by the time the planets inhabitants had re-gained consciousness, they would be waking up to a new world of slavery under the Overlord!

Admiral Coppilia sent the finalised plans to the Overlord and then waited patiently along with all the other commanders at the battle command centre for his response.

While the commanders were waiting, they engaged in some idle chit chat. The subject quickly turned around to whom exactly was the Overlord and from what world did he come from? They chatted about their own downfall and how they were defeated into submission without actually seeing a single Overlord battle ship. They speculated that they had been defeated by one individual and not a massive army.

It was at this point of time that another explosion happened, the virtual battle command centre floor shattered like glass and the two thousand four hundred commanders began falling into a black abyss!

Some screamed, others swore as they accelerated downward but all had just one word when they realised they were falling into an ever narrowing shaft and the shaft walls were lined with millions of long black razor sharp blades. "SHIT" they all shouted as the bodies of the commanders closest to the walls were sliced into small pieces.

Amidst all the darkness and confusion, the tumbling commanders did not see the blackened floor looming towards them. Bones crunched as the survivors crashed into it. They were then crushed as other fell on top of them. Groans and cries filled the air, but one voice roared louder, the Overlords.

"You were brought here to do my bidding" he yelled. "How dare you question me?"

"Coppilia are you still alive?" the Overlord inquired.

A faint "Yes" could be heard as Coppilia tried to wriggle his way out from underneath the bodies.

The Overlord again yelled,

"This is your fault, I left you in command. You have betrayed me."

"My lord it is hard to control the mouths of . . ."

But, before he could finish he was dead, his brain had been vaporised.

Although this was a virtual reality, those who were sliced to pieces by the razor sharp blades or crushed by their fellow commanders also died in reality from catatonic shock. This was due to the uni-net being connected to their neurological receptors.

In total, five hundred and forty seven commanders had died, that was acceptable to the Overlord. He had anticipated that as commanders of armed forces of the Interplanetary Universal Congress they would at some stage start to ask questions about him and his own militias, this little shock tactic would keep them quiet and obedient for a while.

He was also pleased to kill Coppilia, he was way too clever and would have posed a threat to him at some time in the future, but just as an extra precaution and a warning to the other surviving commanders he would also have Coppilia family publically executed!

He then announced in an egotistical way,

> "Commanders, the plans you have put forward are acceptable, without any delay you will now carry them out.
>
> We will also need some new commanders, make the necessary arrangements and send me there names and uni-net link references.
>
> I will also want a new Fleet Admiral, your Planetary Rulers, Sovereigns and Government Leaders will send me a short listing with five of your best commanders.
>
> Now go."

The overlords plan to bully and intimidate the commanders worked wonders, each left and reported straight back to their Planetary Rulers, Sovereigns and Government Leaders. They insisted that the fifty thousand interplanetary congressional battle star ships be in position on the edge of Olotiniums solar system in one of the olotiniums planets rotations and that the fleet would be crewed, armed and ready for war within another planets rotation.

As ordered, the Planetary Rulers, Sovereigns and Government Leaders composed a short list of five new candidates for the position of Admiral of the fleet. These were sent promptly to the Overlord who discarded them all. He suspected that these candidates were not the best but the ones most disliked and expendable and therefore he would have to select one himself.

His choice was another serpent from the planet quzzzuzzz. Most civilisations found this ten to fifteen metre long serpent species with massive fangs and eight, two metre long tentacles to be intimidating and somewhat frightening. He also suspected that in the triloraptor past, similar serpents would have been a predator of them. Quzzzuzzzium venom was extremely lethal, a combat clad triloraptor would have nothing to worry about but, one without its combat uniform made from trilo-r.i.t.s, would be dead in seconds. A scary and a ruthless predator is exactly what he wanted and Zissiani, a female who's file made her sound ruthless but skill full, would be the perfect choice. And if she did not meet his expectations, she was expendable.

Zissiani promotion came to her by royal proclamation; it read 'We the Royal Family of the Quzzzuzzz planet are proud to announce the promotion of Commander Zissiani to intergalactic Admiral of the Fleet. This promotion will take effect immediately. Admiral Zissiani, you will now report directly to the Overlord'.

Zissiani wasn't pleased with her so called promotion, she thought 'Commander Coppilia died within one planets rotation of having this title, this title will also bring death to me; it's now just a matter of time'. She deliberated more, "To live, I need to be a marionette to the Overlord but, any good soldier can do that. But I am Admiral Zissiani; I will please the Overlord with my military brilliance. In glories splendour, I would do his bidding. I will win his trust and if I get the chance, I will kill him before he kills me."

She immediately set about contacting the Overlord by leaving a voice message on the uni-net for him, her message read,

> "Overlord, it is an honour to serve you. I have reviewed the attack plans on the triloraptors and they are flawed."

The message then ended.

'That should get his attention' she thought, and it did. She was summoned to the virtual battle command centre.

The Overlord was in no mood for pleasantries, in his normal bombastic way he waded straight in;

> "You say the attack plans are flawed, how do you come to that analysis?"

Admiral Zissiani came straight to the point,

Triloraptors are no fools; they already know that the Interplanetary Universal Congress has been conquered. By now they know the fleet is being mobilised to hunt them down. If I were them, I would be planning a counter attack."

The Overlord thought for a moment, 'she right, how could I have missed this'

"You have a point" he conceded. "How do you think they will counter attack?"

Admiral Zissiani knew she had the overlord hooked, all she had to do the reel him in. She replied,

"Speculation is of no use, we need good intelligence. I know that you have been doing long range scans of the movements of the triloraptors but with their holographic technology their mother ship could look as if it is in any place at the same time.

I have sent out my own reconnaissance vessels, they have our new cloaking technology, and as it is new, the triloraptors will have not yet developed the technology to detect these vessels. They will be able to advise me on the true movements of the triloraptors."

The Overlord said exasperated,

"You have already sent them and they will advise you."

"Overlord you know a battle cannot be won without decisive action. Time is of the essence, any delay would be costly to the mission. As Admiral I have to make these decisions and gather any pertinent intelligence."

"Yes you do," the Overlord agreed. "Now go and gather your information". "Admiral," he said, "I want immediate updates on any signs of a counter attack."

CHAPTER 6

Zissiani Delight

Zissiani left feeling quite smug, she had just caught the biggest fish in the universe and with that extended her life expectancy by a least one day. That was her plan; survive one day at a time. But an urgent thought popped into her head;

"I'd better get those vessels launched right away."

Under the Interplanetary Universal Congress, interplanetary and inter-galactic peace treaties had been signed and stood strong for hundreds of years. With the law of the way being accepted by all members', life in the universe was until now pretty serene, the only thing that had happened in the last few hundreds of years was a few small skirmishes on individual planets. So when there was a call to war the moth balls literally had to be taken off some of the armaments and inter-galactic battle ships. This was not true of the new Quzzzuzzzian vessels.

From there space docks, the two new Quzzzuzzzian vessels named Cobrasant and Viperious fired up there massive graviton engines and left Quzzzuzzz space at a graviton speed of nine. Each graviton is measured by light speed (299,792,458 <u>metres per second</u>) times ten as one graviton. There maiden flight was a reconnaissance mission of the triloraptor mother ship activities. To the vessels captains and crew members thought it was an excellent opportunity to put the new vessels through their paces and to test out the new cloaking technology.

The heart of these amazing vessels is their graviton engines, each engine uses gravity to super compresses dark matter and this is united with hydrogen using the graviton accelerator. The fusion creates a massive energy field that is contained in the vessels graviton reactors and they in turn supply the vessels with unlimited power.

Through secure channels using the uni-net, the captain of Cobrasant enquired to the captain of Viper;

"How are your engines doing?"

"Running as smooth as a Quzzzuzzzian baby's skin" the other captain replied."

They both laughed. The captain of Cobrasant said;

"I'm just about to turn on my cloaking shield, are your scanners ready?"

"Ready and waiting, I also have a visual of you on our monitors" said the captain of the Viperious vessel.

The captain ordered his number one;

"Engage cloak shield."

"Cloak shield engaged and working within accepted parameters." The number one replied.

The captain then asked the Viperious captain;

"How are we looking from your position?"

"You are completely invisible, our scanners cannot detect you. We are ready to engage our own cloak shield, are your scanners ready?"

"Ready and waiting." the Cobrasant captain confirmed.

"Engage cloak shield." the Viperious captain said to his number one.

"Captain the cloak shield is engaged and instruments show it is working as it should be."

"Excellent," the captain replied, "Captain, What do you see or not see over on the Cobrasant?"

"Space, stars and gas, looks like both or cloaks are working fine. We both have a mission to complete, how about we engage our graviton enrichment drives and let's go see what those triloraptors are up to."

"Sounds good to me," the Viperious captain said, "you go first, I will follow at a safe distance to avoid your bow wave and any spacial turbulence, and I don't want to make the crew sick." He said laughing, "Over and out."

Both vessels had carried out the primary test s with no problems; they then sent a message to Admiral Zissiani of this and that they would be within viewing distance of the triloraptors mother ship within sixteen rotations of their home planet.

While this was happening, Admiral Zissiani had been busy organising the two missions. The ten interplanetary congressional battle crafts had already left for the planet terra; it would take thirty of her planet rotations for the small fleet to get to the terrain solar system. The main fleet had been a nightmare to organise; crews, supplies and armaments were all on board and to her delight the fifty thousand interplanetary congressional battle crafts had now left the edge of Olotiniums solar system in formations of ten thousands. For security, each formation would take a slightly different route but, eventually all would converge as one fleet when the vessels Cobrasant and Viperious confirmed the exact location of the triloraptors mother ship.

Another mammoth task Admiral Zissiani faced was mobilising one billion ground troops and transporting them to the planet known as Notus. She on behalf of the Overlord had had to commandeer thousands of space cruisers, enlist their captains with threats of death and then converted the cruisers into troop and supply carriers. In all fairness to the planetary rulers and governments she had to acknowledge they had co-operated fully but, she and they knew that if they did not co-operate they would die.

Logistically the odds of completing this without raising suspicions from the triloraptors were enormous but it had to be done. As reports came in that the last few cruisers left their planets and were heading for Notus, she knew there would be no turning back or indeed coming back for lots of these vessels and troops.

Admiral Zissiani suspicions were correct; the triloraptors central command had been trying to monitor all spacial activities from planets involved in the Interplanetary Universal Congress. Using long range sensors, they had been able to pick up the convergence of the fifty thousand Interplanetary Universal Congress battle fleet on the edge of Olotiniums solar system and its divided departure. Their sensors had also detected the unusual activity of thousands of other crafts leaving Interplanetary Universal Congress planets. They assumed from this, that the conquered Interplanetary Universal Congress had been ordered by the Overlord to hunt down the only remaining free member of the Interplanetary Universal Congress, the triloraptors.

The fleet of ten battle ships had also caught triloraptors central command attention. From intelligence gathered by eavesdropping on any relevant chatter on the uni-net, they had been able to ascertain that this small fleet was heading to the planet terra. They surmised that its objective was to enslave the planets inhabitants, but why? They are primitive.

With the information at hand, an emergency meeting of triloraptors central command was called. Its central command was headed by one thousand supreme elders; each elder is over 125 trilo-years old. They are a division that are classed as the elite, they are also noted as the shrewdest of all triloraptors, and no other triloraptor would ever question them.

One thing triloraptors are poor at is debating issues, they find it irritating, and when they get irritated they want to kill. To alleviate this and to help the decision process, a simplified process had been adopted hundreds of trilo-years ago. The mother ships supercomputer was feed all the relevant information, then using its superior AI (artificial intelligence) it came up with rational prioritised options that could be voted on. All each elder had to do was consider the options presented on the viewing screen in front of them vote on them and then accept the majority vote.

The trilo-supercomputer considered the overloads invasion of the universe as the number one priority. It addressed this with two options; the first was; seeking out and destroy the overlord. The second option was to try to form an alliance with the overlord and offer him the triloraptors support in his dominance of the universe. Each of the one thousand elders cast their votes and within moments the results were displayed. They had unanimously agreed to option one.

With that vote cast the trilo-supercomputer instantly analysed the direction that the elders had chosen and then brought what it considered as a significance threat to the success of destroying the overlord, the impending war with the Interplanetary Universal Congress battle fleet and other Interplanetary Universal Congress vessels. It addressed this with three options; Counter attack, stand and fight or retreat. Again, each of the one thousand elders cast their votes and within moments the results were displayed. They had unanimously agreed to option one.

Once again the trilo-supercomputer whirled into action, this time its analysis's was more in-depth but still required votes. On the subject of a counter attack, it gave the elders two more options. Option one was a direct attack on the fifty thousand Interplanetary Universal Congress battle fleet using all the triloraptors resources. Option two was small strategic attacks on the fifty thousand Interplanetary Universal Congress battle fleet and other Interplanetary Universal Congress space vessels and a large attack on Interplanetary Universal Congress planets. Again, each of the one thousand elders cast their votes and within moments the results were displayed. They had unanimously agreed to option two.

Over the past hundreds of trilo-years the trilo-supercomputer had assisted the triloraptors in making major decisions but, its AI recognised that the detailed planning of this and every past attack fell on the elder and senior commander, that's what they are good at. So now it paused allowing the elders to formulate their plans. Even as it paused its AI also knew its intellect would be used to co-ordinate the various attacks, so it quietly analysed all the data it had on the overlord, it also looked for weaknesses in the Interplanetary Universal Congress defences, all of this data would be essential as the elders finalised their attack strategies.

One of the elders requested the trilo-super computer to bring up all relevant data on the planet terra. An image of the planets sun and its solar system came up on all of the elders viewing screens. It also added listing of populations of all known species on the planet, registering the 6,816,100,000 Homo sapiens as the most advanced and summarised there technological achievements. Each elder skimmed over the information. They had seen primates before on other planets but they had never developed past their basic evolutionary stages, these had started to develop but, the Homo sapiens technology was primitive.

The same elder asked the trilo-super computers AI to evaluate why the overlord would have an interest in the Homo sapiens on this planets inhabitant? All of the elders shook their heads in agreement at this question but, were not surprised when the trilo-super computer responded that it had no information on this.

Without saying a word, a general consensus of opinion was agreed. To defeat the overlord, they would have to destroy his plans for terra. The trilo-super computer AI sensed that this could lead to a debate, so to save its masters any anguish it then came up with three options that the trilo-elders could vote on. Its analytic brain deduced that if the Homo sapiens were taken out of the equation that would stop the overlord's plans for terra. So logically option one was to kill all Homo sapiens on the planet terra. Option two was to destroy the Interplanetary Universal Congress's small battle fleet and use then Homo sapiens as bait to lure out the mysterious overlord. Option three was simple, let the planet terra fall to the Interplanetary Universal Congress's battle fleet but before this happens abduct selected Homo sapiens for possible future usage against the Interplanetary Universal Congress's and the overlord.

The first two options caused quite a quandary for the trilo-elders; the thought of killing 6,816,100,000 Homo sapiens was to them exhilarating. Collectively their minds raced forward, the planet terra was full of life, they could also kill every other species, and all triloraptors would relish such a killing spree. Trying to put those thought to one side, they also had to look seriously at option two; the triloraptors were under attack, if they were defeated and that was a big if, it could be an end to their civilisation but, option two was not a guarantee that it would lure out the overlord, it would only delay his plans for the planet terra. It also became obvious that if option two was adopted, they would have to deploy time and resources to keep these Homo sapiens and the plant terra safe while they dealt with the overlord.

Most of the elders did not like the third option, abducting hostages was not there way, killing is. They had to accept however, that in light of what was happing, that this option was plausible.

As each elder pondered on what to vote, the trilo-super computer did something that was unprecedented, it aborted the voting procedure. Its AI had sensed the anguish the elders were feeling over the three options. Its next action was to flash up on each elder's screen, 're-evaluating options'; this only took a few trilo-moments. It then came up with a single option that was broken down into four categories;

1. To frustrate the overlord's plans for the Homo sapien species and ultimately the conquest of the universe, they would have to destroy the Interplanetary Universal Congress's small battle fleet heading to terra.
2. Abducting hostages was distasteful but, it would be advantageous as they did not know why the overlord taken an interest in these primates. The hostages could be killed later if they served no purpose.

3. After the abduction, continue to harass or destroy the overlord's plans for the Homo sapiens.
4. When the overlord was defeated they could go back to terra and kill all of its inhabitants.

Triloraptor's have no facial muscles that allow them to smile but, if they had, this option would have made them smile like a Cheshire cat. Each of the one thousand elders cast their vote and instantly their viewing monitors displayed a unanimous agreement in favour of this option.

From the emergency meeting of triloraptors central command the elders now had a constructive direction, the meeting promptly ended. To save time and pointless explanations, the trilo-super computer relayed the voting results to all triloraptors senior commanders. With the super computers working in the background, it would be now up to the elders and the senior commanders to work on the final details to set their plans into action.

CHAPTER 7

Surran

The commander of the fleet and the battle ships captains heading for terra had been on high alert ever since they left Olotiniums space; they had also maintained communications silence. Now with only one day to go before they entered the solar system of terra, everyone's nerves were fraught. The commander though that now we are this far out it would be a good time for a triloraptor ambush. Using its feelers, it reached out and switched on its communication device and addressed all battle fleet captains,

> "This is commander Surran, do complete deep space sweep for any other vessels or any unusual activity." the commander ordered.

Each captain came back with the all clear message. The commander thought where are they? Commander Surran and his crew came from a planet of vast gaseous methane marsh lands; its species was a type of gastropod mollusc known as Slugtonians. Surran was an extremely large Slugtonian who had always had a delicate stomach but, on this day its stomach rolled and pitched like a tiny sail boat would in a gale force storm. What made Commander Surran even tetchier was all Slugtonians are hermaphrodites, having both female and male reproductive organs and the Commander Surran was pregnant and was due to lay its eggs at the same time the fleet hit the terrain solar system!

Commander Surran scanned the three dimensional star chart, the Slugtonian noticed that the next star they would pass was a red dwarf star named Proxima Centauri, they would then have roughly 4.2 light years of open space to terra. The Slugtonian munched on the yellow moss, a delicacy from its home planet and ordered the fleet to do continued sweeps of space. With its stomach rolling and pitching and an unending flow of methane gases being expelled from its anus, it thought, 'if I were a triloraptor, I would use this star system for my ambush'. But it was wrong.

The small battle fleet past Proxima Centauri safely and then made good time to the planet terra's solar system. The three dimensional star chart showed this system has a star that is classified as a type G2 <u>yellow dwarf</u>. Four inner planets called terrestrial planets. An asteroid belt that contains tens of thousands, possibly millions of objects over one kilometre in diameter and finally, the four gas giants, that makes up the outer planets. It also had an assortment of comets composed largely of volatile ices.

Commander Surran had just laid thirty eggs, this was always a traumatic experience but it had not eased the rumbles it felt in its stomach. From the battle ships birthing chamber Commander Surran ordered the fleet,

"Ahead slow, this solar system is a death trap".

Vigilantly the fleet moved forward, it had past the four gas giants and was about to emerge from the final part of the asteroid belt when ten immensely large asteroids broke free, with tremendous acceleration they smashed into the hulls of each of the battleship fleet. Each battleship shook to its core with the impact. Hundreds, possibly thousands of crew members were killed and injured as they were thrown mercilessly around inside their vessels.

"Were under attack." the commander yelled into its communication device.

Using the asteroid belt for cover the triloraptors had used their holographic projector technology to disguise their 1.6093 kilometres long trilo-battle ships as large asteroids. Instantly each trilo-battle ship sealed itself onto the hull of all ten Interplanetary Universal Congress's battle fleet vessels.

The ten trilo-battle ships turned off their holographic projectors and from the Interplanetary Universal Congress's battle fleet vessels viewing ports they could see the featureless gleaming obsidian-black metallic compound the formed the outer structure of the trilo-battle ships. They were no match for these monstrous vessels. Each captain independently tried to break free by firing their main engine thrusters but, size for size; the trilo-battle ships were eight times bigger and immensely more powerful.

Commander Surran tried to use the uni-net to send out an SOS message but the triloraptors had blocked all outward communications from terra's solar system. Each of the ten Interplanetary Universal Congress's battle fleet vessels were now being towed toward the solar systems inner planets by the trilo-battle ships.

In desperation Commander Surran tried to open a communications channel to the trilo-battle ships but it was dead. Then there was a loud explosion, the communication's officer reported,

>"Commander Surran, the triloraptors have breach each of the battle ship hulls, it looks as if they are going to board us."

Instantly using its feelers Commander Surran hit the emergency seal button to the battle ships birthing chamber. The chamber was now sealed; it also had its own filtration system, emergency provisions and nutritious food for the Slugtonians offspring's.

>"Get armed response teams down there on the double and hold those triloraptors back." the commander ordered but there was no reply. "Communication's this is Commander Surran do you hear me?" Again there was no reply.

Surrains stomach was now doing back flips, changing frequencies the Slugtonian tried a ship to ship communication but again, communications had been blocked! The commander's stomach dropped to a new low as the realisation that it and its new borne offspring's were completely isolated, it was trapped and helpless and it knew that the triloraptors would take no prisoners!

From Surrains command console, a warning message flashed up, 'concentrated lethal levels of Metaldehyde gas detected, extraction system malfunction.'

"Holy Slugtonian marsh grass, their exterminating the Slugtonians crew with lethal insecticide!" the commander blurted out loudly.

But it knew it was hopeless. Similar exterminations were happening on board the other nine Interplanetary Universal Congress's battle fleet vessels. The triloraptors had planned there assault with precision, they knew the weaknesses of each of the Interplanetary Universal Congress's members, it was part of their way, from fledglings they were educated in the art of killing. Some choose to specialise in chemical killing, they studied chemical biology and became experts in chemical extermination.

All triloraptors took pride in their killing and the chemicals needed for this mission were very elementary, it was therefore way below an adult triloraptors skill level to get involved in this. So the task was given to the triloraptor juveniles to organise, administer and then vent away the poisonous gases later.

Sombula the chair elect had sent two Interplanetary Universal Congress's battle cruisers on this mission. Her specie is a type of highly intelligent ant but, they are easily killed with a high concentration of borax gas and H_2O steam. The triloraptors flooded both vessels with this lethal combination and within ten trilo-seconds they had killed every formicidae on board.

From the planet Quzzzuzzz, Admiral Zissiani had sent one battle cruiser. In comparison with the other tasks she had at hand, this should have been a fairly easy mission so she sent its oldest but in all fairness; the junior triloraptors found the Quzzzuzzz battle ship the best of a bad bunch and its crew was the hardest to kill. They however resorted to an age old chemical weapon, hydrogen cyanide gas. The weapon was banned under an Interplanetary Universal Congress treaty but like many such treaties, they were broken when the need to use them arose. HCN is in abundance as an interstellar medium and hydrogen cyanide gas is a simple by-product, therefore for the nomadic triloraptors this is an easy weapon to manufacture. All the junior triloraptors had to do is mix hydrogen cyanide at a concentration of 7500 ppm; this is a lethal dosage, even for the ten to fifteen metre long serpent species.

A quick life form scan showed that most of the Interplanetary Universal Congress's battle crew were dead. The lethal gases were vented out of each vessel and then it was now time for the one thousand triloraptors clad in their trilo-combat uniforms and with their trilo-trons at their sides to board each vessel. There orders, killed the small pockets of survivors, upload all computer data from the numerous on board terminals to their own trilo-super computer and seize all usable armaments and supplies.

From the safety of the birthing chamber, Commander Surran observed the triloraptors boarding party as they plundered its command vessels armaments and supplies. As they had not blown up the fleet vessels, a small glimmer of hope crept into the Slugtonians mind, it thought, 'they know they cannot breach the chamber, so once they have what they want they might leave me and my offspring's alive'.

Commander Surran was a highly experienced commander but to presume clemency from the triloraptors was foolish and in a second a more startling thought the Slugtonian thought;

> "I am the commander of this fleet, the triloraptors are going make an example of me, my death will be a warning for the rest of the Interplanetary Universal Congress's battle fleet".

With that thought, its stomach went into overdrive, it's started to shake its body ferociously and this promoted at violent eruption of gases from the Slugtonians mouth and anus!

Commander Surran had every right to think this, the ten Interplanetary Universal Congress's battle vessels were still being towed deeper towards the solar systems sun! Within a few trilo-minutes they passed the planet mars and then terra. To avoid detection from the Homo sapiens space telescopes, ground-based telescopes and observatories, the twenty vessels passed terra's orbit on the opposite side of the sun. They then continued on passed Venus and mercury, it was at this point of time that the internal temperature in the Slugtonians birthing chamber began to rise!

Slugtonians don't like heat, they like a moist atmosphere and an artificial moist undergrowth, in that climate they can manoeuvre around they battle ship easily. All of this was now drying up along with the Slugtonians and its offspring's skins. In desperation Commander Surran used its feelers to hit the communications button and tried to open a communications channel with the triloraptors, it said,

> "This is Commander Surran, under the Interplanetary Universal Congress's convention, the offspring's on-board these Slugtonian battle cruisers are protected by the rules of engagement, that also applies to the parent. I therefore wish to surrender."

But there was an eerie silence. The triloraptor boarding parties had now vacated all of the Interplanetary Universal Congress's battle fleet and had just released the sealing clamps; all ten Interplanetary Universal Congress's battle fleet cruisers were without power and just entering the outer corona of this solar system's star!

All ten Interplanetary Universal Congress's battle fleet vessels had self-regenerating exterior bio-ceramic casings that can withstand extremely high temperatures. This star classified is a type G2 yellow dwarf was a white star. Most stars of this classification average temperature of the outer corona and solar winds are about 1 million-2 million Kelvin's. At a push and with some heavy exterior damage and extreme discomfort to the crew the Interplanetary Universal Congress's battle fleet vessels could withstand this. The triloraptors knew this and therefore released the fleet over a hot region where the temperatures were 8 million-20 million Kelvin's; at these temperatures, the battle fleet would simply melt into oblivion!

As Commander Surran's battle cruiser tumbled into the fiery abyss, it could not move its body, its underside had started to melt and the rest of its body was now one mass of blisters! The pain was unbearable but, as the heat became more intense the Slugtonian tears boiled as it saw it's young shrivel and die. Its own death was now just a few moments away, in that moment Surran knew that the monster that had sent them to this horrific death, the Overlord had greatly underestimated the triloraptors, this small fleet had been easily destroyed. Surran also knew that many more lives would be lost in trying to defeat the triloraptors.

At the virtual battle command centre Admiral Zissiani had been informed immediately that communications had been severed from the terra bound fleet, she knew that there was only one reason for this,

"The triloraptors!" she hissed out loudly.

She then thought, 'this will be my death unless I think of something fast' and with that a plan started to form in her head.

Admiral Zissiani immediately contacted the Overlord;

"Overlord, I have some bad news, we have lost contact with the fleet sent to terra." she paused "I fear the worst, they are probably all dead but all is not lost" she said reassuringly. "In my battle strategy, I made contingencies for the triloraptors interception of this fleet, so as a backup, I sent a covert second fleet of four vessels. They are ordered to take a longer but stealthier route to terra and should arrive at the planet terra's solar system shortly."

There was a long silence from the Overlord, Admiral Zissiani knew her life was hanging by a fine tread, she started to shake uncontrollably.

He then said scowling,

"This backup fleet; has it the equipment and expertise to follow through on my plans for the Homo sapiens?"

"Yes" Admiral Zissiani replied.

"That's all I need to know. Go and keep me informed the moment they arrive."

Admiral Zissiani immediately broke contact and thought, 'That was close, if the Overlord finds out that I have been lying through my fangs he will kill me but this has just bought me a little more time. Her thoughts deepened, 'one day at time was a little presumptuous, it's now down to, every second counts.'

Trying to recompose herself Admiral Zissiani then let her thoughts drift on how she would set the plans into action to send four battle cruisers to terra as quickly as possible. Her only realistic option was to take four battle ships from the main fleet and deploy them to terra. The first thing she would do is bring them up to speed on the overall invasion plan of terra and the failure of the last fleet under that incompetent slimy slug, Commander Surran.

She would also have to conscript as many experts as possible for the uni-net installation and scrounge the equipment needed. Ground troops and armaments would have to be packed to the rafters as they would only have four and not ten vessels. Food and water would also have to be rationed until they arrived on terra. On the way to terra the battleship labs would have to work around the clock to manufacture the Propofol gas missiles needed. With a plan devised, she sent her orders with a lethal proviso: get there as quickly as possible and complete the mission successfully. Failure would result in the immediate execution of all on this mission, along with their families. 'Curse that slug' she said out loud.

CHAPTER 8

Abduction

With the Interplanetary Universal Congress's small battle fleet out of the way, six of the triloraptors battle ships left the terrain solar system, three were used on a covert mission and the remaining one set about the abduction plans for the Homo sapiens.

Terra or earth as it is known to its inhabitants meets with all the criteria as a life supporting planet. Most similar planet's that the triloraptors encounter when hunting have specie that have not developed there intelligence or intellect above the basic needs for survival. These Homo sapiens have however had developed highly complex social cultures, multi-national food industries and distribution centres, multi-national industries, a mind boggling financial system, a space program where they launch themselves into space inside rockets that contain highly inflammable fuel and an array of quite basic but extremely destructive weapons. The latter was the only thing that slightly impressed the triloraptors.

These Homo sapiens had an obsession with clothing garments; most species used such items to combat the environmental conditions. These two legged apes had numerous different clothes for socialising, work and for sleeping in? All in all, the triloraptors surmised they were on the road to destroying their own planet. It also inspired the triloraptors into thinking; in the not too distant future the triloraptors would return and complete the job for them!

One homo sapien weakness that stood out from all the rest was there obsession with recreational pursuits. Everywhere the triloraptors scanned homo sapiens where running, swimming, riding self-propelled bikes and boards, kicking and hitting different sized round objects called balls.

Some of the Homo sapiens socialised and drank large volumes of alcohol substances. Others while socialising took a cocktail of chemical based drugs. To pursue all of these recreational activities the Homo sapiens had built large arenas, pitches, and domes and had even designated numerous coastal beaches and large land masses as pleasure resorts.

But they did not confine these recreational activities just to the planet's surface. For their pleasure, they had just constructed a number of recreational space stations (RSS). Each space station housed a working crew of thirty five and had luxury quarters and superb leisure facilities to accommodate two hundred guests. Five were now up and running and another five were still being constructed.

The five that were in operation and the five that would be completed in approximately two earth years orbited Terra (the earth) in a low earth orbit (LEO) They followed geocentric orbits ranging in altitude from 160 kilometres' (100 statue miles) to 2,000 kilometres (1,200 mi) above mean sea level. At 160 km, one revolution takes approximately 90 minutes, and the circular orbital speed is 8,000 metres per second (26,000 ft/s).

There initial designs were based on the now obsolete International Space Station (ISS) that was completed in the earth year 2011. The new RSS's were now twenty times larger, the space stations, including their large solar arrays, span the area of twenty U.S. football fields and appeared as extremely bright stars from the planet's surface during the night. To add a nice touch and for advertising purposes they could also put on an impressive nightly laser light show. To the triloraptors the RSS's were a folly, an unsightly design, but would be the perfect targets for their mission.

Virgin Galactic's, two hundred seated, Virgin space shuttle 1 had just docked bay after an uneventful flight from Spaceport America. As the passengers disembarked from the shuttles airlock, the RSS's captain and crew stood in line and warmly welcomed their new guests. The guests were excited; this was their first trip and vacation into space, they were ushered to the upper decks impressive space dome foyer, the foyer also doubled as the entertainments area and bar.

As the guests gazed through the large transparent dome, they could see the planet earth in all its splendour, to them, this was breath taking. Each were offered light refreshments and then given an RSS orientation and safety talk. With the boring bits over, they were then shown by the entertainments manager, a 3D holographic video of the scheduled entertainments on offer. The space walk, weightless football and the space bungee jump seemed to be the most popular among the more energetic guests. For those who wished to conserve their energy, luxury spars, whirlpools, weightless massage rooms, a small casino and an all inclusive bar were also available. Each facility had a million dollar selling point, they all had a panoramic view of space and the planet earth.

Once the talks and video were over, the guests were directed to their luxury suites. The suites were reasonably spacious; all had the luxuries of a five star hotel. Each bed faced a large floor to ceiling curtained viewing port, so if the guests wished they always had a spectacular view of the celestial heavens.

The crew's job descriptions were open ended; they were on hand twenty four hours each earth day to pamper their paying guests. Each guest had paid one hundred and fifty thousand US dollars for a seven day trip. Each suite has occupancy of two guests, the suites also had bed settee that was used for younger guests. Each RSS has one hundred suites, that is a cool two million, one hundred thousand dollars turn over every seven calendar days. The guests also paid extra for the children, space walks and other special activities that were on offer.

Dr Elaine Laurence woke with a start! She was instantly dazed by an extremely bright light, her ear drums filled with sounds of people shouting and screaming. She tried to move but realised, restraints had been placed on her arms and legs. To her horror, she also realised she was naked! Without warning, jets of freezing cold water hit her body.

Out of shock she too began to scream and then suddenly the water jets stopped, the lights went out and she fell directly back to a deep sleep.

Elaine woke yet again with a start, all over again the bright lights blinded her and she could hear the yells and screams of people. Over all the voices she could hear someone screaming, it was her! The jets of icy cold water blasted her body.

She screamed 'help, somebody help me' but her plea's was lost by the sounds of four hundred and fifty nine other people who were also shouting similar pleas of help. The water jets stopped, the lights went off and all four hundred and sixty nine people went instantly back to sleep.

What Elaine hadn't notice was the Intravenous drip in her left hand, this had been inserted by the trilo-android's. The drip was delivering an isotonic solution for the replacement of fluids. She and all four hundred and fifty nine other RSS guest and crew were now prisoners of the trilo-raptors and were been looked after by the remaining trilo-attack crafts computer. They had been abducted nine earth days ago.

There abduction plan was executed with triloraptor precision. Using the Propofol gas missiles taken from the ten interplanetary congressional battle star ships, two were dismantled and modified into much smaller units. The units were fitted with a target guidance system and at a pre-arranged attack time, each small missile was fired at the air purification pipes on two of the RSS's. For effective delivery of the Propofol gas, the trilo-raptors had to minimise damage to the fragile air purification pipes. To this end, each missile was remotely controlled and guided in, on impact, the needle sharp pointed nose cone punctured the air pipe, it them automatically sealed itself to the air pipes outer shell and the gas was then pumped into the RSS's air systems. Within seconds, all of the crew and guests were completely unconscious.

The removal of the abductees was as easy stealing sweets from a baby. The trilo-battle ship approached each RSS with its holographic projector on. All that could be seen from each RSS was the normal view of space. The trilo-attack ship then docked, blasted open the RSS's airlocks and used its pre-programmed trilo-androids to removing the abductees clothing and then bring the unconscious crew and guests to the prepared holding chamber.

The trilo-raptors knew the planet terra had various satellites in space. So while the abduction was taking place, a trilo-distraction was also arranged. This distraction was really to appease the trilo-raptors. It seemed pointless not to kill something while they were in the neighbourhood. Up until the declaration of war, they had observed the rules of the inter-universal congress and did not kill anything that was classed as an intelligent being, but not anymore. That was their way.

From the stockpile of missiles plundered from the ten interplanetary congressional battle star ships, they had numerous ones that looked like small meteors. At the pre-arranged attack time, hundreds of these were fired into terra's atmosphere. By design some detonated and exploded, others followed on an exact trajectory plan set by the trilo-raptors and ploughed into the other eight RSS's. The crew and guests onboard the three occupied were killed instantly! Work crews on the other five also died. Just to make this look like a celestial accident, other meteor missiles collided with numerous other communications and spy satellites, instantly destroying them.

None of the meteor missiles fell to the planet's surface; they had all been designed to burn up or explode before then. But, hundreds of tons of wreckage from the destroyed RSS's and satellites would plummet indiscriminately down to terra's surface.

The trilo-raptor attack ship undocked and accelerated away from the scene but, if anyone would have cared to look back, they would have seen last two RSS's blow apart into thousands of pieces. They too had been destroyed by the meteor missiles.

As the trilo-battle ship reached 353 miles (569 km) above the surface of terra. A second small volley of meteor missiles were fired, they instantly destroyed the earth's largest space telescopes known as Hubble and James Webb! The battle ship then accelerated and headed for its next mission.

CHAPTER 9

Trilo-Raptors Fleet And Mother Ship

Cobrasant and Viperious, the two Quzzzuzzzian vessels had now been travelling at nine gravitons for fifteen of their planets rotations of their home planet. Both inter-galactic battle ships slowed to half a graviton. There cloaking system were on and working perfectly. Ship to ship communications and internal ship silence was now imperative. Both had already calibrated their long range sensors to home in on the unique drive signatures given by all trilo-raptors vessels.

For the next rotation of their planet, both vessels slowly crept forward and then as if it were a surprise, the sensors suddenly jump to life, indicating trilo-raptor vessels had just come into sensor range. What they saw sent the crew's emotions off the Quzzzuzzzian scale, they were stunned, excited and if honest, even the captains were a little frightened.

Quzzzuzzzian sensors were highly sophisticated. They could analyse data and then covert it into an accurate holographic image of what it had detected. The hologram showed 3D images of one thousand and sixty trilo-raptor ships plus one massive ship that would be the trilo-raptor mother ship. This was way more than any of the Interplanetary Universal Congress had envisaged.

The Trilo-raptor fleet of one thousand flew in a perfect Hexagon formation that spanned 1,609,300 kilometres (100 miles) with the mother ship at its centre. This was the standard formation of the trilo-raptor fleet. Each trilo-raptor vessel was spaced out precisely,

71

this allowed small trilo-shuttle crafts to manoeuvre and dock without unnecessary space turbulence.

The other frightening part was the other sixty vessels; they were colossal battle ships that covered a buffer zone extending a further 804650 kilometres (50 miles) outside the perimeters of the six sides of the hexagon formation. The sensors also detected and displayed numerous other triloraptor-ships of various sizes that came, docked with the mother ship for a while and then set of back into space. These, they presumed were the all important supply ships.

Both Cobrasant and viperious captains drew the same conclusion, the triloraptors fleet and resources were way more than had been anticipated. They also thought that the trilo-raptors knew the Interplanetary Universal Congress fleet was coming but were not overly concerned. They came to this assumption by the fact that the triloraptor fleet was just cruising in space and going about their business as usual.

After scanning the trilo-raptor fleet for one rotation of their planet, both the Cobrasant and viperious captains felt that they had gathered all the necessary information. They also felt they had been pushing their luck at not been detected, so with cautionary haste, they changed course and accelerated to nine gravitons. As soon as the Cobrasant and Viperious had put a safe distance between them and the trilo-raptor fleet, a secure communications channel was opened and a full report was personally given by captains to Admiral Zissiani.

Admiral Zissiani uploaded the holographic imagery supplied by the Cobrasant and viperious into the virtual battle hall computers and then spent a rotation of her planet going over them in every detail; she also created numerous battle strategy scenarios. She concluded that the original plan was still the best of an okay bunch.

To win, the Interplanetary Universal Congress fleet would sustain massive losses; deaths will be in the millions, if not billions. Admiral Zissiani pondered for a while on thoughts of more peaceful resolutions but, with her own life hanging on the line, she did what all survivalists do. She sent the exact co-ordinance of the trilo-raptors fleet and mother ship to Interplanetary Universal Congress fleet with orders to continue as planned. She also sent orders to the cobrasant and viperious captains to change their heading and start attacking and destroying the trilo-raptor supply vessels. Her last job before she left the virtual battle hall was to update the Overlord.

The uni-net call to the overlord was to say the least, short!

Admiral Zissiani started, 'Overlord, I have a full update for you on the . . .' but was then cut short.

"You know where the trilo-raptors fleet and mother ship are, correct?"

"Yes." Admiral Zissiani replied

"Then get on with my orders and stop wasting time' the overlord yelled, and ended the uni-net call".

The battle begins.

Cobrasant and Viperious captains had done as they were told, but using a bit of initiative they plotted two separate courses to intercept trilo-raptor supply ships. Cobrasant would cover vessels approaching the front of the fleet and Viperious, the rear. For safety, they would only intercept vessels that still had one day's rotation on their planet to travel. That way, they would not have to worry about the main fleet sending re-enforcements.

The Quzzzuzzz race had for a long time distrusted the trilo-raptors. At numerous Interplanetary Universal Congress meetings they had voiced their concerns over what they classed as 'trilo-raptors, flaunting the law of the way'. While the Interplanetary Universal Congress chose to do nothing, the Quzzzuzzz had built the Cobrasant and Viperious. They had also been secretly developing new weapon technology; preliminary test had been carried out with outstanding results.

These new weapons utilise one of the most natural forces in the universe, gravity. On certain planets, the developing life forces believe gravity is the god of universal creation. On other planets, gravity it is the mother of all things known. But irrespective of what these beings believe. All sentient life forces that have knowledge of gravity, know of its dark side, its destructive nature and its ultimate name, death.

Both Cobrasant and Viperious had been equipped with the new G.R.I.M weaponry. G.R.I.M, stand for, gravitational rotation inversion missile. A, G.R.I.M missile is fired at its designated target, on impact it explodes and in less than a nano second (A nanosecond (ns) is one billionth of a second ($10-9$ s) a gravitation field envelopes the target. The gravitational field's strength is numerically equal to the acceleration of objects under its influence. The gravitation field accelerates the designated target so fast that, the matter it's made of inverses in on itself. The collapsed matter becomes so dense that atoms collide and become destroyed; this is turn triggers, multiple atomic explosions.

The Viperious long range scanners picked up a small fleet of five trilo-raptor supply ships on a heading towards their mother ship. With its cloak system on, Viperious captain set a course to intercept the supply fleet. At a range of 16,192,000 kilometres (1000 miles) the Viperious came to a dead stop.

The captain then ordered a G.R.I.M to be locked onto each supply vessel. The captain thought,

> "Up until now, these new weapons that up until now had only been field tested. Now, on their first outing, they are taking on the impressive trilo-raptor ships with their latest technology."

Robo-matic inter trans-dimensional substance or as it is known trilo-r.i.t.s was an enigma to the Interplanetary Universal Congress scientific community. To a lowly Quzzzuzzz captain and his crew who were now on the front line, it was downright frightening.

Another thought entered his mind,

"I'm glad the Viperious is also armed with numerous other long and short range missiles. We might need them!"

"Armed and ready." called the first officer.

"Fire." the captain boomed.

And with that, five G.R.I.M's silently left their missile bay. Each had cloaking technology built into them, so to the naked eye they were invisible; they ran at zero silence and gave off zero heat from their propulsion systems. But, the big but was; could trilo-raptor ships scanners detect them before they detonated.

It would take just under three Quzzzuzzz seconds for the G.R.I.M's to travel the 16,192,000 kilometres (1000 miles) to their target. To the Viperious captain and crew it seemed like a life time. And then, the Viperious scanners light up. They displayed all five G.R.I.Ms hitting their targets and in a nano second the trilo-raptor ships had gone! The shock wave sent out from all five detonations was enormous, even at 16,192,000 kilometres (1000 miles) away they had to brace themselves for heavy impact. The crew were ecstatic; they had just achieved their first victory over the trilo-raptors.

Within two quzzzuzzz hours the battleship Cobrasant had also had a similar encounter. It too had destroyed five trilo-raptor supply ships.

For security, Admiral Zissiani had not allowed the Cobrasant or Viperious to have any contact with the main Interplanetary Universal Congress fleet. But, upon receiving news of their victories, she took upon herself to let the fleet them know of what had happened. Eagar to boost the fleets morale and for her own ego, she contracted her fifteen metre long body and slipped into her fully scaled, blue and silver admiral uniform. The uniform was made of a silken Kevlar that hugged her long body and eight tentacles like a second skin. Glancing at her reflection in her glass tiled command centre, she thought;

"Zissiani, you are an impressive sight, now you gorgeous Quzzzuzzz, let's get down to business."

In her opening uni-net address to the fleet, she elaborated on how the Quzzzuzzz battle ships had struck the first of what will be many devastating blows with this new weapon.

Now with defiance in her voice, she declared that;

> "This will lead them to ultimate victory against the trilo-raptors."

She also stated;

> "The production of the G.R.I.M's was now at full speed and as soon as possible, other Interplanetary Universal Congress battle fleet ships would be fitted with them."

While her mouth was running away from her, her mind was quite clear.

The G.R.I.M's were only going to be supplied to Quzzzuzzz battle ships.

The icing on the cake for Admiral Zissiani was been able to announce;

> "Intelligence has shown that as soon as the attack was over, the trilo-raptor fleet began to disburse. From a thousand strong, the main fleet has been reduced to half."

With ridicule in her voice she said;

> "The mighty trilo-raptors are now on the run".

And with that she ended her address to the Interplanetary Universal Congress battle fleet.

Her address to the overlord was a little more conservative,

> "Overlord the Cobrasant and Viperious has destroyed ten triloraptor supply ships. Both ship captains have reported as soon as this happened, the trilo-raptors fleet started to disburse."

"And what do you make of that" inquired the overlord.

"They are coming" she quietly stated.

There was a moment's pause and then the overlord said,

> "Well then, I hope you and the Interplanetary Universal Congress planets are prepared."

He continued;

> "What is happening with the four Interplanetary Universal Congress battle ships heading towards terra?"

> "They are entering terra solar system as we speak." Admiral Zissiani replied.

> "Good," he said, "I will expect more good news soon."

And with that, in his normal abrupt way, he ended the call.

The universe has perplexed the mind of many scholars. One of the earlier thoughts of these inquisitive minds was; are we alone in the universe or are their other intelligent being out their? Individuals on each planet have painstakingly worked out formulas for the recognition of potential life. The criterion for these formulas has been calculated on what they observe and their own intelligence. They have taken into account the size and classification of a star. The number and position of planets in its system and the distance of a planet is from the sun/star.

It was thought by certain species that, if a planet were too close to its sun and it would be too hot. At the other end of the scale, if it was too far away, it would be a gas planet and that too would not sustain intelligent life. But, life is in abundance throughout the whole universe. Planetary "habitation zones" are for the recognition of certain species but do not take into account the full meaning of life.

Co-habitation on board the four Interplanetary Universal Congress battle ships had become unbearable. This was due to cramped conditions; thousands of intelligent beings were now reduced to arguing, fighting and in some cases, some came close to actual murder!

To accommodate each life form, the four ships had separated the life forms into numerous atmospheric chambers. This in itself wasn't too hard; the problems arose when several life forms had to share the same chamber. The largest group and the most problematic were the life forms that breathed in a combination of nitrogen, oxygen, and argon, known as air. Although these life forms were the key to success for this mission, they were testing the patience of the other crew members and each of the ships captains.

To stay alive, they needed all hands on deck. Each ship's captain made a call to their heads of security ordering them to empty the make shift brigs. The detainees had all been warned that if any more incidents arise, they would all be ejected into space!

The four Interplanetary Universal Congress battle ships had just entered terra solar system, each ship was on maximum alert. Their long range scanners had informed them that the majority of terra's communications, weather, leisure and military satellites had vanished? A good guess would be trilo-raptors. However, if plans worked out, this could work to their advantage as they would have had to disable them anyhow.

The lead ship was the battle ship Chela. Whose captain was an arthropod of the spider crab species. The ship was from his home planet, takaashigani. The same planet was known to the Homo sapiens on terra as Gliese 581 d that resides approximately twenty light-years away from terra in the constellation of Libra.

Captain Obersani stood a little over six metres tall, with a leg span of over sixteen metres from claw to claw. His chelipeds were two metres long and he and his species had orange, with white spots along the legs. Despite their ferocious appearance, Captain Obersani and his entire specie had a calm temperament.

"Chief weapons officer, this is your Captain."

"Go ahead captain." the chief weapon officer replied.

"Activate the deflector weapons shield."

The chief weapons officer was also an arthropod from takaashigani, touching her command screen with her chelipeds; she activated the deflector weapons shield.

"Activated captain they should be online in a few moments. I have also brought all main weapons are on line."

"Good." replied the captain.

With that, the battle ship Chela shuddered momentarily as the neutron reactors engaged, within moments, an oval energy field formed around the whole of the ship. It glistened as particles of space debris bounced off it. The deflector weapons shield would not stop a full blast from a trilo-raptors battle ship but it would cushion several blows and give them a fighting chance.

The only problems with the deflector weapons shield were, once it was engaged the ship could only travel at cruising speed. That would mean that it would now take a half takaashigani day to get to terra! It also restricted the ships long scanners, so the Chela would have to rely on the three other battle ships for that crucial information.

The other three ships did not have the deflector shield technology but, wished they did. In the event of a trilo-raptors attack, the plan was to use the battle ship Chela as a temporary shield, while they used a barrage of guided missiles to try to destroy the trilo-raptors ships.

At cruising speed, each ship cautiously crept forward; each life form had forgotten the cramped conditions and their petty grievances. Friend and Foe now stood together, anxiously waiting for some kind of trilo-raptor surprise attack. Finally, after what seemed like a life time and without incidence, they made it to their planned initial assault point on the opposite side of terra's moon.

Since leaving the Interplanetary Universal Congress main fleet, the four battle ships had run several virtual simulations of their plan on how to overthrow the planet terra. It was now time to instigate the plan for real. The meteor weapons were armed and ready, all four battle ships had synchronised their battle computers and on an automatic countdown from three, all four ships launched several hundred thousand meteor missiles towards terra.

Each missile had its own onboard guidance system; the guidance system had been programmed so that missile would hit its targeted area with one hundred percent accuracy! To compensate for atmospheric conditions, rain and high winds, each missile had a built in disbursement analyser that would compensate for poor conditions and evenly distribute the Propofol gas. Some also had super bunker buster capabilities for underground targets.

CHAPTER 10

Earth

Although several earth days had passed, the inhabitants of earth were still in shock at what had happened to the ten RSS's and the hundreds of other man made satellites that orbited the earth. The science community, Astrologers and religious bodies all put forward theories on how these meteors suddenly appeared, but in truth, it was all speculation, nobody knew.

The leaders of earth governments, monarchs, and dictator rulers from all nations meet at the Headquarters of the United Nations, New York for crisis meetings. After a televised tribute to all those who had died, the first priority on their busy agenda was how to stop this from happening in the future. While some fantastic ideas where put forward, the one big stumbling block and where negotiations became tetchy was, who was going to finance this and who would have control over it? Another priority was a fast track program to build new satellites. On this, it was agreed by all, that private companies would have to be brought into the negotiations however, this too was a testy area, as each leader had their own hidden military agenda.

Earth day three of the United Nations meeting was about to start. All world delegates were seated when the President of the General Assembly announced hurriedly,

> "Ladies and gentlemen, we have just had reports coming in of thousands of meteors similar to those that had struck earth satellites were heading towards earth". She continued,

"We must start emergency evacuation protocols immediately."

With that, she and the world leaders were ushered away to reconvene in the UN safe bunker.

As the various dignitaries jostled for evacuation priority, a guided meteor missile crashed through the UN building roof and exploded! The missile had been specially modified; its blast radius was limited to 0.8046.5 kilometres (half a mile). It was known by Interplanetary Universal Congress that it is custom and practice in such building to have bunkers, so the missile was also fitted with the equivalent to a super bunker buster. The blast on this one would penetrate downwards for 0.4022.25 kilometres (quarter of a mile)!

The destruction of the meteor missile was enormous; Most of the Turtle Bay area where the UN building was located had been vaporised! The adjoining east rivers bank had also been destroyed. The blast threw its waters high into the sky and as the waters fell, it drenched most of New York. When the river settled, its waters flooded into the void that once was Turtle Bay and the UN building. Globally all other UN buildings around the world had also been targeted, they too came to a wraithlike end.

To maximise on the disruption and destruction of governments around terra's globe, numerous other targets were obliterated. The Pentagon building is the home to the United States Department of Defence, its location, Arlington County, Virginia, U.S.A that too was destroyed. Scans had revealed The Pentagon had a warren of bunkers deep into the earth; the missiles super bunker buster was modified to compensate for this, its downward blast superseded 0.8046.5 kilometres (half a mile)! In Washington D C, the Whitehouse, home to the president of the U.S.A and the Senate building were deemed as viable targets and also destroyed.

Just a little over 4.828 kilometres (3,000 miles) away from the USA land mass is a the small island known as the United Kingdom, the UK Island is split into three domains, England, Scotland and Wales. In England the Houses of Parliament, the Prime Ministers House at Downing Street, MI5 Headquarters Thames House and Buckingham Palace, London were targeted and destroyed. Another UK strategic target was GCHQ headquarters in Cheltenham; that too had an extra special super bunker buster to compensate for its deep bunkers.

In Scotland, the main target was the Scottish Parliament Building, Holyrood, and Edinburgh. It had been noted that in past historical wars with the Scots that they were and can be troublesome bunch, so the city centres of Dundee, Aberdeen and Glasgow were also targeted.

Wales had caused a small problem; it did not seem to have a large central government building so the government offices at Merthyr Tydfil, Aberystwyth and Llandudno were all targeted and instantly destroyed.

From space if one looks at the United Kingdom a small divide exists that is known as the Irish Sea, on the other side of divide you can see another small island that is known as Ireland. Ireland has two land borders, north and south. North is governed by the Northern Ireland Assembly; their meeting place is, Parliament Buildings in the grounds of the 224 Acres Stormont Estate. The building is designed in Greek Classical tradition, constructed by Stewart Partners Ltd under the guidance of architect Arnold Thornley, from Liverpool. He was a man who paid great attention to detail with many of the features in Parliament Buildings having symbolic reference. One example of this detail can be illustrated by the length of the building for it measures exactly 365 feet wide, representative of one foot for each day of the earth year. Much of the interior of Parliament Buildings is constructed from marble. The Great Hall is made entirely from Italian travertine marble. The meteor missile that hit it vaporised this magnificent building and the surrounding area in a nano second.

To the south the President elect official residence is the Áras an Uachtaráin, a beautiful building constructed in 1780. It has ninety-two roomed and is located in the Phoenix Park in Dublin. That too was hit by a small but destructive meteor missile.

The Interplanetary Universal Congress had for hundreds of years knew of terra. The planet had been scanned and mapped on numerous occasions. As its civilisations developed, radio and television broadcasts were occasionally monitored. From these broadcasts, Interplanetary Universal Congress linguists toiled, trying to decipherer the numerous and sometimes complex languages. The main reason for this was it was hoped that in the future terra would become part of Interplanetary Universal Congress. For that to happen, the Interplanetary Universal Congress would have to have some insight into the homo sapien species culture, their strengths and weaknesses.

In the Interplanetary Universal Congress opinion, one of their major weaknesses was too many multi governments, monarchs, leaders and dictators. Again to the Interplanetary Universal Congress this was what was called the 'large tribal stage'. To destroy the will of each Homo Sapien, all you had to do was destroy their cultural heritage, tribal leaders and their habitats. And that what the meteor missiles were doing.

On terra, large tribes of Homo sapiens live in area's known as continents. A continent is one of several very large landmasses on Terra/Earth. They are (from largest in size to smallest): Asia, Africa, North America, South America, Antarctica, Europe, and Australia. Each continents heads of governments, monarchs, leaders and dictators meetings places, home land security/Intelligence gathering buildings, palaces and homes were targeted and destroyed.

As the meteor missiles fell on terra the battle ship Chela and three other Interplanetary Universal Congress battleships had closely being monitoring their progress.

Captain Obersani requested an immediate update on the distribution of the Propofol gas from his number one.

"Everything is as planned." replied the number one. He continued;

"Sensors show all air breathing species on terra's surface are now unconscious."

For the first time since his battle ship was conscripted into this small fleet, Captain Obersani felt a twang of excitement.

> "Excellent", he said. "I will contact the other three battle ship's captains and move the fleet into terra's orbit. Have all landing parties standing by, once we establish orbit, I want my crew to be the first to put down on terra's surface."

The number one replied enthusiastically;

> "Captain, the crew are drilled and ready."

In earth's time, it took ten minutes for the four Interplanetary Universal Congress battle ships to move from the opposite side of the moon into earth's orbit. Once there, the battle ship Chela immediately launched hundreds of shuttle crafts. The three other Interplanetary Universal Congress battle ships were a little more cautious and held back until they determined it was safe. To them and Captain Obersani and his crew, the thoughts of a trilo-raptor trap were still relevant. However, as reports came in that the Chela's ground crews had landed safely thousands more shuttle crafts followed and the invasion of the earth began!

Each shuttle craft had a tactical destination; some put down and had to make safe the thousands of military, navy and air force bases and installations on terra. This was not an easy job as the Homo sapiens had billions of weapons that range from bladed weapons, simple guns that fire multiple bullets, short and long range missiles, numerous lethal gas and biological weapons, laser blasters and at the other end of a gigantic scale, atom bombs!

Anything that had nuclear capabilities was taboo for Interplanetary Universal Congress. In the history of the universe, hundreds of species had at some stage developed nuclear energy but, it had been to their detriment. Countess wars and horrendous accidents had happened that had but only one outcome, billions dead and in most cases the destruction of that species planet! Terra was heading down this destructive path, the planet was already scarred with nuclear tests sites and it had hundreds of nuclear energy plants dotted around its globe, some of them had already malfunctioned, making large areas uninhabitable for decades. Others were so unstable; a complete meltdown was just around the corner!

The Interplanetary Universal Congress landing teams would have deactivate them, this was a perilous job but one that had been tackled numerous times before. They would isolate and contain the reactors in a special force fields designed for this, each reactor would then be transported into space where it would be released and allowed to fall into the suns gravitational field, the sun would then naturally consume the nuclear reactors.

Another problematic area was the numerous nuclear and other power driven submarines, they had their own onboard life support systems, and this caused a problem as the Propofol gas had not affected them. Initially they were dealt with, with a gravity containment field. This was fired directly at the submarines; the field gradually adjusted the gravity within the field pulling the vessel towards the sea bed. Once anchored, the submarines were cut with high powered precision lasers into pieces and the reactors and nuclear missiles removed for disposal. As too the crew, they would be killed in the process but, that seemed a small price to pay.

Another portion of shuttle crafts had to deal with the global installation of the uni-net. This was another task the Interplanetary Universal Congress had dealt with many billions of times. The uni-net technicians from the previous failed mission had already set up a relay of uni-satellites that spanned from terra to its closest hub on Gliese 581 d approximately twenty light-years away. So the hardest task the uni-net landing teams technicians had to do was implant the uni-net into over 8 billion homo sapiens brains on the planet terra.

While these numbers sound daunting, the actual installation task itself was down to uni-bots. The uni-bots resemble a female mosquito; they fly at speeds of up to 241.39 kilometres per hour (150 miles per hour). They are genetically engineered, being part organic and part android. Each uni-bot is programmed to seek out the recipient life force, in this case Homo sapiens. Each uni-bot has a micro laser injection system and has a pay load that can inject one hundred individuals. The pay load is uni-nanomites: once injected into the recipient's blood stream, the uni-nanomites make their way to the synaptic brain pathways and build from bottom up the uni-link device. Once they complete the installation, they then attach themselves to the device for future upgrades and maintenance.

One upgrade that was going to be installed was the overlords disintegration sub programme, just like the rest of the Interplanetary Universal Congress, the Homo sapiens were to have a link to their synaptic brain and neurological receptors, if they failed to submit to the overloads demands, they too would have their brains vaporised!

At strategic points, the uni-technicians released one billion uni-bots across terra's globe, it was estimated that they would have injected the whole population within a couple of earth days! In fact, this was such a fast and reliable system, with small modifications, whole Interplanetary Universal Congress populations can be treated for the control and extermination of infectious diseases. Sadly, the uni-bots were not originally developed for the good of the Interplanetary Universal Congress; they were used as mass air born assassins!

While the uni-bots sought out their recipients, the uni-technicians busied themselves setting up the pre-fabricated buildings to house their uni-net super computers and other essential uni-net equipment. When constructed, the two hundred metre wide and sixty meters high uni-net buildings are domed in shape and have an ultra smooth bomb proof exterior that is made from a modified form of titanium. The uni-net domes are all fortified with ten multi directional/pulse adjustable, graviton pulse cannons. Each cannon can fire a graviton pulse as small as ten millimetres and as wide as one metre, they are one hundred percent accurate, with a kill range of 8.04672 kilometres (5 miles). With a little forethought, it was also decided that as the Homo sapiens were a warring species, each dome will have one hundred elite Interplanetary Universal Congress guards on duty around terra's clock.

Another assignment for the uni-technicians was installation of public uni-net display screens. The screens are made of two films bonded together, the first of a transparent synthetic polymer that is roughly 0.5 mils, or 12.5 microns, thick, the same thickness of cling film. The second film is the same thickness and is a transparent self repairing organic polymer film that has superb micro electrical and conducting qualities; this is impregnated with billions of super compressed crystallised argon and plasma particles that produce a stunning 3840×2160 resolution in 3D. When charged, each crystal reverberates and acts as a micro speaker, as there are billions the sound quality is superb.

Screens come in rolls, ten metres wide and have two hundred metres of screen on each roll. The uni-net technicians just unrolls the desired length from its packing box, cut the length with the serrated edge tool provide in the lid of the packing box, peel off a thin backing film to reveal a super self adhesive backing and then, carefully places the screen onto the chosen area. Once positioned, the technician's attach the all in one micro computer, sender, receiver and power cell; they then run diagnostic tests to see if everything is working and if satisfied, set the anti-tamper device and then move on to the next installation.

With all of the screens installed the uni-net technicians set about their final task before the Propofol gas wears off and the Homo sapiens wake up is, setting up thousands of virtual meeting arenas. This was another task that had been done hundreds of thousands of times before and one that the uni-net super computers handle. A basic template is always used and the arena can hold a comfortable one hundred thousand beings, all the uni-net technicians add is the specie specifics. In this case, to show total dominance, they reset the arena's parameters to an uncomfortable five hundred thousand! And each homo sapien would enter as white cube, with have no vocal input. This was done so all they can do is listen and obey!

CHAPTER 11

A New Day

When you gas over eight billion Homo sapiens with Propofol gas, the affects are almost instant. Normally after seven days the affects start to wear off, some would recover quickly; others would wake a day or so later and would feel drowsy for days. This however was not normal; it was the waking from a content slumber into a living nightmare.

One thing that would become instantly apparent to every being on the planet terra was, what was, was no more. Each individual had prior to the gassing been going around doing their normal daily business, now as they woke from their enforced sleep they were surrounded by death and devastation!

Those in transit in the various modes of transport on the planet were the hardest hit. Across the globe, millions of motorised vehicle accidents had happened; killing many thousands instantaneously. Others again totalling hundreds of thousands could have lived but died because they did not receive immediate medical treatment. Those who were lucky enough to have survived this motorised bloodbath, with mild or no injuries, were not so lucky, they lived and had to witness the reality of the mangled wreckage of bodies and vehicles left.

It is estimated that during day light hours 100.000 air planes are in the skies globally around terra. At night these numbers fall to approximately 35.000. Aeroplanes vary immensely in size and that reflects on how many crew and passengers would be on board. As terra's atmosphere filled with Propofol gas, these airborne Homo sapiens were to be added to the number of instant fatalities. Quite simply, the air craft's fell from the sky, but they didn't just kill those on board, these airplanes were scattered across the worlds skies so while some crashed into mountains or into the sea, the majority plummeted into highly populated areas!

Earth's total land mass is 148,939,063.133 km2 (57,505,693.767 sq mi) which is about 29.2% of its total surface. Water covers approximately 70.8% of the Earth's surface. Like many evolving specie, the Homo sapiens were curious. Over two thousand earth years ago they looked at these vast expanses of water and wondered to what lay beyond the horizon, so these early pioneers built boats. The first were crude and made primarily wood although reed, bark and animal skins were also used. But over a period of time they became master boat builders, now they have millions of splendid wood, metal, fibre glass and carbon vessels. The scale and size of these is astonishing, cruise liners can be 360 metres (1,181 ft) long and 72 m (236 ft) above the water line and can have up to 6,300 passengers. Commercial ones, like an oil tanker, can be 380.00 m (1,246.72 ft) long, with an average 275,000 gross tonnage. Container and bulk vessels can be even longer at 397.71 m (1,304.8 ft). At the other end of the scale there are many hundreds of thousands, perhaps millions of pleasure boats. They too can vary in size, and if you are wealthy they can be extremely grand or if your pockets are not so deep, fairly basic.

As there are so many vessels, globally certain seaways are extremely busy. The Straits of Dover is the busiest international seaway in the world. In just one earth day, the straits are used by over four hundred commercial vessels. On the day the Propofol gas was dispersed into terra's atmosphere, the shipping lanes of the world were as normal, very busy! Now after seven days, the waking Homo sapiens were stunned by the maritime devastation.

With their engines still running and the crew's unconscious at the helms, oil tankers had run aground; their hulls had split wide open, spilling their precious cargo. This black liquid gold had swamped numerous coastal waters and river estuaries, the ecological catastrophe it brought would remain for many decades to come.

Out at sea and especially in the narrow straits of Dover and other major seaways, numerous gigantic tankers, container and bulk carrying vessels had smashed into each other. As metal tore through metal, there hulls split, spilling out thousands of gallons of inflammable diesel fuel, as it ignited, it set fire to the cargo. Now all that could be seen as one looked globally around the oceans and seaways were a raging watery inferno. Before this watery cataclysm happened, the crews of these blazing hellholes were mercifully unconscious from the affects of the Propofol gas. The heat was so intense, that their bodies were burnt to cinders!

While deaths were high from these tragedies, the main maritime fatalities came from the cruise liners. These towering giants of the seas had either run aground and capsized, or had collided with other sea fairing vessels, The outcome was catastrophic, on the capsized liners the unconscious passengers that had been trapped below the waterline as the indoor areas, restaurants and cabins flooded with water, they had drowned instantaneously. As fires swept through the decks above the waterlines other helpless victims had been burnt to death. But out of all the maritime accidents brought about by the Propofol gas a large proportion of these cruise liners that had collided, had now sunk, taking the passengers and crew members to a watery grave.

On the subject of watery graves, others who died this way were all those enjoying swimming in the sea, outdoor, indoor pools or in one of the hundreds of lakes and rivers on the planet. This may not sound like it might total many but when you tote the figures up globally, the body count fell into several thousand!

Homo sapiens or as they call themselves human beings have been in existence on the planet they know as earth (terra) for about 200,000 years. Over that period, natural climatic changes have happened. In present time, the humans believe that the current climatic changes are due to their planetary interference. Their populations have swelled to every corner of the planet. To feed these billions, they have had to cultivate vast areas that were once great forests. There demand for minerals, ores, coals and fuels and numerous other material possessions have been enormous. It would be fair to say they, like many species in their universe, have raped the hell out of their own planet.

Now with the stratospheric ozone layer damaged, staying out in the sun for any length of time is considered harmful to the human's skin. Those that had visited one of the thousands of beaches dotted around earth's coasts, or were doing a spot of sunbathing seven days ago, were now waking up seven days later with third degree burns!

Humans are a member of a species of bipedal primates in the family Hominidae. Everyone on earth (terra) is a homo sapiens. This is Latin for the term, "wise human". As humans, they have a highly developed brain, a bipedal gait, and opposable thumbs.

While they have highly developed brains, on the day of the awakening, all humans were in a traumatised state. It was difficult to take in all what had and is happening. Trying to comprehend all the disasters that they had woke to was one thing, but seeing alien beings and their crafts around their planet was almost beyond belief!

Captain Obersani knew that first contact with new species was difficult; the first contact protocols rules were simple. Establish contact by simple non threatening codes and messages and then gradually over time exchange information on your own specie, that way you can build a mutual non threatening relationship. Face to face contact would only be used after all basic protocols had been used and each of the species knew what the other looked like.

Captain Obersani allowed his mind to ponder on the various species the humans would encounter.

The first was his own but, perhaps he was a little biased a he thought all arthropods from the planet takaashigani were the most handsome creatures in the universe. Most stand a little over six metres tall, with a leg span of over sixteen metres from claw to claw. There chelipeds are a minimum of two metres long and they have orange, with white spots along the legs.

But then he reflected;

> "While I might see my own specie as beautiful, we will probably terrify the humans."

But then another thought hit him;

> "Wait until they see the quzzzuzzz, serpent species, from the planet quzzzuzzz. At fifteen metres long, massive fangs and eight, two metre long tentacles, and they too can be intimidating and extremely frightening."

Captain Obersani mind was now having a full debate;

> "Humans have seen ants before, but not a few hundred that are winged, one metre tall and have the tale of a scorpion that discharges a blast of highly concentrated formic acid that would melt the human skins!"

He paused, for what started as a sobering thought;

> "The humans would not see these immediately, on the day of the awakening they were the elite soldiers that stand guard around the uni-net installation buildings'. But he thought they would eventually have to come face to face with these highly intelligent ants. Would they appreciate that these early pioneers had set up colonies on numerous Interplanetary Universal Congress planets? No he doubted it. What they would see was, ferocious, genetically enhanced soldier ants with orders to kill all humans on sight!"

> "Try to think positively." he said out loud. Obersani then thought;

> "The humans like technology; the uni-net is highly advanced technology and with the uni-net language translators online, they can now converse with all humans. That's good."

But then a big negative thought came into his head.

> "Would they want to converse with Interplanetary Universal Congress members who have just invaded their planet and particularly the uni-net technicians who had planted the device in their heads, the Amozo's.?

Each Interplanetary Universal Congress planet has its own Uni-net technicians but for this mission, the Amozo's were chosen for their size, speed and agility

Obersani physically shuddered and continued with his thoughts;

> 'They will hate us all but, when they see the Amozo's, who could like a giant twenty metre long black legged, centipede? Their reaction will be worse when they find they are carnivorous, eat large mammals and then discover that, the modified claws called forcipules which curve around their heads and can deliver venom into their prey."

His thoughts now hit an all time low;

> "The venom of these Amozo's is extremely potent and contains acetylcholine, histamine and serotonin (pain mediators), proteases and a cardiodepressant factor. Bites are painful to most Interplanetary Universal Congress specie and cause severe swelling, chills, fever, and weakness. For humans the bites are likely to be fatal!"

Captain Obersani thoughts were disturbed by his second in command;

> "Captain, you have an urgent uni-net call from Admiral Zissiani."

The captain answered immediately;

> "How can I help you Admiral Zissiani?"

> "Are the homo sapiens waking up?" the admiral inquired.

"Yes, some are coming around as we speak." the captain replied.

"Captain Obersani, I have been ordered by the overlord to make first contact with the Homo sapiens via the uni-net display screens. To this end, I have recorded a brief communication. I have attached this in a file to you, have the uni-net technicians upload it immediately and then play it on a constant loop for the next twenty four earth hours."

Captain Obersani did not hesitate with his reply;

"I will do it immediately."

And with that Admiral Zissiani ended her call.

Within a few moments the uni-net had uploaded Admiral Zissiani file and it was then broadcast to the entire planet earth.

Without any fanfare, Admiral Zissiani appeared in her fully scaled, blue and silver admiral uniform, she looked cool, calm and collected and above all, completely menacing to her human audience as her message began;

"Human beings of the planet earth, I am Admiral Zissiani of the Interplanetary Universal Congress. On the order of the overlord of this universe, seven of your earth days ago, four of the Interplanetary Universal Congress battle ships began a plan to conquer your planet. That plan has now been implemented. You like all Interplanetary Universal Congress planets and the beings that reside on them are now slaves to the overlord.

Over the seven day period that you have been unconscious, your military capabilities have been neutralised. Key buildings and government installations have been destroyed.

Each human being has also had a device planted into the base of your brains. The device will be activated shortly and will give you access to the uni-net. The uni-net is similar to the internet but this one connects you to the whole universe.

As like all Interplanetary Universal Congress planet members, that totals trillions of beings. The uni-net device we and you have also has a hidden disintegration sub programme in your synaptic brain and neurological receptors. This can be detonated at my will, causing your brains to be vaporised completely!

I cannot emphasise enough how fruitless it will be if you try to defy the overlord. Defiance will only bring death to you and many others!

Your orders for now are; Sort out what needs to be sorted and then go or stay at home and wait for the interface uni-net links to be turned on. You will then be given your next orders."

With that the communication ended. It was then continually repeated for the next twenty four of earth's hours.

Throughout the universe, the thought of slavery to most civilised being is unacceptable, so within a few earth minutes of the first broadcast, the humans were already beginning to protest. At first, it was just individual rumbles. Then, though the media, land and mobile phones and the internet, the humans of earth had united in to one voice, and that voice began to fill the city streets, towns and squares around the world.

The first line of protest was to attack the uni-net monitors. This however was fruitless, as each monitor had an anti-tamper device with its own AI built into its system. Any objects thrown at the monitors were automatically deflected by an electrical force field. The same energy source then fired a small but effective bolt of electricity at the attacker or attackers. Should the attacks continue the onboard AI would increase the bolt power each time by a percentage factor of ten.

Captain Obersani and the other three battle fleet captains had been monitoring the situation carefully. After a short uni-net meeting it was agreed that Admiral Zissiani should be contacted for clarification on how to handle the human's uprisings.

Her response was immediate and precise; use non lethal force for the first twelve earth hours and thereafter, lethal force!

All four battleships captains had already anticipated Admiral Zissiani response and each had five hundred drone attack crafts on standby. The one metre in diameter attack craft were designed to be used in space and planetary atmospheres. For stealth, they have a mirrored pearlescent outer skin that allows them to blend almost invisibly with their surroundings.

The orders were given, and two thousand drone attack crafts were launched into earth upper atmosphere. It only took a few earth minutes for these silent, super fast and highly manoeuvrable craft to deliver the non lethal weapons.

Tiananmen Square in Beijing was the meeting place for thousands of protesters, this hostile crowd were thrown into utter confusion by the fact that moments earlier they were all standing and chanting 'Out with all aliens, the Earth is ours,' and now they were all slipping and sliding on the floor. Across the other side of the world the same was happing in Trafalgar Square London. Zero friction silicon had been sprayed into both squares.

In the Main Market Square (Rynek Główny) in the Old Town in Kraków, Poland and in the Zócalo Square Mexico the story was completely different. The thousands of protesters were now all vomiting violently. They had been sprayed with highly pungent odour; the foul smelling odour would last for days and could only be removed by a special chemical detergent.

Although the Vatican had been destroyed, crowds still gathered at Saint Peter's Square. They and the crowds at the Plaza Mayor Madrid Spain and Times Square, U.S.A were treated with a spray of Lysergic acid diethylamide, abbreviated LSD or LSD-25. A psychedelic drug, whose primary action is to alter cognition and perception and induce hallucinations! Each individual reacted differently to this drug, for some they were walking around in a blissful haze while others were living their worst nightmares!

Despite the Interplanetary Universal Congress use of non lethal weapons, the twelfth hour deadline was looming and crowds were still forming. The humans had not calmed down; to the contrary their chanting had now turned to too full blown rioting! Vehicles and building where been set alight, looting and robberies were taking place globally and in some cases they were attacking their own people. It was now time for lethal force!

The drone attack crafts swooped in once more, this time individually targeting thousands of humans. The results were horrendous, thousands lay dying or dead. Those who were witness to this began to screamed uncontrollably, the carcases of the victims lay motionless, their entire skeleton had been removed, all two hundred and six bones in their human bodies has been vaporised! Death this way for countless humans was not instant; the hearts of the victims were still beating. Their brains cognitive ability was still functioning and some still could see though their eyes but, they could move. Eventually they would all die but for some, this long death was not over yet.

It was the Amozo's and the quzzzuzzz, serpent specie, who had developed this gruesome weapon. As both species are carnivorous, it is easier on the digestive system to remove the bones of your prey before you swallow it whole! The weapon uses an ultra sonic wave that is tuned to the same frequencies as the outer surface of bone is called the periosteum and the many inner layers called cancellous. As the ultra sonic wave hits the bones, it atomises them.

The Interplanetary Universal Congress had seen planetary riots before; and in their dark past protesters were subject to all kinds of abuse; they were captured, horrendously tortured and sometimes Killed. This all changed with the introduction of the Universal convention, the rules state all specie had a right to protest. In the case of the humans and with the Interplanetary Universal Congress member's lives at risk for the overlord, the rule book was thrown away.

As a further shock tactic to stun the rebellious humans into submission, the drone attack crafts swooped in again. Several chained grappling hooks shot out from each craft, their razor sharp hooks tore into the flesh of the boneless dead or dying. With the carcasses snagged, they were dragged around the major cities, squares, roads and streets. As the flaccid skins of the humans made contact with the abrasive concrete, tarmac surfaces and obstacles they struck, they became shredded into small bloodied fragments. By any species standards, defiling a body in such a way is classed as deplorable. As shameless as it was, it did the job.

Within one hour of this attack, the squares had emptied, the cities centres became ghost towns. For the first time in human history, all of humanity wept as they watched their fellow humans being callously de-boned and then torn apart. Humanity now cowered behind locked doors with their spirits completely broken.

Sadly, for a few, the horror wasn't over yet. While the humans were fleeing for their lives' both the Amozo's and the quzzzuzzz used the terror and confusion to snatch a few live de-boned humans. In both cultures, live food was far better than dead. However, to eat live food in this day and age was unspeakable as it did not fit in with Interplanetary Universal Congress ideology. But on this day, the boundaries of what is civilised had been crossed. In the total madness that surrounded them, who cared? So they openly gorged themselves on the live humans!

Over the next few hours earth's humans did exactly as they were told. They stayed indoors and waited patiently but apprehensively for the next phase, the turning on of their personal interface uni-net device.

The interfaces turn on required every human being on the planet to register and set up a virtual account. Statistically getting almost eight billion humans to register all at once is unworkable. The interface turn on was further complication by the humans one or more children. The parents had to register for each juvenile family member and then the child's interface uni-net link would automatically turn on. While the registration process sounds complicated, it is as easy as thinking. Each human is notified mentally that the uni-net link is active. It then pops a series of simple questions into the recipients mind, name, address, date of birth and if they have any children they then supply the same information. The human answers each question by thought, each answer is verified by the uni-net computers and with all the information supplied and the registration is complete and an account is opened.

Uni-net technicians had completed planetary interfaces turn on hundreds of times before. So, in order for the uni-net turn on to be smooth and not to overload the uni-net computers, the uni-nets technicians stuck to the same logical geographical rule, The teams closest to the planets north and south poles start first, then geographically uni-net teams worked their way inward until the last turn on was done along the planets equatorial line.

Remarkably within twelve earth hours all human uni-net interfaces were active and Admiral Zissiani was advised that all was ready for the overlord. She immediately contacted him and was taken by surprised at his enthusiasm.

> "Admiral Zissiani, you have done an excellent job. Congratulate the terra fleet for me; you must be extremely proud of them". He stated in a loud but almost sincere way."

> "Oh", she said stumbling for words. "I am, I am, and I will, of course."

> "Good, now I must address the homo sapiens."

> "Overlord, may I make a suggestion." Admiral Zissiani said gingerly.

> "Go ahead."

> "In your address it might be a good idea to call the Homo sapiens human beings, they like that title."

Even as she said it, she thought,

"Oh no, you should have kept your mouth shut."

But it was too late. With a roar, the overlord replied;

"I already knew that."

Then his tone changed and he sounded calm;

"But you have a point; they will be more receptive if I speak to them as human being."

The overlord ended the uni-net call ended but Admiral Zissiani stayed online as she wanted to hear firsthand what the overlord plans were for the humans.

As for the humans, the uni-net call came for them all to assemble in their various virtual uni-net arenas. This was a new experience for the humans but as they started to amass into their designated virtual arenas, they began to realise that there were far too many of them for the area provide. This resulted in them instantly having virtual claustrophobia. Out of frustration they tried to jostle and push each other but as there virtual avatar was a square cube, they just ended up jamming each other tighter together. In some parts of the arena the white cubes were now stacked up five high! Another frustrating factor was they could not communicate with each other. Inside each humans head, they were screaming, shouting and cursing at the other cubes but, inside the virtual arena there was nothing but silence.

After what seemed like hours, that silence was broken as the overlord began to speak. In his normal style, he opened to speech by bellowing;

"Human beings of the planet earth!"

This made everyone jump. There was then a full earth minutes pause before he continued;

"I am the overlord of this universe. You and all being of this universe are my slaves!"

Again, he paused but came back with the same gusto;

"The lives you once lived are over, now you will live or die for me!"

There was another timely pause; then he continued;

"It has already been pointed out to you that installed in the base of your brains is a device that I can activate to kill you. Test me or any of the Interplanetary Universal Congress forces and you will see your family, friends and thousands die. Finally I will kill you!

Your governments, leaders, military and many of the building they once use have been neutralised and destroyed."

His tone changed and there was enthusiasm in his voice;

"This is a new age, a new beginning for you. The human race does not have any need for governments or leaders. As I intend to rule your planet!

Any government leaders, monarchs, religious leaders and their families that have survived until now, have just been killed!"

In every virtual arena, virtual screens flashed on displaying these people just dropping dead, their brains had been vaporised! The screens stayed on as he continued to speak;

"All financial institutes will cease trading immediately. In the new order, individual wealth will be of no importance.

Human beings, your world needs fixing, under my guidance, the Interplanetary Universal Congress will help you rebuild it.

But more importantly, you the human race needs fixing. You as a race are physically and mentally weak and prone to all manner of illnesses. I will instruct the uni-net technicians to send out uni-bots with a super vaccine that will destroy most of your common illnesses. However, lots of illnesses are self inflicted! To eradicate these, all junk food, cigarettes, alcohol and the social use of drugs is banned immediately. Anyone seen or caught using these banned food or substances will be killed instantly!

Adults will not be able to have babies without official approval; a virtual global department will be set up for this, initially this will be managed by the Interplanetary Universal Congress. Further, all new born humans of the future will be genetically enhanced, to this end, a long term genetic re-programming will begin. Any children born without official approval will be killed along with their parents!"

In the overlord's normal abrupt way, he yelled;

"Now, go!"

CHAPTER 12

Human Vessels

As a race, humanity formed several different views on the overlord's speech. Some declared him a modern deity who has come to cleanse the earth of corruption and all sinners. Other's thought he was a reincarnated oppressor of their dark past, Adolf Hitler. For most however, who just wanted to live, they just accepted this was now the way.

Admiral Zissiani had been listening closely to the overlord's speech, her first thoughts were;

> "He's as cunning as a quzzzuzzz fox, all this talk and he still has hasn't revealed anything about himself or his actual interest in these Homo sapiens."

At that, Admiral Zissiani had a uni-net call from the overlord. He began;

> "Admiral Zissiani, you have heard my speech to the humans. For the time being, I am putting Captain Obersani in charge of terra's operations. He will put into operation my instructions. Give him the good news; also inform him if he fails me, Obersani, his family and the terra fleet will die.

> My primary assignment for the captain is to select five hundred male and five hundred female humans. Each must be twenty earth years old, be in extremely good health and have a good family medical history of health and longevity. I want this done now!"

On the issue of the human selection, Admiral Zissiani had what she thought was several essential questions but, before she could open her mouth, she was cut off! All she could do was convey the *"good news"* to Captain Obersani and let him know of his new mission.

Captain Obersani was first and foremost a soldier, so he did not deliberate on his new promotion or orders; he just got the job done. He contacted an organisation on earth known as the world health organisation at its headquarters in Geneva, Switzerland and told them they have six earth hours to select the suitable human candidates or they would all die!

His next priority was to contact the uni-net technicians to see if they had started the human vaccination program and was pleased to hear that this had already been done. He was advised that it was in fact normal procedure for all new contacts to be super vaccinated. It stopped the transmission of viruses and any other nasty bugs to Interplanetary Universal Congress personnel.

Arthropods like Captain Obersani from the planet takaashigani found it difficult to understand why the humans would take substances that they could become addicted too and put their personal health at jeopardy? But as he browsed at earth's internet, he realised that the humans were not only killing themselves they were also paying multinational companies and certain unscrupulous individual's large amounts of money for the privilege!

Obersani decided that the only way to conform with the overlords orders to eradicate the problem was to destroy the cigarettes, alcohol and drugs at it source. He quickly gathered the information and co-ordinances he needed on the crop sites, production factories and laboratories, and then without hesitation, he ordered his and the three other Interplanetary Universal Congress battleships to use a few surplus guided meteor missiles to destroy them.

Satisfied that two major tasks had now been dealt with, Captain Obersani thought it was time to chase up the progress on the one thousand humans. He again contacted the world health organisation.

Within moments of his call he was astonished to find that they had not only selected one thousand humans, they had chosen them from different places on earth and sorted then into race, IQ, education and had all medical reports at hand. He thought;

> 'They are sending their young into the unknown and maybe to their death. It's amazing what they will do to save their own lives'.

But then another thought jumped into his head, one that he did not like;

> "Look at what you are now doing to live, and how low the mighty Captain Obersani has stooped on his eight legs."

Throwing that thought aside, he contacted Admiral Zissiani and gave her a full update on his progress. She in turn contacted the overlord with the news of the one thousand humans.

In an uncommon jovial tone, the overlord stated;

> "Well, this is indeed excellent news, have their uni-net ID's and particulars sent straight to me."

The details were sent within seconds and the overlord; he immediately summoned the one thousand to a special virtual assembly chamber that he had been designed for this occasion. Security was extremely tight; to enter the main chamber, each virtual human had to go through a ten security doors that took them to one of ten inner chambers. It was a slow process but each door and inner chamber was a virtual fire wall and antivirus scanner. As each entrant went through each door, they had to answer some basic random questions like; uni-net ID, Christian and Maiden name, exams past and what school they attended. Each virtual human was then scanned and allowed to move to the next door.

As each person entered the main chamber they paused as the lighting was exceptionally dim. In this eerie environment they could not see the shape of the chamber, nor could they see if there were any seats or obstacles that they might trip over. What made it worse was the total silence. So each person literally groped around in the dark. With all one thousand assembled the ceiling, walls and floor suddenly light up to a brilliant white. This caused a moment of alarm but then the lighting changed to an agreeable sky blue. As the one thousand eyes adjusted they could see raised beds all around the edges of the chamber. A voice seems to surround them and said;

> "Please do not be alarmed, in an orderly manner make your way to one of the beds and lie down."

What they did not realise was that the beds were highly sophisticated physical and neurological scanners that was linked to a virtual super computer. All one thousand did as the voice commanded; as they lay down, each bed then did a preliminary scan of its subject. In a calm way, the voice then said;

> "Relax and look at the ceiling, various virtual objects will appear all you have to do is mentally recognise them. As you see the objects, try to remember everything about that object. If it is a tree, flower or plant, try to picture where you have seen it. Then let your mind sense its smell and texture and if edible its taste."

To everyone's delight, the first virtual flower everyone viewed was a single red rose; to help stimulate the brains neuron network that helps store and retrieve memory, the aroma of roses was added. Immediately the humans began to recall roses in bloom in the spring and summer months. But then other memories began to emerge, ones of romance, Valentine 's Day, birthdays and that of love ones. Some also visualised rain, water, plant food and those who have a thorny experience, blood and pain.

Different flowers stirred different memories to each individual but when a wreath was shown the general memory consensus was one of sadness. Each person began to remember a loved one that had passed away, the funeral and the grief suffered.

Before the one thousand became to melancholy, the voice then interrupted their thoughts;

> "You have all done well, clear your minds; the next range of objects is food."

And with that a large chocolate cake appeared. On earth chocolate is one of nature's most concentrated sources of theobromine, a mild, natural stimulant. The group had mixed mental reactions, some wished they could eat this delicious delight and mentally started to crave for the taste of chocolate. Other's instantly thought of the consequences of eating rich food, far too many calories and putting on weight. Then as the brains unmyelinated fibres linked more neurons, more thoughts came into their heads. The thought of chocolate had stirred up thoughts of their childhood, the birthday's parties they had had and then the brands of chocolate they either favoured or disliked.

Give or take a few million, the human brain consists of about one billion neurons. Each neuron forms about one thousand connections to other neurons, amounting to more than a trillion connections. The next virtual item certainly light up a large sections of the brains neurons.

A large cow grazing in a field was presented to the captive audience. Within seconds, the cows head exploded! To help stimulate the cerebral neurons and as many memories and mental reactions as possible, all one thousand were simultaneously spattered with virtual cow brains! The virtual picture then changed to an abattoir, where the cow was sliced into joints. As the saws cut through the cow's carcass, virtual blood, flesh and fat spayed out onto the now shocked and disgusted onlookers. Finally, everything disappeared, and then there was a faint smell of cooking and slowly a large juicy cooked steak materialised.

It was already known that the cerebral cortex is where the information processing takes place and that it plays a key role in memory, attention, perceptual awareness, thought, language, and consciousness. However what was required was to pinpoint the exact points where past and present memories and emotions are stored. It was a lengthy process that took over twelve earth hours but at the end of this the overlord virtual super computer had all the information it required.

Its next procedure was extremely delicate, the super computer had to remove the human memories, neuron by neuron and replace them with the overlord own peoples neural memories. In the first instance, each of the one thousands uni-nets hidden disintegration sub programmes had to be disabled. A highly complex coded disarm command was sent to the uni-nanomites and within a nanosecond all devices were deactivated. Now that the recipients brains would not exploded, the super computer started the eraser and upload programme, it would be a long process that required the bare minimum brain activity so all one thousand were heavily sedated.

CHAPTER 13

Help Me!

While the one thousand humans slept, in another part of the universe one of their fellow humans being was just beginning to wake up.

Dr Elaine Laurence started to wake up but felt drowsy; all she wanted to do was go back to sleep but, a not too distant noise keep repeating it's self? She forced her eyes open but the brightness of what seemed like sunlight stunned her eyes. She clenched her eyes closed and then so that her eyes would adjust to the light, gradually opened them. To her amazement she was on a beach, the noise she could hear were the waves gently lapping onto the shore.

As she was lying on stomach, she reached out with both arms to push herself up but was stunned to see that both her arms and hands were covered in a hard nut coloured material that she could not identify? Although she was an intelligent woman and a medical doctor her mind could not grasp what had happened. She began to panic, with her heart racing; she quickly checked the rest of her body and found that every inch of her body was covered in the same hard nut coloured material. Hoping that it would tear or rip, she clawed at the material but it was hopeless, the substance seemed to be her skin!

In a blind panic, Elaine ran to the water's edge and tried frantically to wash this hideous skin covering away but as she tossed the salted water over her face and head she realised that she no hair! She carefully ran her fingers over her bare scalp, dropped to her knees and then began to sob! As she sobbed, she began to repeat the same words;

"Help! please help me!"

At first the words were just a mumble but then the mumble steadily got louder and louder until they became a hysterical roar but, no one came, Dr Elaine Laurence was alone!

Despite the fact that Dr Elaine Laurence's solitude was an enforced one, Captain Obersani decided he needed to get away from the hustle and bustle of life onboard a battleship for a few earth days. His chosen place for his solitude was earths Mariana Trench in the western Pacific Ocean. He had read that because of its depth 10.91 kilometres (6.78 miles) (35,800 ft) and with a water pressure of 1,086 bars (15,750 psi) it was virtually unexplored by the humans. But for him, a six metre tall arthropod from the planet takaashigani it would be a peaceful walk in the park.

Obersani ordered ones of his battleship shuttles to fly him to the east of the Mariana Islands. From there they travelled along the 2,550 kilometres (1,580 miles) long trench until they reached its deepest point and then as the shuttle hovered two metres over the ocean, Obersani took the plunge and gradually descended 10.91 kilometres (6.78 miles) (35,800 ft) to the bottom.

Even for an arthropod of his size the descent was slow, but he was in no rush. While travelling in space has its merits, for Obersani there was nothing finer than being back in his natural habitat, the sea. Obersani hadn't eaten a good meal for days so one of the things on his agenda was food and in this environment the menu was definitely to his liking. He like all arthropods are detrivores, they will consume dead or alive fish and animals as well as plant matter (algae, etc.). Obersani jovially thought to himself;

"I had better not eat too much or I might not be able to swim back to the surface."

As Obersani approach the sea bed he felt something hit his back legs, as he turned around his back legs floated passed him, they had been cut off! Before he had time to react, the same happened to too his other four legs and his chelipeds. Obersani main body dropped onto the sea bed, dying and in agony Obersani looked up to see a trilo-raptor. The triloraptor was clad from head to toe in obsidian-black metallic trilo-combat uniform and at his side was the razor sharp lethal weapon, the trilo-tron!

Being a true soldier and battleship captain, Obersani's dying thoughts were too try to alert the Interplanetary Universal Congress and his small fleet of the triloraptor earthly presence. This however proved fruitless as his uni-net link was not working? In deaths grip he lay helpless but then the full magnitude of this situation hit home. Just metres from where he lay, the triloraptor enormous battleship turn off its holographic field and launched four trilo-missiles. Obersani instinctively knew the missiles targets, the four Interplanetary Universal Congress battleships. He did not see them exploded or see their debris fall from the sky; Captain Obersani never wanted to die in space, he died where all arthropods from the planet takaashigani should die, at sea.

The launching of the four trilo-missiles was not a random attack; it was indeed part of a highly covert and well executed offensive by the triloraptors. The triloraptor trilo-craft had used the destruction of earth's space stations and satellites to covertly enter the planet's atmosphere. It then dived into the depths of the Pacific Ocean and used a proton energy beam to cut a rift half a kilometre wide the sea bed. It then lower its self into the rift and used its holographic technology to make the rift look as Mariana Trench had looked for hundreds of thousands of years.

Being experts predators, the triloraptors knew that the Interplanetary Universal Congress battleships would return and ultimately conquer the planet terra. What the Interplanetary Universal Congress battleships would not expect was for the triloraptors to counter attack from the sea below! All they had to do was wait and with the excitement of was to come, killing, they were in triloraptor heaven.

At precisely the same time as the four trilo-missiles hit their targets, numerous electric magnetic missiles struck every earth uni-net installation. All of the uni-net supercomputers were instantly destroyed along with uni-net earth. These E.M Missiles had been fired from another triloraptor trilo-craft. This one had been stealthily hiding in the 8046.72 metres (5 miles) deep South Pole-Aitken basin crater on earth's moon. This is the biggest and deepest crater on the Moon, an abyss that could engulf earths United States from the East Coast through Texas.

Before the triloraptors destroyed earth's uni-net computers, the moons hidden triloraptor trilo-craft had been carefully monitoring all uni-net activity. It wasn't long before they discovered the overlord's virtual program. While their own onboard ships computer was not powerful enough to crack the ten layered fire wall, they felt confident that given time, their mother ships trilo-super computer would be able to do this. So they utilised a ghost cloning programme to replicate each virtual fire wall and its central chamber. For security all this data was backed up and then sent onto the mother ship.

Approximately twenty light-years away from earth a third triloraptor trilo-craft had been waiting patiently for the signal to attack. It too had used its holographic technology to invisibly hid it's self, this time as an asteroid. At the synchronized time its missiles struck and destroyed the major uni-net hub close to the planet Gliese 581 d. Without a nano second to lose the triloraptor trilo-craft raced towards earth, its mission on route was destroy all the uni-net satellites.

As soon as the humans witnessed the destruction of the Interplanetary Universal Congress battleships and uni-net installations they began to rebel. They turned out into the cities, towns and streets in their thousands. The fortunate ones had small hand guns and knew how to make petrol bombs however, most had to make do with just the bricks and stones they tore up from the road surfaces, kerbs and paving's. Irrespective of what weapon or weapons the humans had, each fought courageously.

From the onset of earth's occupation those who had been in a position of power and were fortunate to be still alive had been planning a serious of strategic revolts. To this end they had hidden away some serious weaponry, they saw themselves as the saviours of the earth and were the new revolutionary armies of the planet earth, for them, it was now time to go to war!

As like the triloraptors, the earthlings took the Interplanetary Universal Congress ground forces by surprise and in numerous bloody battles, the humans individually or in small armies slowly began to take back their planet.

Without any encouragement from the triloraptors and with the full co-operation of the World Health Authorities, the 'one thousand' selected humans were immediately rounded up for debriefing and if need be some 'military' interrogation! Within a few earth hours they has all been transported and were all held in a specially made area at Guantanamo Bay detention camp, Cuba.

The de-briefings and interrogations started immediately. What was found was a little startling, most if not all of their basic human memories had been wiped, they could not recall their names, parents names, home address's, schools they had attended and most of earlier life experiences. What they could recall was faint but similar memories of another person's identity that could only come from one place, an extraterrestrial race!

Each of the one thousand was instantly deemed as a threat to the planets global security and in view of what had happened on the planet earth over the last few weeks they were also classed as extremely hostile aliens.

Although the governments of the earth were in disarray, a unilateral agreement was signed by the joint chiefs of all the armed forces on the planet earth that all one thousand should be promptly executed! It was also agreed that the executions be made to look as if the invading forces from Interplanetary Universal Congress had been mentally and genetically experimenting on the one thousand and these experiments had gone disastrously wrong! As a result of these failed experiments, the Interplanetary Universal Congress then took all one thousand brave earthlings and callously executed them!

Had the triloraptor had time, they would have truly loved to have taken part in the executions one thousand humans. And being triloraptors they would have been very creative in the way they killed them. However, for the time being the triloraptors had achieved their earthly goals and now it was time to move on to their next objective.

CHAPTER 14

Rage And Vile Mood

Five earth minutes ago the overlord was feeling ecstatic; he was on the threshold of his life's ambition. Now he was in a rage and totally frustrated, his plans were in shreds and he had one thing on his mind retribution! He immediately contacted Admiral Zissiani;

> "Zissiani, he yelled, 'what has happened on terra? What has happened to my one thousand humans?"

Admiral Zissiani had only a moment ago been informed by uni-technicians that the uni-net from the planet Gliese 581 d to terra had gone down. She had also tried to contact Captain Obersani but communications to all four Interplanetary Universal Congress battleships had been severed. She replied;

> "Overlord, I suspect the triloraptors have destroyed terra's uni-net link. Further, I have not been able to contact the four Interplanetary Universal Congress battleships; I therefore believe that they have been destroyed. Overlord with communications down, I have no idea what has happened to the one thousand humans."

This news just compounded the overlord's vile mood, he screamed;

> "Zissiani, mark my words, I want all triloraptors dead! This deed will be done within the next five rotations of your planet or I will kill everyone within the Interplanetary Universal Congress!"

At that, he severed his uni-net call.

For Admiral Zissiani, she knew how volatile the overlord was; since this nightmare began, she had been living one rotation of her planet at a time. So for her, five rotations was a nice extension, but she had quickly calculated it may not be enough time to save the Quzzzuzzzian's and Interplanetary Universal Congress!

With no time to lose, using a secure communication band that is used only by the Quzzzuzzzian's, Admiral Zissiani contacted both the cobrasant's and viperious captains, her commands were precise and to the point;

> "I want you both to desist in your present mission. Your new mission is to head at maximum speed to terra's solar system.
>
> On route and when you arrive, do not engage the triloraptors.
>
> You must not use the uni-net for any communications and when you arrive at terra's solar system you must use your cloaking technology.
>
> Do not contact me until you both arrive at the outer edge of terra' solar system.
>
> Only use the Quzzzuzzzian secure band. I will give you your next orders."

At that she ended her message.

The Cobrasant and viperious changed course immediately. They had calculated that if they travel at ten gravitons it would take two of their planets rotations to reach terra's solar system however, the new orders stated at full speed. It was now time to put their new graviton engines to the test.

The highest speed ever reached by any Interplanetary Universal Congress vessel was ten gravitons; both vessels reached ten gravitons with ease. In a joint agreement both the Cobrasant and viperious increased acceleration a graviton at a time and then carried out a system check to see if all was running smooth, the new engines performed amazingly. At an astonishing fifteen gravitons both captains made the decision not accelerate any faster, the engines seemed to have endless power and structurally both ships were in great shape. The problem was there long range sensors had detected three triloraptor battleships and they were approaching terra's solar system and would need at least a half rotation of their planets to de-accelerate.

As soon as the Cobrasant and viperious reached the edge of terra's solar system they engaged their cloaking devise. Together captains then opened the Quzzzuzzzian secure band contacted Admiral Zissiani. Both captains could not contain their excitement and informed Admiral Zissiani of their speed achievement.

> "Congratulations, she replied. 'This is a fantastic achievement for all Quzzzuzzzian's and when the time is right you; your crew and all concerned will be officially congratulated. However for the time being this is a covert operation.

> Your orders for now are is to turn off your cloaking devices. There are three triloraptor battleships close to your location; they will be in contact with you. You are under direct orders from me to do exactly as they ask."

At that, Admiral Zissiani ended the call.

Within a few Quzzzuzzzian minutes the three triloraptor battleships came into view. A message came in over the Quzzzuzzzian secure band, it was the triloraptors! The message was short and to the point;

> "Cobrasant and viperious, we are sending over two shuttle crafts, prepare to be boarded."

The Captains couldn't believe this; they and the Interplanetary Universal Congress were at war with the triloraptors! They, the Quzzzuzzzian's had the best two battleships in the Interplanetary Universal Congress.

And, and this was a big and, they, using Quzzzuzzzian's technology were the only Interplanetary Universal Congress battleships that had destroyed some of the triloraptors trilo-ships. They huffed and puffed but as they were under direct orders from Admiral Zissiani had to concede and replied;

> "Triloraptor trilo-crafts, we are ready to be boarded and are under direct orders from Admiral Zissiani to co-operate fully."

Both the Cobrasant and viperious kept the Quzzzuzzzian secure band open and waited for a response from the triloraptors but, the triloraptors did not reply. After what seemed like an eternity, the Cobrasant and viperious scanners picked up the two trilo-shuttle crafts the heading towards them. They did not request docking information; they just flew straight into the docking bays and without a word, ten combat clad triloraptors exited each of their shuttle crafts. In silence and un-escorted they marched up to the ships bridge, there they were greeted by the ships captains; each captain repeated his orders from Admiral Zissiani and this time on each battleship one of the triloraptors spoke;

> "We require access to your computer data base, the schematics for your gravitons engines, cloaking device and your G.R.I.M missiles.
>
> You will then take us on a tour of the engine room and armoury!"

After that was said, the triloraptors shuttle teams never uttered another word. They didn't have to; through their visors, each triloraptor was interconnected to each other and all were interconnected to the battleship central computer. As they viewed the data bases of the Cobrasant and viperious and inspected their engine rooms and armouries all information was automatically upload the battleships central computer, this information was then sent to the triloraptors mother ships trilo-super computer. In all, the whole affair lasted less than one Quzzzuzzzian hour and then as abruptly as they arrived, the triloraptors left.

With the two trilo-shuttle craft back on board there trilo-craft, another triloraptor message was sent;

"Cobrasant and viperious, you will proceed towards the planet terra and take up the co-ordinances sent. We shall all convene around terra."

All the Cobrasant and viperious could do was, comply. It only took fifteen Quzzzuzzzian minutes for all five battleships to assemble at their allocated co-ordinances. Then another triloraptor message was sent, this one really stunned the captain and crew of the Cobrasant and viperious.

"Cobrasant and viperious, you have in your armoury several hundred pressure bomb missiles. Arm all your pressure bomb missiles. Confirm when they are armed."

Jointly, both captains feared the worse but again complied. Each captain independently replied and asked the same question;

"This is the Captain of the Cobrasant, pressure bomb missiles are armed. What is their designated target?"

"This is the Captain of the Viperious; all pressure bomb missiles are armed. What is their designated target?"

The triloraptors replied promptly;

"Cobrasant on our order, you will fire on the targets; San Andreas Fault, San Jacinto Fault Zone-United States West Coast (California). Calaveras Fault-United States West Coast-California, Chixoy-Polochic Fault-Central America. Motagua Fault-Central America.

Viperious on our order, you will fire on the targets; Itoigawa-Shizuoka-Japan. North Anatolian Fault-Turkey. Liquine-Ofqui Fault-Chile. Macquarie Fault Zone-Pacific Ocean from New Zealand to Indonesia. Chaman Fault-Pakistan and Afghanistan."

A mutual rage engulfed the Cobrasant and Viperious captains! They were not just being asked to destroy a civilised race that had already undergone several horrendous ordeals at the hand of the Interplanetary Universal Congress and triloraptors; there action would also tear the planet terra apart killing all life on the planet! It was the Cobrasant captain who spoke first:

"Triloraptors, I am sure I speak for both the Cobrasant and Viperious. We will not fire on these defenceless beings."

It only took the triloraptor a moment to reply;

"Cobrasant and Viperious, your orders from Admiral Zissiani are your orders. If for any reason you do not carry out these orders, we have authorization from Admiral Zissiani to destroy you!"

That really put the cat amongst the pigeons; a verbal response was quickly fired back from the Cobrasant captain;

"Triloraptors, as you are aware, we have G.R.I.M missiles. If, on your part there are any signs of aggression, we will use them!"

At that, to show the triloraptors that this was not idle talk, the captain ordered his weaponry sergeant to arm all G.R.I.M missiles and target the three trilo-crafts. In a show of solidarity the Viperious captain did the same.

The weaponry sergeants of both the Cobrasant and Viperious came back with the same response;

"Captains, the G.R.I.M missiles are off line! Our weapons security protocols and weapon commands have been overridden!"

"Triloraptors," hissed the Cobrasant captain.

"Agreed," responded the Viperious captain. He continued;

"In the interests of our ships and crew's safety, I think it time to withdraw before thing get worse,"

"That's a positive yes from me."

The Cobrasant and Viperious captains then commanded their first officers to set a course out of terra's solar system as fast as possible. Within moments the first officers of both the Cobrasant and Viperious came back with the same response;

"Captains, the graviton engines are off line! All our security protocols and engine commands have been overridden!"

'Triloraptors,' hissed both captains!

"How is this possible?" The Viperious captain inquired.

With disdain, the Cobrasant replied;

"They accessed our computers when we allowed them to board our vessels, from there; they uploaded all our security protocols and systems commands. Now we are at their mercy!"

It would seem that Cobrasant and Viperious were not the only ones at the mercy of the triloraptors. Over one third of the triloraptor fleet had converged around Interplanetary Universal Congress planets and had started to attack them. The Slugtonians were the first Interplanetary Universal Congress planet to feel the wrath of the triloraptors. To their detriment, they like all Interplanetary Universal Congress planets had sent all of their battleships and troops to either engage the triloraptors main fleet or to the planet Notus. The Slugtonians high council sent out a uni-net word distress message to Admiral Zissiani, it read;

"Admiral Zissiani, we are under heavy attack from the triloraptors. We have limited weapons and resources and cannot hold out much longer, please send re-enforcements as soon as possible."

Using the uni-net virtual conference facility, Admiral Zissiani tried to respond to the distress call but there was no uni-net connection. She immediately ordered the uni-net technicians to investigate the problem. After a quick but meticulous systems analysis, the head of uni-net for Quzzzuzzzian came back to her;

"Admiral Zissiani, our analysis has shown that the Slugtonians uni-net system is and has been completely off line for some time. I would speculate that all uni-net satellites and uni-net installations have been severely damaged or destroyed. At present, the Slugtonians have no way of contacting us and we have no way of contacting them."

Admiral Zissiani inquired;

"Do we have a backup system?"

"No." The head uni-net technician replied. "As you are aware, the uni-net has been our main source of communications for many years. We and the Interplanetary Universal Congress have grown to rely solely on this."

Admiral Zissiani asked another pertinent question;

"How quickly can you re-install a uni-net system for the Slugtonians?"

"If we had all the resources at hand, it would take fourteen rotations of our planet". "But", the uni-net technician went on to explain, "It would be suicide to go near the Slugtonians planet with the triloraptors in the vicinity."

Again Admiral Zissiani asked another relevant question;

"A few hundreds of Quzzzuzzzian years ago, long range communications were done through a hyper channel, are any of those systems still in functional?"

There was a pause before the head uni-net technician replied;

"I have heard of this but it was well before my time Admiral. I will have to investigate this and get back to you."

He paused again;

"Just a thought Admiral, the triloraptors have a unique system that allows them to constantly communicate with their fleet, mother ship and each other but we have never bothered to examine their technology."

Before Admiral Zissiani could finish her discussion with the uni-net technician another emergency call came in;

"Admiral Zissiani the Takaashigani Empire is under attack from the triloraptors! We have no option, we are immediately recalling all of our battleships and . . . . !

The uni-net call ended abruptly! Over the next few Quzzzuzzzian hours, Admiral Zissiani had several similar uni-net calls that all ended the same way.

CHAPTER 15

Notus

Notus is situated at one of the furthest galaxies in the universe and therefore it is believed to be one of the oldest. To reach this galaxy known as primus one, it took the Interplanetary Universal Congress fleet designated to this part of the mission fifteen rotations of the Quzzzuzzzian planet. Now many of them had been ordered to do a u-turn and head back at top speed to their own planets as quickly as possible. As many of the vessels were in close proximity of Notus, the Interplanetary Universal Congress leaders decided to hedge their bets with the overlord and drop off the one billion troops, land, air craft's and munitions in readiness for the impending ground battle with the triloraptors.

Proportionately, Notus is the largest of the life bearing planets in the known universe. Its actual mass is five hundred times bigger than terra. Two thirds of this giant planet is covered by water with fifteen massive oceans and three hundred and thirty nine seas. Life has flourished on the giant for over a billion years but, as there has been no evidence of intelligent life and its remoteness, the Interplanetary Universal Congress, they never took much notice of this planet.

To determine the best landing points the Interplanetary Universal Congress's fleet used their long range scanners. However this proved problematic as the scanners could not give out accurate readings due to a massive solar storm that had started too erupted from the solar systems star. Solar storms of this magnitude are quit common especially when you consider the star itself known as Saulė Majoris is a Interplanetary Universal Congress class O. Class O stars are rare, very hot and shine with a power of over a million times of a G2 star like terra's sun. Saulė Majoris is veritable giant compared with terra's sun; it is approximately 1,500 times larger!

Saulė Majoris solar system is again gigantic compared with terra's solar system. It has ten planets, five inner terrestrial planets and then five super gas giants that make up the outer planets. It also has an assortment of comets composed largely of volatile ices. On the outer limits of the solar system, there is a vast asteroid belt that also contains at least five dwarf planets. The asteroids in this enormous belt vary vastly in size, some are just one metre in diameter but others exceed one hundred kilometres in diameter. While some of these asteroids are composed of frozen volatiles, others are primarily composed of rock and metal.

For a single vessel, navigation through such asteroid belts is normally not a problem but, as the fleet had hundreds of vessels, it was left to the onboard computers to work on the safest routes and then let the computers autopilots guide the fleet ships safely through this labyrinth of ice, rock and metal.

It only took a few moments for all the Interplanetary Universal Congress fleets computers to come back with the same conclusions. They could not find a safe passage through the asteroid belt; this was due to high magnetic fields being omitted from the asteroids composed of various metals.

Each computer illustrated that the metallic asteroids were being charged by high energy particles from the solar storm, making them a positive pole. Although each Interplanetary Universal Congress's fleet vessel was been bombarded with the same particles, the exteriors of each ship was registering as a negative pole? If they tried to navigate through the magnetised asteroids, they would risk the metallic asteroids being attracted to them and then automatically crashing into them! While the smaller ones would just bounce off them, the larger ones could crush them!

In a general consensus of opinion, the Interplanetary Universal Congress's fleet captains decided that they did not have time to solve this magnetic puzzle, so they just backed off, armed there neutron and proton cannons, and blasted a safe passage through the asteroid belt!

It only took half a Quzzzuzzzian hour for all of the Interplanetary Universal Congress's fleet to pass to safely through the asteroid belt. Without any time to spare, they charted the fastest route towards Notus. These new bearings brought them close to the first of the gas giants in the Saulė Majoris solar system. It was at this point that some of the older vessels experienced a major problem, they were been pulled severely off course.

The problem was immediately identified and blamed on the age of these vessels. Most of the older vessels hulls were made from a metal alloy and that had now been coated with a layer of negative high energy particles from the powerful solar storm. The gas giant causing this problem is known as G-G1. G-G1 is a cold hydrogen-rich gas giant but has a liquid metal core. The fleets heading was crossing the cores magnetic pole on its positive side and that was pulling these older vessels off course.

Before changing course, the vessels affected by these phenomena ran a quick computer simulation of their path to Notus. It was found that two of the other gas giants and two of the inner terrestrial planets would also cause similar problems! In fact, these other planets magnets poles were hundreds of times more powerful than G-G1.To continue on the same heading could be disastrous, the worst case scenario shown on their computer simulations was that they could be pulled so far off course and into the planets atmospheres, their they would have with no hope of escape!. Frustrated but not defeated, a new route was charted; the only problem was it would take several more Quzzzuzzzian hours to get to Notus.

Dr Elaine Laurence decided that feeling sorry for herself was not the answer to her problems. She got herself up from the water's edge and started to explore her surroundings. The beach was long and flat but she could see in the distance some large sand dunes, she spoke out aloud to herself;

> "Elaine, that looks like a good vantage point to see from, get yourself over there and let's see what you can see from the top."

Elaine started to sprinted across the sand but then realised she was running at quite a fast speed, she continued to sprint and commented to herself;

> "Wow girl, when you get home you'd better get into the Olympic team!"

She increased her pace and found she could accelerated and accelerate. She had no idea how fast she was running but within less than a minute she found herself on the edge of the dunes. She looked back to the sea shore but then realised it was several miles away!

Being a medical doctor Elaine automatically reached for her wrist pulse to check her heart rate but with her new had exterior skin she could not feel anything. Without thinking, she laughed out loud but then realised that while her mouth could open and close, she hadn't got any facial muscles to smile. She commented to herself;

> "Elaine you and this day are getting stranger and stranger."

The sand dunes in front of Elaine were just over fourteen metres high and for some reason that Elaine could not explain she just felt inclined to jump up the sand dune, to her amazement she did it in one leap!

> "Bloody hell" she yelled, "I must have turned into some kind of super grass hopper."

Elaine nearly jumped out of her new skin as a voice said;

> "Not a grass hopper."

Shocked but trying to rationalise just what happened, Doctor Elaine Laurence scanned the area but could not see anyone. She said out loud;

"Dam it Elaine, now you are hearing voices, get to grips with yourself!"

"You are not hearing voices." the voice replied.

Despite trying to compose herself, Elaine was again taken aback by the voice, with a tremor in her voice, she called out;

"Where are you? I can't see you."

"You are standing on me." the voice replied.

Well that was it for Elaine, that revelation literally bold her backwards. She was so shocked; she lost her footing and tumbled down the sand dune!

The voice inquired;

"Are you alright?"

Slightly embarrassed, Elaine stood up and said;

"Yes, I'm fine."

But then looked around to see who was talking to her, again she could not see anyone.

"Look," she said, "you are scarring the hell out of me, show yourself."

"Sorry to frighten, you are standing on me, I am in underneath you!"

Puzzled Elaine looked, but all she could see was a sand dune in front of her and sand under her feet? She knew it sounded stupid but she had to say it;

"You are the sand?"

"No, you are on the planet Notus and I and the planet are one."

Elaine could not comprehend this strange explanation as in her mind she was on earth! Annoyed by this foolish reply, Elaine said;

"What are you talking about, this is earth."

"Elaine" the voice replied; "You are not of this planet. You are from the planet terra, known as earth. A race known as triloraptors dropped you onto this beach."

Elaine's legs seemed to buckle under her and she sat with a thump on the sand. Tiers swelled in her eyes. Her mind was racing but none of what she heard made any sense.

"Elaine, I know you are upset and what you have just heard has come as a great shock to you. But it is all true."

The voice paused for a moment and then spoke gently:

"Would you like me to leave you alone for a while, we can talk later."

Wiping the tears from her eyes, Elaine said sobbing;

"Please, don't leave me."

She then started to shake, trembling she said;

"I'm frightened and confused."

Compassionately the voice replied;

"Of course I will stay with you, my name is Notus."

Crying and trying to laugh at the same time, Elaine replied;

"Hi Notus."

Then Elaine inquired;

"Are you really part of the planet?"

"Yes" Notice replied, "As I already said, I and the planet are one."

Still puzzled by Notus's answer, Elaine asked another question that in her mind she thought was foolish, but she had to ask;

"Are you some kind of deity or God?"

From Elaine prospective and all that had happened to her, Notus could under why she asked this question. Without sounding condescending Notice replied;

"I am not God or any kind of God; I am just the same as you, a living being."

Elaine took a few moments to look up at the sky, then beach she was on and the distant sea. She then inhaled the fresh sea air and said:

"Notus, that's a bit of an understatement. I have only seen this beach on this planet, but from where I am sitting, it looks beautiful. I don't understand how you and the planet are one. I have no idea how you can communicate with me. In fact, I have millions of questions in my head."

Notus interrupted her;

"Elaine, let me try to answer one question at a time. I can communicate with you because I open a door in your mind that has allowed you to become a telepath; Telepathy is the way I communicate. The conversations you and I are having can only heard by you. I also had to explore your mind and extract the words your race use for communication."

Elaine dint say anything, she just thought her response;

"So I really don't have to talk a reply, I could just think it?"

Notus laughed and replied;

"Just like what you have done."

Excited by this, Elaine telepathically said;

"Wow, that's cool. Now that's out of the way, I know this is vane but, could you explain what had happened to my skin and what is this hard nut coloured material?"

Notus could feel Elaine was starting to mentally relax and replied;

"You are not of this planet and the sun here compared on terra is very powerful. I had to change your DNA structure to an adaptive DNA; your body can now adapt too many different environments. If I left you as you were, you would have possibly died from sun burn or heat exhaustion. You body core can only cope with temperatures up to 40 C (104 F). The air temperature on the beach is 60 C (140 F) and rising. With your new skin, your core temperature will remain a healthy 37.0 °C (98.6 °F) and it will not burn in the sun."

As a medical doctor, Elaine had listened intensely to what Notus had said, she commented;

"You have the ability to change a living persons DNA, Wow! What did you base my new skin on?"

Almost embarrassed, Notus said;

"The sand ants, like the ones running up and down the dune. They have been living in this hot environment for over a million years."

Elaine looks around her and could see numerous little ants with a hard nut coloured exoskeleton. She scoop one up, examined for a moment and said out loud;

> "Hello little ant, I'm Elaine, I'm not a grass hopper but I could be your Ant-tee."

Spontaneously, she and Notus began to laugh. Once the laughter subsided, Elaine asked another telepathic question;

> "Notus what is adaptive DNA?"

Drolly, Notus replied;

> "To put it in a nut shell . . . . no pun intended. If an environment or situation puts you in danger, you can change physical form so that you survive."

> "So" Elaine said, "I am no longer human."

Notus paused and then responded;

> "You are what you want to be but as a species you are new. Perhaps a 'Newman being' instead of human being."

Elaine laughed at this and thought;

> "Notus you have a wicked sense of humour."

Chuckling Notus said;

> "I do indeed but, when you are as old as I am you need one."

Elaine enquired;

> "How old are you?"

"That's a good question," Notus replied, "your home planet earth or as I know it terra is about 4.54 billion years old, I was around to see it borne. I was also living when this solar system and planets were being formed, that's a little over eight billion years. Before that I was living in another universe and I and another planet were at one for over ten billion years."

Shocked by this revelation, Elaine gasped and said;

"Oh my god, you are over twenty two billion years old."

Notus began to laugh and said;

"I am over twenty two billion years young . . . . and a bit more."

Elaine laughed but Notus had made her curious, she asked;

"You said you were at one with another planet before this one and it was in another universe. What happened to the planet and the universe you were in and why did you come to this one?"

Sounding like a school teacher, Notus replied;

"So many questions but I shall try to answer them. The existence of my specie is dominated by us searching out a solar system that is just forming and the individually moulding that system so planets like your earth or the planet Notus can the flourish. It is not just a matter of finding such a planet, it is then a long process that can take at least a billion years to stabilise that planet. Once a planet is stabilised it can them start to support aerobic organisms. At present, on Notus and earth there are over one million different life forms.

A planet life expectancy will depend on its star, most stars remain stable for about seven to ten billion years and then they start to get old, as they get old they start to expand and become red giants. It is at that point of time that all life on the planet will has ceased and sadly this is where we say our goodbyes and also depart. That is what happened to my last planet."

Notus paused. Elaine could telepathically feel a genuine sadness in Notus.

"Are you ok?" she inquired.

Quietly Notus said;

"Yes, I still feel sad when I think of my last planet. We were at one for a long time."

Bouncing back, Notus said;

"I shall continue with my answers to your questions.

The universe I travelled from is still there, it is quite old and universally established."

Notus asked a question;

"Have heard of the goldilocks zone or the circumstellar habitable zone, abbreviated CHZ?"

"Yes," Elaine replied. "They are one and the same; CHZ is a zone that is classed as a habitable zone around a star. Theory has it that if a planet is in this zone and has the right atmospheric pressure to maintain liquid water then it could support life."

Notus answered back in teacher mode;

"That's a good answer, ten out of ten."

Trying not to be to pretentious, Notus continued;

"Although CHZ it is not a theory, it is a fact. As you are aware there are trillions of stars in a universe but only a few fit into the goldilocks zone. I spent millions of years in the other universe searching for another new solar system that would support a potential planet that would ultimately have life on it. With no luck, I decided to look further afield and came to this one. Within a short period of time, that is a few million years, I found this system and the rest is history."

Telepathically Elaine said;

"Notus, I think you missed out a few billion years of this planets evolution. I take it that when you find a system it is in an infantile state, possibly just gas, metal and rock. How do you and it join together and then what happens?"

Elaine could feel Notus was pleased with her latest questions. Enthusiastically Notus replied;

"Infantile is an understatement, when I arrive it is total chaos! The systems star has just formed and its gravity has begun to gather the left over gas and dust into small clumps. Before these small clumps form into a protoplanetary disks, I select the one that fits into the goldilocks zone and enter into its nucleus.

My own species have several unique abilities, one of them is being able to attract or repel gases and dust particles. My first objective is to help create a solid inner core that contains iron and nickel. As this is forming, gravity is already present and starts to compress this. The temperatures at the centre of the core can be as high as 9500 K, that's hotter than the surface of Notus's Sun!

Gravity and I now work hand in hand; together we begin to attract material to form an outer core. The outer core is composed of iron mixed with nickel and trace amounts of lighter elements. The outer core naturally liquefies as it comes into contact with the extremely hot inner core. At this stage large quantities of other gases, dust particles, ice and debris are also drawn in and can be counterproductive to the cores creation, so

I drive back what is not needed and delicately hold the what is needed in the protoplanet outer disc, some of this material will be used later for the planet's primordial atmosphere.

Now comes the difficult part, to hold the outer core in place, a mantle needs to be composed. The depth of the mantle can vary and this depends on the overall size of the planet. On terra the mantle is about 3,000km on Notus it is 6,000km. The mantle is made of silicate rocks that are rich in iron and magnesium. Again, I help attract these metals and rocks and until the mantle is stabilised, I help hold the mantle in place.

On the top of the mantle a crust is formed from an assortment of metals and rocks. The metals are iron, magnesium and aluminium and the rocks are silicate rocks, like basalt and granite.

The crust can range in a depth of 5 to 150km and is very volatile. Because of it size and the area it covers, it naturally forms into several areas that are known as tectonic plates. If allowed, these plates can slide and reshape vast areas of the surface of the planet. Although this is a natural planetary process, I do my best to try to hold them together and try to minimise the effect there movements have on the surface."

Notus paused for a moment so that Elaine could absorb this part of the protoplanetary jigsaw puzzle. Notus inquired;

"Are you Ok so far?"

"Oh yes," Elaine replied enthusiastically; "this is fascinating, please continue."

"Ok", Notus said, "the next part is the formation of the planet's atmosphere. You must appreciate that this did not start happen until the planets crust was formed and even then it was in a primordial state. The planet was still very hot and the atmosphere at that was mostly made up of hydrogen and helium. I helped to cool the planet by attracting hundreds of thousands of small to medium ice asteroids into the upper atmosphere; they melted upon entry, raining down H_2O (water) and other organic compounds onto the hot planet surface, eventually the planet's surface began to cool and fundamental changes began.

The lighter gases, the hydrogen and helium were drawn into the exosphere and most of these gases drift off into space. On the surface, vast amounts of gases were being produced from high volcanic activity, these gases began to dominate the lower atmosphere, they are; H_2O (water) as steam, carbon dioxide (CO_2), and ammonia (NH_3). The steam from this and my melted ice contribution started to form dense clouds and consequently it began to rain. As the rain cascaded down, it began to pool into the lower land levels of the planets crust, and this started to form the earlier oceans and seas.

High levels of carbon dioxide (CO_2) were present but as the rain was globally torrential, it forced the (CO_2) into the seas and oceans where it was dissolved. In due course, a simple form of bacteria developed that could live on energy from the Sun and carbon dioxide in the water. Now this is the exciting bit, this bacterium produces large amounts of oxygen as a waste product. As a consequence, oxygen levels begin to build up in the atmosphere and aerobic life forms begin to develop. I then monitor the evolution of these life forms and from time to time give them a little DNA nudge to help them develop to their full potential".

"Wow and double wow" Elaine said breathlessly. "That is one fantastic account of the evolution of Notus. Could I ask you another question?"

"Of course." Notus replied.

"Does your specie help and become one with all planets that fit into the goldilocks zone?"

"Not all. Sometimes we arrive too late and cannot join with the inner core and sadly these planets have great difficulty in producing aerobic life forms."

Notus knew that Elaine was now thinking about her own planet Earth and continued;

"Earth or terra as I know it has one of my specie in its core; in fact terra is one of my offspring's."

Almost gasping, Elaine verbally said;

"You have children".

With pride of a parent Notus said;

"We do not give birth as you do, I and my specie do not have a gender as you do, and we also do not have to seek a mate. It is rare for us to have offspring's but under the right conditions we do produce offspring's. One of those conditions is moving from one universe to another.

That is why I was hesitant to move, however, shortly after I entered this universe, I had several offspring's, terra being one of them."

Notus continued in a more sombre mode;

"You may have heard of this; four and a half billion years ago when terra was quite young another juvenile planet named Theia collided with terra. The collision almost killed terra but my little offspring was strong, I think you would say 'a chip off the old block' but now Elaine terra is under threat of destruction from forces far stronger than a rogue planet!"

For Elaine this had been a true roller coaster of a day but this latest revelation truly stunned her. Before she could think or say anything Notus continued;

"Elaine, I am sorry to have to burden you but there is more; one of my offspring's, Olotinium has recently been killed and I am about to be invaded by a massive force!"

Elaine was overcome with anger, she had been torn from her planet, turned into a 'newman' and now her planet earth was going to be destroyed!

"Notus," Elaine irately declared; "from what you have told me, you and your specie must be the most powerful in every universe! Surely you can and your kind can stop this

Notus knew it would be hard for Elaine to comprehend and answered;

"I understand how you feel, I too feel angry. The forces we are encountering have over many thousands of years developed into highly intelligent beings. In some case their intellect is equal to mine. What they have also development is weapons of mass destruction; these weapons are so powerful they can tear apart whole planets and obliterate stars!"

Calming down a little, Elaine verbally asked;

"Did one of these weapons kill Olotinium?"

With distain Notus said;

"Not one Elaine, several hundred thousand of these despicable things. It was a callous attack that not only killed Olotinium; they also killed several billion of a species known as Olotinium's and all other life forms on this planet!

Elaine had only one question;

"Why"

Notus felt Elaine needed and full explanation and said;

"In this case, it was a show of power and to gain dominance. The specie behind this heartless act lives in another universe, and their universe is classed as a micro-verse. Many years ago this micro-verse was vibrant and full of life. Now thanks to one species that is dominated by a malevolent but super intelligent being called the 'Overlord', this micro-verse is almost barren of life. His plans are now to conquer this universe, enslave all intelligent beings and re-colonise it with his own specie!

To re-colonise his species, the overlord has had to overcome some major obstacles, the first two being comparative size and distance. The overlord's universe is only the size of an almost flat one metre balloon but, everything in it is proportioned to fit, just as we fit into this one.

To overcome these factors, ingeniously, the overlord used a serious of microscopic wormhole; these micro-wormholes are portals that link one universe to another universe. They can also link vast amounts of space together, for example if you enter a micro-wormholes in one part of space, you will exit maybe millions if not billions of light years away!

The problem is they are very unstable, but the overlord overcame this with a substance known as R.I.T.S, (robomatic inter transdimensional substance). He used R.I.T.S to stabilise both ends of the microscopic wormholes. Once stabilised and tested, he manufactured micro-shuttle pods out of the R.I.T.S and sent an army of atom sized nano-bots from his universe to this universe. This army was virtually undetectable as atoms in the overlord's universe are approximately one million times smaller than they are in this one!

Some of these atom sized nano-bots were programmed to infiltrate a universal communications system known as the uni-net, this is similar to the internet you have on earth, but on a much grander scale.

Once the nano-bots gained access to the uni-net, they reprogrammed a device known as a uni-link; the re-programming placed a hidden disintegration sub programme in the uni-links root directory. This device is connected to the brains synaptic pathways of billions and billions of beings that are part of the Interplanetary Universal Congress. Once re-programmed, the overlord used this uni-net device to conquer almost all of the intelligent life forms in this universe!

Resistance was something the overlord had planned for, he used several hundred thousand atom sized nuclear armed nano-bots to attach themselves to the core the planet Olotinium. Sadly, these atoms were so tiny, Olotinium did not notice them. When the Interplanetary Universal Congress refused his demands to become his slaves, he detonated the nuclear nano-bots!"

Elaine mind was in a spin, she closed her eyes and words like, micro-universes, overlords, microscopic wormholes, atom sized nano-bots, Interplanetary Universal Congress and robomatic inter transdimensional substances filled her head. Without thinking she blurted out;

"What a bloody mess!"

Even with her medical training, trying to compose her mind was difficult but one thought did come in;

"What has the planet earth got to do with this?"

Notus picked up on this thought immediately and answered;

"The overlord species DNA is identical to your homo sapiens DNA. I believe he wanted to use your physical bodies, erase your minds and replace them with his own people consciousness."

Now, Notus began to elaborate;

As I have pointed out the overlord is a genius; proportionally his universes population are microscopic compared with yours. But he wants to re-programme your brains neuron by neuron and replace them with the overlord own peoples neural memories, he is going to do this with the aid of a super computer, highly sophisticated software and the uni net communications system!

Elaine, under direct orders from the overlord, several earth days ago your planet earth has been conquered by an invasion force from the Interplanetary Universal Congress. Your people were globally rendered unconscious; this was done by introducing a gas called Propofol into terra's atmosphere. When they were all unconscious, the uni-net device was installed by uni-bots into every human being"! In addition, they all now have the hidden disintegration sub programme connected to their brains synaptic pathways!"

Notus waited for Elaine's response but all emotions and words had been drained from her. She just sat, starring into thin air.

Trying to cheer her up, Notus said;

"Elaine, I know all what I have told you is bad but, all is not lost, the universal tides are about to turn."

CHAPTER 16

Cobrasant And Viperious

Although a few earth hours had past, both the Cobrasant and Viperious were still furious at their predicament. With no engines and the G.R.I.M missiles of line they were sitting ducks! Rather than do nothing and face possible destruction from the trilo-raptors, they had instructed their technical teams to work on a solution to this problem.

The Viperious weaponry sergeant called directly though to the ship's captain;

> "Captain, we have a serious problem, I have been trying to get the G.R.I.M's back online and they have started to malfunction!"

The captain was in no mood for indecisive statements, he yelled back;

> "Malfunction, what in name of a Quzzzuzzzian do you mean by that?"

With a panic in his voice he replied;

> "Captain they have just armed themselves, we have only a ten Quzzzuzzzian minute before they detonate!"

Before the Viperious captain could reply, a SOS call came in from the Cobrasant;

"Captain, our G.R.I.Ms seem to have mysteriously armed themselves and we have no way of disarming them. We are about to engage emergency protocols to abandon ship."

Now calm and decisive the Viperious captain replied;

"Captain of the Cobrasant, it seems that we are in the same position, have you contacted the triloraptors for assistance?"

"Captain of the Viperious, an SOS has been sent out on all channels. I would recommend you abandon ship as soon as possible."

Without hesitation the Viperious captain gave the order to abandon ship. He and his crew then made a hasty but orderly exit to the life pods. Each life pod held twenty Quzzzuzzzian's. As the last Quzzzuzzzian strapped itself in, the life pods jettisoned themselves away from their mother ship at one fiftieth of a graviton. This however was not fast enough to escape the blasts from the G.R.I.M missiles and numerous other weapons onboard both the Viperious and the Cobrasant. As sturdy and as robust as the life pods were, they were no match for the shock waves they felt, they were colossal! Inevitably, numerous life pods were severely damaged and as for their occupants, the only chance for survival was a rescue mission from the triloraptors or a return to the planet terra where they would have to fall on the mercy of the human beings . . . the same being their fellow Quzzzuzzzian's were eating alive a few earth days ago!

The destruction of the Cobrasant and Viperious had a massive knock on effect, as battleships, their stockpiles of onboard weaponry was extremely impressive but, these weapons were not all meant to explode at the same time and in the same place!

As they were primed, the G.R.I.M.'s were the first to detonate, G.R.I.M's by their design use gravitational fields to inverse any matter or spacial material that happens to be close at hand. Once captured in this swirling gravitational field, the matter or spacial material becomes so dense that the atoms they are made of smash together and become destroyed. These weapons on their own are awesome but, when you throw in a combination of neutron and photon missiles along with graviton blasters and the two ships graviton engines, you get an explosive cocktail that would impress any weapons technician.

Despite their nature for sophisticated destructive tactics, the triloraptors were not impressed with this! Prior to the explosions, they had received an SOS from both battleships and were trying to establish why the G.R.I.M's on board both the Cobrasant and Viperious had armed themselves? Their emotions were void of any feeling as they watched the Cobrasant and Viperious being destroyed. The only logical reaction was to issue a major warning to brace for impact as the blast waves from the destroyed ships spread outwards. Now they themselves were in deep trouble, without warning, three of the G.R.I.M's gravitational fields had mysteriously travelled in the blast waves and had enveloped the three trilo-crafts!

In less than a nano second, the integrity of the trilo-crafts ships that were made from R.I.T.S, (robomatic inter transdimensional substance) began to collapse. All three ships immediately imploded and subsequently exploded; again shock waves and disproportionate amounts of radiation filled the voids in space in terra's solar system.

On the planet terra, the homo sapien were busy restoring order, they were oblivious to what had happened in their solar system. Terra had protected them and then shielded them from the disproportionate amounts of radiation with its atmosphere.

Frustrated, annoyed and confused, that's what Admiral Zissiani was feeling. She had just got news through SOS signals from some of the survivor's pods that the Cobrasant and Viperious had been destroyed; she had also been informed that the three trilo-raptor craft had also been destroyed. Her mind was racing; she ran the same question over and over again in her mind;

>"What in the name of Quzzzuzzzian's fang had happened to the pride of her fleet? Had the triloraptors destroyed them? Did the Cobrasant and Viperious destroy the three trilo-crafts?"

The reality was, she did not know but, she did know that she would have to face the consequences and for her, they would be grave! It was time for her to use some of her Quzzzuzzzian cunning. She still had a few Quzzzuzzzian days left before the overlord's ultimatum. So Admiral Zissiani concocted a story that three triloraptor crafts had ambushed the two Quzzzuzzzian battleships as they entered into terra's solar system. In the ensuing battle, the Cobrasant and Viperious successfully destroyed the three triloraptor crafts but both the Cobrasant and Viperious had sustained irreparable damage and the crews had to abandon ship. A rescue mission would be sent to extract the courageous crew members.

Admiral Zissiani conceitedly thought;

"Even by my standards, that sounds rather convincing."

And with that, she sent a uni-net video message of the details to the overlord. Just to make it a little more convincing, when she was recording the message she shed a few tears and wept as she said she was going to sent a rescue mission . . . of which she had no intentions of doing!

Now, she had deal with her collaborators, the triloraptors! She had secretly formed an alliance with the triloraptors to depose the overlord. Using a secure Quzzzuzzzian channel, she sent a message to the triloraptors mother ship. It said;

"I thought the triloraptors were an intelligent race. Yet you have foolishly set off the G.R.I.Ms anti-tamper device when you deactivated them. Did you not think that we would have added these as a necessary precaution in case you tried to destroy the Cobrasant and Viperious.

As a result of this transgression, you have now put our terra mission in serious jeopardy!

I however have kept my side of the bargain, you have our G.R.I.M technology, the schematics for our cloaking device and graviton engines; now keep your side! Time is running out, let me know the moment you decipher the uni-link destruction code."

At that, Admiral Zissiani ended her transmission. Although this was a serious situation, and it could have ended her alliance with the triloraptors, she began to laugh and though the laughter she said;

"Zissiani, if you are still alive when this is over, you should go into politics, you my gorgeous Quzzzuzzzian are the best fabricator of the truth that I know!"

CHAPTER 17

Emergency Meeting

On board the triloraptor mother ship an emergency meeting of triloraptors central command was called. They had just received Admiral Zissiani latest message and their trilo-supercomputer had some important information for them. Each of the one thousand elders positioned themselves so they stood in front of their communications monitor and for security; the super commuters AI did a recognition scan on each triloraptor. With that out of the way, the first item on the agenda was Admiral Zissiani latest message.

It was already common triloraptor knowledge that the uni-link destruction code has been deciphered by their super computer a few trilo-days ago. So a vote was taken on if or when they would release this information. A small debate took place where the majority of elders said they did not trust Admiral Zissiani and on the issue of G.R.I.M anti-tamper device, they all believed she was lying through her venomous fangs. Others stated that the triloraptors are still at war with the Interplanetary Universal Congress and felt the triloraptors would be better off without them. But, in the throes of the final debate, all agreed that they had to stop the overlord. The vote went in favour that if all went according to plan; they would release the deciphered code one trilo-hour before the overlord's deadline!

Next on the agenda was a progress report on the G.R.I.M's. A three dimensional image popped up onto their screens. It was an image of a 'super G.R.I.M' with an R.I.T.S exterior body that is 2953 metres long. It had been constructed in record time by the triloraptor weapons technology division and the image showed that it was attached to the under body of the trilo-mother ship.

One of the assembled elders asked the trilo-supercomputer if this was ready to be launched and the reply was, "affirmative!" The screen then changed to show several thousand G.R.I.M missiles that had also been constructed by the triloraptor weapons technology division. The trilo-super computers AI anticipated the next question and on their screens a message flashed up reading, "all G.R.I.M's are ready to be launched."

In the middle of meeting room the trilo-supercomputer brought up an enormous virtual display of the planet Notus solar system. All one thousand elders turned away from their communication monitor and looked at the planets solar system slowly turning in front of them. The super commuter then started a simulation of a planned attack; first it pinpointed the position of the Interplanetary Universal Congress forces fleet. Then it showed hundred hundreds of G.R.I.M's being launched from numerous trilo-crafts that had entered Notus's solar system. Within a few trilo-seconds the G.R.I.M's hit and destroyed the whole of Interplanetary Universal Congress forces fleet! The simulation then showed the aftermath of the blasts from the G.R.I.M's. One terrestrial and two of the gas giant planets that the Interplanetary Universal Congress fleet were in close proximity to would be severely damaged!

Next, the trilo-mother ship entered the outskirts of Notus's solar system and launched the super G.R.I.M, and then at maximum speed, the mother ship exited. Within a few trilo-seconds the super G.R.I.M approach the planet and divided into two separate missiles, their targets were the planets north and south poles, simultaneously the super G.R.I.M's hit both poles. What happened next was, the planet began to spin faster and faster, this caused its atmosphere to disintegrate and spill out into space. Subsequently Notus's crust shattered and its fiery inner core burst outward. Now the gravitational pull was so great that the Notus began to shrink and shrink, within a few trilo-minutes Notus imploded and then fiercely exploded. Trillions upon trillion of atoms had been destroyed, as the blast expanded outward, it consumed every planet in the solar system, each in turn was destroyed! For a few moments all that remained in this solar chaos was gases, dust particles and its sun, Saulė Majoris but, even this mighty giant could not stand such a blast, Saulė Majoris went super nova!

For a moment the assembled body were silent . . . . and then;

"Thump, thump, thump, thump, thump, thump, thump, thump, thump, thump, thump, thump, thump, thump, thump, thump, thump, thump."

In an unprecedented action, they all began to stamp their feet, it was a show of extreme excitement and solidarity for what they had seen!

Back on the beach on the planet Notus, Elaine had decided that a swim in the warm ocean might calm her down. The swim was exhilarating, at first she just splashed about in the briny water, then she dived under a small wave, surfaced and swam as hard and fast as she could. Even under pressure her heart didn't race and her breath was controlled, she thought;

"Adaptive D.N.A, it seems to have made me stronger."

As she left the warm waters, she noticed that her finger and toes had grown about twice as long and in between each finger and toe a web had formed! She said out loud;

"Adaptive D.N.A, Dr. Frankenstein."

Notus laughed and said in a Swiss accent;

"Should I call you Eve or my fallen angel?"

"Ha, Ha," Elaine said sarcastically.

Elaine pointed to her webbed toes and asked;

"Is this permanent?"

Notice relied rhythmically;

"Nope, the webs and the toes they goes."

Notus then added;

"Don't worry, as your hands and feet dry in the sun they will return back to normal. You have a lot to learn about Adaptive D.N.A."

Notus continued in a more serious voice;

"Elaine, I have some good news for you, your planet Earth, my offspring terra is safe. The battleships in terra's solar system that had been deployed to destroy terra have been destroyed.

Elaine inquired;

"How were the battleships destroyed?"

Notus paused, Elaine sensed Notus needed reflect for a few moments and then answered;

"You must understand Elaine, Terra, like me and all of my specie embraces all life. The overlord, along with the Interplanetary Universal Congress and the triloraptors, have all put terra and your species the Homo sapiens in severe jeopardy. Reluctantly terra had to fight back; terra used their technology to turn the weapons they had on themselves. They effectively destroyed each other!

Now, I too have to fight back, unfortunately my fight back will be on a much grander scale and if you are willing will also involve you!"

"Me!" Elaine exclaimed. "I am a meagre human or . . . newman. How can I possibly contribute to a galactic war?"

It was now time for Notus to reveal something that had been in the planning for some time;

"Elaine, look out to sea."

Silently and slowly, from below the blue waters an outline of a crystal blue Marquise-Cut boat shaped Diamond began to emerge. Its size, an amazing 2953 metres long and 1476.5 metres wide! As the diamond shape rose out of the water, spectacular rainbows formed where the sun light hit the sea water as it cascaded of the brightly polished surface. It continued to slowly rise until it was about one thousand metres above sea level and then it just stopped.

Elaine was breathless, it was stunningly beautiful. Elaine used her telepathy and said;

"Wow and triple wow, that's some rock, what exactly is it?"

Notus replied in prideful manner;

"That Elaine is some of the atomised remains of Olotinium that I have slowly been gathering to me from the Olotinium solar system. Olotinium the being is made of pure energy, as am I. While the being Olotinium may have died, the pure energy that makes Olotinium's atoms lives on.

I took Olotinium's gathered atoms to a depth of about 150km into Notus's mantle and tetrahedrally bonded Olotinium atoms with four pure carbon atoms that normally make diamonds. The result is a super strong pure energy structured diamond. Then under the extreme pressure the mantle provided, I bonded billions and billions of the new diamond atoms together to form one big crystal exterior. What you are looking at is N.O.T.U.S 1 the spacecraft!"

Elaine just couldn't stop looking at it, it was astonishing. Without taking her eyes off it she asked;

"A spacecraft, what do you 'the great Notus' need with spacecraft? Oh, Ok while I am asking, why have you called this magnificent vessel N.O.T.U.S 1?"

Laughing, Notus said in an echoingly deep voice;

"The great Notus will reply."

Dropping the deep voice, Notus then continued normally;

"In answer to the first part of your question, I don't need a spacecraft, but for you to help me and to get back home, you do.

Immediately Notus sensed Elaine wanted to ask another question but swiftly carried on talking so that Elaine would not interrupt;

"As to the name N.O.T.U.S, it is the same as mine and has two significances, one it stands for, 'Not of this universal system' and the second is, the N stands for Notus, Notus is the parent and the offspring's are; O for Olotinium, the T for Terra, the U for Ulysses and S for Slugtonian. Finally the spaceship is the first I have built, hence number one."

Elaine was bubbling with questions, jumping in she said;

"Notus you are one deep individual, now that you have explained it, the name is very appropriate and I guess you gave the planet your name as well?"

A simple reply came back;

"Correct."

With that small mystery sorted, Elaine had another question but this was a big one;

"I couldn't help notice that you seem to have shot past the bit about me helping you and for me more importantly, getting back home, come on Notus, I need answers!"

Notus took Elaine's verbal scolding on the chin and bounced back in a James Cagney accent;

"Ok, ok I'll talk, Elaine, you should've have been a cop."

Elaine started to laugh and allowed Notus to continue;

"As I explained before a massive force intends to invade Notus. The invasion force is the Interplanetary Universal Congress. They are being forced by the overlord to fight a war to eradicate a race called the triloraptors. While the triloraptors have every right to a place in this universe they by their nature a borne killer's, they have no home planet and are nomadic space wanderers!

Killing is what they do well at and they are on their way to battle with the Interplanetary Universal Congress forces in this solar system, a battle I think the triloraptors will win. But, their plan is to destroy the whole of this solar system including Saulė Majoris this systems sun!"

Elaine just couldn't hold the words in, she said out loud;

"Oh My God! Almost breathless she continued; "Just how many are coming?"

"This Elaine will be Notus's Alamo, we are outnumbered and outgunned but if I can count on your support, we could just win."

Elaine's reply was meant to be humorous but, a little truth waned through;

"Can't we just get out of Dodge?"

Being a telepath Notus new exactly what Elaine was thinking and said;

> "Elaine if you want to go now, that's okay, you can take Notus one and go now. You have truly been through enough."

> "Notus." Elaine said stubbornly; "you have scanned my brain, you know all there is to know about me. I am not a quitter; I am Doctor Elaine Laurence, the same Doctor Elaine Laurence who campaigned against the culling of seals, the murder of whales and the destruction of the Amazon rain forests. Yes I am scared but, I will see this all the way through to hopefully a triumphant end."

Notus felt proud of this little plucky Newman, but Notus knew what lay ahead was going to really test Elaine. Notus said;

> "Elaine, I will bring Notus one on to the beach, you might like to look around inside."

Notus one silently cruised over and landed gently on the beach. One of the lower angled facets opened outward to reveal an entrance. Elaine walked through the entrance and into an arched corridor that lead her upward to a large empty crystal chamber. The walls of the chamber were completely transparent and Elaine could see the sea and beach below her.

Elaine was a little puzzled; she had expected to see the spacecraft packed with equipment, to the contrary there wasn't even a chair. Trying to be polite, she said out loud to Notus;

> "Notus this is very nice, in fact it's amazing but, you said it was a spacecraft, where is all the equipment?"

Notice had been expecting Elaine's response and said;

> "This dear girl is not one of your earthly Apollo tin cans; this is a highly sophisticated star ship. Everything you need is here."

Notus said "chair" and in the centre of the chamber a large crystal chair rose from the chambers floor. Notus then said; "control panel" and just in front of the chair a crystal control panel that rose up. Notus then requested that Elaine take a seat and he would explain the controls.

Elaine sat on the crystal chair and looked at a rather attractive, highly polished clear blue crystal that was completely transparent control panel. This time, she took the initiative from Notus and said "display on". The diamond display light up with the colours of different gem stones. Elaine said half laughing;

"Don't tell me the green is for go and the red is for stop."

Laughing back but also being serious Notus said;

"Yep," I thought I would keep it simple. I have incorporated a colour coded gyro control system that links in with the gyro chamber you are in. You can also fly Notus by telepathic control, voice commands and when necessary by auto pilot.

Oh, before we go any further, you might want to take a look at your skin."

Elaine looked down at her hands and her skin they were beginning to become reflective and the same colour as Notus one, crystal blue. A quick inspection of the rest of her body revealed the same was happening. Without saying a word she though;

"Adaptive DNA."

Notus explained;

"Elaine as you are no longer on the beach your body will adapt to its new surroundings. This is your space look and if I may say so, it's very becoming."

Laughing Notus added;

"You look a real gem! Now, would you like to take Notus one for a spin?"

Elaine was it little distracted, she was busy pocking and prodding her new skin, so Notus repeated his request;

"Elaine would you like to take Notus one for a spin?"

This time Notus had caught her attention and she enthusiastically replied;

"Oh yes, back home I have a commercial aircraft pilots licence but you had better put the L Plates on for this big baby."

Notus laughed and said;

"Sit in the command chair 'Captain Elaine Laurence' and prepare yourself for the ride of a life time."

Staying in the Planet atmosphere and just below the speed of sound, Notus flew Notus one for the first few earth minutes, and then the controls were handed over to Elaine. The controls were a lot easier than any aircraft Elaine had flown before, and Elaine seemed to be a natural at the helm. Pleased with Elaine, Notus said;

"It's time to leave the planet's atmosphere, let's head off into space and really see what Notus one can do."

With that, Notus one gently left the planet's atmosphere and then began to accelerate. Within a second they had taken a high orbit altitude around the planet Notus. As they orbited the planet, Notus proudly pointed out the various oceans, seas and land masses with their mountain ranges and other geographical points of interest.

For Elaine, this experience was overwhelming, tears of absolute bliss filled her eyes, and the views from space were just amazing. For Notus, it was a stark reminder that a battle to save this beautiful planet and

Notus' solar system were only a few earth hours away! Without any further distractions Notus said to Elaine;

> "It's time to go and meet with the Interplanetary Universal Congress Fleet."

Elaine's coolly inquired;

> "What's the plan when we meet them?"

But her heart began to race as she heard Notus's answer;

> "We politely ask them to leave, if they don't leave, we will have to destroy them!

Elaine knew the answer but she still had to ask the question;

> "Are you serious?"

Notus replied positively;

> "Absolutely, Elaine, this is life or death, in this and every other universe it is classed as, the way."

On their route to Notus, the Interplanetary Universal Congress was still experiencing planetary magnetic pull problems when suddenly their long range scanners picked up a single vessel heading towards them. Computer scans could not identify this vessel. So adopting normal protocols, they sent out a message in all known communications asking that this vessel indentify itself.

In a whisper Elaine said to Notus;

> "What shall I say?"

Almost whispering back, Notus said;

> "Just make something up but, make it sound convincing."

It wasn't long before they got a reply;

> "This is Captain Elaine Laurence of the planet Notus; you are violating the space of the Newman Empire. Turn back immediately!"

This really threw the Interplanetary Universal Congress fleet. They did not know that Notus had intelligent life forms and had never heard of the Newman race? Without delay, they sent an urgent message to Admiral Zissiani. Her response was calculating and merciless, these Newman's had only sent one vessel and scans could not detect any weapons! They, the Interplanetary Universal Congress had hundreds of ships that were busting with armaments. Her orders; destroy this vessel without delay and proceed as planned.

Notus had intercepted the message and immediately informed Elaine;

> "They are going to attack!"

To Elaine surprise Notus called out;

> "Weapons panels activate and turn on!"

At either side of Elaine's command chair two clear blue crystal panels rose from the floor. The tops of each panels had a diamond display that was light up with the colours of different gem stones. Notus then said to Elaine;

> "Reach out and touch the two black ones together."

Without hesitation Elaine did as requested and Notus one flipped onto its side so its underbelly was showing to the approaching Interplanetary Universal Congress fleet. Its underbelly then slowly began to changed colour from crystal blue to black.

Confused by what was happing, Elaine asked;

> "What's Just happened?"

With no time to spare, Notus said;

> "We are now in attack mode one. That means Notus one has flipped onto its side, its gyro chamber controller has kept the command chamber upright and we have just engaged the dark matter crystal compressor; the crystals are now charging themselves up by drawing dark matter from space and then are super compressing them. In one earth second it will be released."

Notus one shuddered as the compressed dark matter burst from the angled facets on the underbelly of the ship. Elaine didn't pretend to understand what Notus had just said or done. And if she was little puzzled, the Interplanetary Universal Congress fleet were absolutely mystified. They were about to fire a barrage of missiles when the alien craft flipped onto its side. The order to fire was in its final countdown, three, two, o . . . . when an invisible but enormous wave, 80467.2 Meters (50 Miles) high and 321868.8 Meters (200 Miles) wide of compressed black matter hit them. It could only be described as been hit by a colossal spacial tsunami.

The frontal formation of the Interplanetary Universal Congress fleet took the heaviest hit; the mammoth wave destroyed them instantly! The second line of ships was thrown thousands of meters backwards. Consequently they crashed into the fleet's third line and all were either crushed or destroyed by their own onboard weapons as they detonated!

For the lucky ones at the rear of the fleet, they managed to escape with heavy to light structural damage. Logically, they decided to back away and regrouped. The remaining fleet commanders sent an SOS message to Admiral Zissiani of their situation and asked for emergency medical supplies to be sent as quickly as possible.

Admiral Zissiani was not in the mood for another failure! She ordered the remaining fleet commanders to do an immediate investigation into what had happened and to do an inventory of what was salvageable.

They however did not have time to answer as Notus one had pursued them and for the second time they were issued with an ultimatum;

> "This is Captain Elaine Laurence of the planet Notus; you are violating the space of the Newman Empire. Leave this space immediately!"

Without hesitation the battered fleet sent a message saying they would comply and started to withdraw immediately. Elaine was ecstatic, using her telepathy she repeatedly said;

> "We've won, we've won, we've won."

Notus could not allow her to continue and stopped her in her tracks;

> "Elaine!" he shouted. "Stop, we have not won anything yet."

Notus then continued in a lower tone;

> "This was just the first battle; the war is far from over. Our next enemies are on their way and they are hardened killers, the next battle will not be this easy."

Elaine had instantly calmed down and asked;

> "Your referring to the triloraptors, aren't you?"

Coldly Notus said;

> "Yes I am."

The triloraptor main fleet had made good time and was fast approaching Notus's solar system. They like the Interplanetary Universal Congress fleet were having problems with their long range scanners, this again was due to the solar storms been throw up from Saulė Majoris.

One thing the long range scanner did notice was that one third of the Interplanetary Universal Congress fleet had turned around and was heading back towards them. Their conclusion was that they had detected the triloraptor fleet and were going to make their first battle stand on the edge of Notus Solar system. Perhaps they were even planning to use the solar systems large asteroid belt as addition cover? This for the triloraptors made the forthcoming battle even more exhilarating, the enemy was actually going to put up a serious fight!

As final preparations for the battle took place, the triloraptors detected the strong positive magnetic fields given off by thousands of metallic asteroids. They had also detected that Saulė Majoris solar storms were bombarding its solar system and the Interplanetary Universal Congress's fleet with negatively charged particles. Without delay, a plan was drawn up so that they could capitalise on this unusual but potentially useful phenomena.

Within a few trilo-days of acquiring the Quzzzuzzzian cloaking technology, numerous trilo-crafts had been equipped with the new cloaking technology, now it was time to put this neat bit of technology to work. Six trilo-crafts engaged their cloaks and slipped unnoticed though the solar systems asteroid belt. Once past the hazardous asteroid belt, they travelled at top speed and stealthy positioned the six cloaked trilo-crafts to the rear of what remained Interplanetary Universal Congress fleet.

Along with the mother ship, the main triloraptor fleet waited 1609.3 Kilometres (1,000 miles) outside Notus's solar system. Their on board computers had plotted the movements of each metallic asteroid and they designated one hundred trilo-crafts to locked their graviton beams onto the asteroids they wanted to target.

As the Interplanetary Universal Congress fleet approach the asteroid belt, one at a time, the one hundred tri-crafts fired a solitary graviton beams at the targeted metallic asteroids. The graviton beam was just powerful enough to apply a serious punch to the asteroid, this punch then sent it crashing into an Interplanetary Universal Congress vessel. The force of the collision shot the Interplanetary Universal Congress vessel backwards and into an invisible proton grid field that the six cloaked tri-craft had set up! The Interplanetary Universal Congress vessel was then instantly destroyed!

With no escape, the Interplanetary Universal Congress fleet were being picked off one at a time by this game of space pool. In desperation they sent a distress signal to Notus one. It simply said;

> "Citizens of the newman race, we are under attack and are unable to defend ourselves. Please show compassion for us and provide help."

Elaine and Notus did not say a word to each other; they both knew they had to help.

Notus then said to Elaine;

> "On the weapons display, reach out and touch the two yellow gems together."

Elaine enquired;

> "Attack mode two?"

Notus replied and explained;

> "Yes, this is hydrogen and helium fusion, Notus one picked this up on its maiden voyage into Saulė Majoris core!

The central band of crystal facets began to glow a yellow white, this band began to rotate and the hydrogen and helium from the band began to expand outward until it was twenty five times the circumference of Notice one. The band was designed so that it narrowed down to a sharp razors edge. Looking out the from the Interplanetary Universal Congress fleet viewing ports, Notus one polished crystal exterior reflected the light and now looked like a mini star with a large fiery belt around it!

Notus had calculated the positions of the six cloaked trilo-crafts and accelerated Notus one straight at the trilo-craft holding one of the central positions. The trilo-crafts detected the approaching fire ball but they could not react quickly enough!

Notus called to Elaine;

"Brace yourself for impact!"

One earth second later, Notus one crashed into the mid-section of the trilo-craft, it's extended rotating fire band had cut straight through the first tri-craft, the trilo-craft instantly exploded. Without pausing, Notus one headed straight for the second trilo-craft. It only took an earth second for it to again crash into the mid-section of the second trilo-craft and that too was severed in half and instantly exploded. The proton grid field immediately collapsed. Seeing what had happened and fearing that they would be targeted next by this kamikaze pilot, the four outer trilo-crafts turned off their cloaks and in unity they powered up and individually fired a G.R.I.M, their only target was Notus one!

Before Elaine could recompose herself from the two trilo-craft impacts, Notus called out another order;

"Quickly, hit the green coloured gems!"

Elaine reacted immediately and in a heart stopping moment Notus one came to an abrupt halt. Instantly, the fiery central band of crystal facets stopped glowing and every angled facet on its crystal exterior began to give out an individual but enormous alternating gravitational field. This confused the four approaching G.R.I.M missiles sensors. Without a positive lock on a target they then malfunctioned and mistakenly the missiles locked onto a more positive source of matter, the other trilo-crafts! Within moments, all four trilo-crafts imploded and then exploded!

As all four trilo-crafts and their onboard G.R.I.M.s exploded together it caused several massive spacial shock waves, most converging centrally, and that's where Notus one was situated! Notus immediately increased each crystal facets gravitation fields tenfold and they deflected the incoming shock wave outwards. The space in and around Notus one seemed to boil and whirl, so Notus though it sensible to take Notus one and Elaine out of harm's way, at top speed Noutus1 accelerated and paused at safe distance.

Some of the already damaged Interplanetary Universal Congress fleet vessels were not so lucky; they did not have time to move and the colossal shock waves crashed into them. In desperation the onboard crews scrambled for their life pods but it was too late. The already damaged structure of these ships could not sustain any more damage they literally began to fall apart, a few moments later they just disintegrated and all the crews died with their ships!

The triloraptors fleet were not perturbed by these events, they actually the crew admired the technology of this unknown spacecraft, True to form for the triloraptors; they also accepted that their own trilo-crafts had not been as cunning as this unknown enemy, therefore they deserved to die!

Triloraptors do not like making mistakes; in view of what happen; they abandon their playful game of graviton space pool and resorted back to their original plan. Their whole fleet began to advance towards Notus's solar system!

Notus had expected this line of attack and said to Elaine;

> "I think we have just rattled the triloraptors cage, they do not want to play any more games. Would you be so kind and hit amber coloured gems."

In the last few hours Elaine had gained a lot of confidence and respect in this powerful being. Without asking why, she did as requested. .

Notus one flipped onto its top side and began to glow vivid amber. The crystal space craft was now facing towards the asteroid belt and immediately it began to radiate a colossal negative magnetic and gravitational field. Slowly, thousands of metallic asteroids of all shapes and sizes began to move toward the space craft. In harmony with Notus one, Notus increased the magnetic and gravitational fields power two hundred fold and one small planetoid composed mainly of metals, granite and ice began to move slowly toward Notus one.

It only took a few earth minutes for all of this to happen, and in that time none of the asteroids collided, they were been controlled by the immense magnetic and gravitational fields from Notus one's individual crystal facets and the enormous power that Notus the being was using. In all of Notus's billion of years of life, Notus had never exerted this much power and for the first in the life of this being life, physical and mental fatigue began to set in.

With so many asteroids drawn towards Notus one a vast openings appeared in the asteroid belt. Seeing what was happening, the triloraptors seized the opportunity and the triloraptor fleet armed all weapons and at top speed lunged forward.

What happened next shook every cell in Elaine's and surviving Interplanetary Universal Congress member's bodies. Notus the being drew on its vast source of energy and gave out a battle cry, the roar was so powerful that the restrained metallic asteroids held by Notus one shot forward at almost the speed of light! Each asteroid seemed to be guided and they accurately crashed into the advancing triloraptors fleet.

Although the trilo-crafts were made of R.I.T.S (robomatic inter transdimensional substance) the impact on the trilo-crafts was colossal; it pushed each trilo-craft backward into deep space, and then, one by one the trilo-crafts and their armed on board munitions and G.R.I.Ms exploded into space dust!

For the triloraptors, the destruction was immense, all that remained of the triloraptors fleet was its mother ship; however in the mass destruction, that too was badly damaged. In a final stand, the triloraptor mother ship's crew armed the super G.R.I.M. and tried to fire it! It was then that they realised the coupling attaching it to the underbelly of had been damaged! The triloraptors had no time for repairs!

Notus had detected what was happening with the triloraptors mother ship and in one last endeavour Notus summoned up all of its remaining power. The roar was almost fifty times more powerful than the last! The planetoid with a diameter of 965.606 kilometres (six hundred miles) and made of metal, granite and ice was instantly released from Notus's and Notus one's magnetic and gravitational grips; the planetoid shot past the asteroid belt and into outer space at almost the speed of light! Within less than a second the planetoid crashed into the triloraptors mother ship sending it hurdling backwards into deep space. The impact instantly broke the super G.R.I.Ms coupling and as it was armed, it immediately split and attacked the planetoids magnetic poles. Within a nano second the triloraptors mother ship and planetoid where in a deadly gravitational spin. A few nano seconds later the triloraptors mother ship and planetoid imploded and then dramatically exploded.

Both planetoid and triloraptors mother ship had been driven far enough away from Notus's solar system so that when the G.R.I.M and they exploded. The immense blast waves and hail of debris from the planetoid only caused minimal damage to the outskirts of the solar system. The explosion did however light up a small part of the far reaches of the universe and for the next few million years the same pin point of light could be observed by universal astrologers.

Notus then just said one word quietly;

"Elaine."

Notus voice seemed to be drained of energy and then said wearily;

"We, my planet, Notus's solar system and Saulė Majoris are now safe."

Elaine couldn't help it, she began to cry. Why, she wasn't sure but she sat on her crystal chair and for a while she sobbed. Thoughts of what had happened over the past day flew into her head, she then remembered one of her first thoughts when she on the beach on Notus.

"Elaine you and this day are getting stranger and stranger."

And it had, but it was not over just yet.

A call came in to Notus one from the from the remaining and battered Interplanetary Universal Congress fleet;

> "Captain Elaine Laurence of the planet Notus and the Newman Empire. We of the remaining Interplanetary Universal Congress thank you for your help and assistance. Without this, we would have been slaughtered. We will be leaving your space as quickly as we can. Before we leave, we have a request for you; Admiral Zissiani of the Interplanetary Universal Congress would like to talk to you. Please respond."

Using telepathy Elaine composed her thoughts and then spoke with Notus;

> "I take it that you heard the communication, what do you think we should do?"

Still sounding mentally weary, Notus replied;

> "It was a call I was expecting, we will of course reply. Before we do, I have just acquired the triloraptors mother ships equivalent of a black box. It was ejected just before the planetoid hit it. Its main contents are the triloraptors backup files for their trilo-super computers data base. I am accessing the files as we speak and have the code that will disarm the hidden uni-net disintegration device.
>
> It is time to speak with Admiral Zissiani, but only tell her that you have been able find the code. More importantly do not trust her!"

Elaine had no idea what to say so she thought it would be better if she played it by ear, Elaine started;

"This is Captain Elaine Laurence of the planet Notus and the Newman Empire. Your words of thanks have no meaning. The battles in and around Notus could have been avoided!"

Before Elaine could continue, Admiral Zissiani butted in;

"Captain Laurence this is Admiral Zissiani of the Interplanetary Universal Congress, I agree with you that this battle around your noble planet could have been avoided but we were driven by a madman who wants to take over this universe!

Normally we at the Interplanetary Universal Congress are civilised and peaceful but we have been gambling with our lives to try to appease this tyrant. If your race would consider . . . ."

Elaine now butted in;

"Admiral Zissiani shut your mouth and listen! I have the code to disarm the uni-net disintegration device. It has just been sent over to your battered fleet. Advice the Interplanetary Universal Congress and the triloraptors to end your war now! Also, stay away from Notus and the planet earth. You, the triloraptors and the Interplanetary Universal Congress have been warned!"

With that Elaine ended her transmission.

Notus started to laugh and said a little sarcastically;

"Captain Elaine Laurence of the planet Notus and the Newman Empire, that was not very diplomatic but, I think she got your point."

Elaine relied;

"Notus, you said don't thrust her." Elaine continued; "This has been one long day for both of us. How about we head on home, you can rustle up some food for this hungry and tired newman."

CHAPTER 18

Madam Chair Elect

Looking rather stunning in her new snug fitting fully scaled gold outfit, Admiral Zissiani entered the virtual congressional halls on the Uni-net. The entire delegation stood and cheered.

The speaker for the Interplanetary Universal Congress said;

> "Welcome Madam chair elect."

The new chair elect gracefully moved up to the podium and waited for the applause to die down, when they did, the new chair elect Zissiani addressed the entire Interplanetary Universal Congress and all its members by a virtual uni-net link.

> "Members of the Interplanetary Universal Congress, we have all been through a terrible ordeal. We have been mentally violated and dishonourably used as instruments of mass destruction. That nightmare is now over!"

Applause filled the virtual congressional halls. Madam Chair elect Zissiani again waited for the applause to die down, she then continued;

> "The uni-net has now been modified and new security protocols have been put in place. We can all now rest assured that this will never happen again."

She then declared in a loud encouraging voice;

"The uni-net is now safe!"

The virtual congressional hall erupted with applause. Zissiani raised all eight tentacles to halt the applause; she then waited a full Quzzzuzzzian minute for all everyone to be silent, took a slow gulp of air and continued;

> "Since disarming the hidden uni-net disintegration sub programme device that was maliciously planted in every individual's synaptic brain and neurological receptors. I have had only one conversation with the despicable being who planted it there, we know him as the overlord. I recorded that conversation and it will be broadcast now on the uni-net for all to hear."

In a threatening voice the overlord spoke;

> "Admiral Zissiani, you and the Interplanetary Universal Congress have let me down. I ordered you to capture the planet terra, you failed! I ordered you to kill all the triloraptors, you failed! I ordered you to capture triloraptors mother ship, you failed.
>
> Now, I gave you the next five rotations of your planet to get these deeds done or I would kill everyone within the Interplanetary Universal Congress. Your time is up!"

With that and without hesitation, the overlord then tried to detonate the uni-net disintegration device!

Calmly Admiral Zissiani said;

> "Overlord, it is not I or the Interplanetary Universal Congress that has failed, it is you!
>
> I have had the disarm code for some days, and all the members of the Interplanetary Universal Congress are now safe.

The war between Interplanetary Universal Congress and triloraptors that you forced both parties into is now over.

Be advised that we are hunting you for war crimes, cold blooded murder and genocide against members the Interplanetary Universal Congress. For this, every resource from the Interplanetary Universal Congress will be used. We will get you and you will pay!"

The overlord did not respond but, the whole of the Interplanetary Universal Congress did with rapturous applause for their saviour, Chair elect Zissiani.

Chair elect Zissiani stood on the podium and in her true form, she forced a few tears from her cunning eyes. The applause got even louder, still playing to the audience; she lowered he head and let out a little sob. Now she had a standing ovation! Wiping her eyes with two of her eight tentacles and she thought;

> "Zissiani, these events have really tested you, but you are a brilliant soldier, a masterful politician and above all a great leader. The Interplanetary Universal Congress is really lucky to have you."

As the applause died down a question was asked from one of the invited delegates from the planet takaashigani;

> "Madam Chair Elect what plans do you or the Interplanetary Universal Congress have for the planet terra or as the humans call it, earth."

Chair elect Zissiani had expected this question and had an answer prepared;

> "I thank you on behalf of the Interplanetary Universal Congress for your legitimate concerns, a concern we all share. This race of beings has been severely wronged by the Interplanetary

Universal Congress forces but in our defence, we were being held as universal hostages by that evil being, the overlord.

Sadly, and may I say understandably, the human race may never trust us again. I suggest for the immediate future that we leave these good people alone. Because of what we did to them, they need to rebuild their lives, cultures and their world. When we bring the overlord to justice, we can invite them along to observe and hear all what had happened."

Then Chair elect Zissiani played her ace card. She burst into tears, crying with her tentacles wrapped tightly around her body as if she were trying to console herself, she said;

> "Hopefully in time, the humans will find it in their hearts to forgive us."

Zissiani the brilliant actress's little plan worked, around the universe tears filled the eyes of those who cold cry, others just held their heads low and Chair elect Zissiani thought;

> "Yes, I really do deserve this, just as the overlord will deserve what is coming to him when the triloraptors get to him!"

CHAPTER 19

Cease Fire

Once their mother ship and main fleet had been destroyed, the trilo-crafts attacking the Interplanetary Universal Congress planets agreed to a cease fire. The cease fire was reinforced by the message sent out by Captain Elaine Laurence of the planet Notus and the Newman Empire.

The triloraptors held no malice against the Newman Empire, on the contrary, for the exquisite way the Newman Empire destroyed their main fleet and their mother ship, they admired and respected them. That respect increased when they got a message that they could come and retrieve the mother ships black box from just outside Notus's solar system.

The retrieval of the black box brought both a welcoming surprise and a revelation. In with their mother ships backed up data files were the exact co-ordinances for the overlord's universe and more importantly, the co-ordinances for the micro-worm holes that lead to this universe.

The revelation came in another data file; this file contained the routes the triloraptors had taken on their universal nomadic travels. A cross reference had been added that showed that a few trilo-years ago, the triloraptors fleet had stopped for general repairs. They had undertaken these general repairs within ten trilo-miles of the co-ordinances of the overlord's micro-worm holes! A foot note was added to the file that said that the overlord had by chance been able to stabilise the micro-worm holes with discarded R.I.T.S (robomatic inter transdimensional

175

substance) material. It had been the triloraptors technology that had allowed the overlord to enter this universe!

As a cease fire was now in place, the triloraptors informed Admiral Zissiani, now Chair Elect that they had the co-ordinances for the overlord's universe and also the co-ordinances for the micro-worm holes that lead to and from his universe.

Knowing that they were not very popular and the blame for what had recently happened had not yet fallen on to anyone other than the overlords shoulders, they conveniently neglected to mention to her that it was through their space litter that all of this started.

In an unprecedented gesture of good will they further said that they would personally deal with the overlord and it would not be necessary for the Interplanetary Universal Congress to deploy any more forces. For Admiral Zissiani, that was a deal made in the celestial heavens and one that when it was over she could take full advantage of!

For the triloraptor their unprecedented gesture of good was a polite way to keep the Interplanetary Universal Congress out of what could be an unrestricted and spectacular killing spree!

CHAPTER 20

Adaptive DNA

After all that had happened sleep came easy for Elaine. She had found that her crystal chair in Notus one could fully recline and with the aid of a built in gravitation cushion, it was surprisingly comfortable. So on her way back to the planet Notus, she closed her eyes for forty winks and for the first time in weeks, she had a natural 'drug free sleep', that sleep lasted a full eight hours!

Elaine woke up feeling refreshed but ravenous. She walked outside into the fresh air and filled her lungs with a few deep breaths. The morning air felt good and helped clear the remnants of sleep from her body. She noticed instantly that as she walked further away from Notus one her skin tone was changing, this time it was a light green colour. She thought;

"Adaptive DNA, I wonder what critter I am similar to now?"

Looking around, she could see that Notus one had landed in a clearing on the edge of a large forest. The trees closest looked like tall palm tree on earth. She sprinted over and at the top of the palm trees was large green nuts; from where she stood they resembled coconuts. She bent down and jumped upward, the jump thrust her high into the air and she easily cleared the eight metres to where the cluster of green nuts hung. She grabbed at one and then began to drop to the ground. As she dropped, she let nut go and it hit the ground with a thud. The nut cracked just enough for Elaine to prise it open. Inside was a liquid that tasted identical to coconut milk. Elaine gulp that down and then tasted the white flesh inside the nut, this again tasted identical to coconut.

Her breakfast was disturbed when Notus said;

"Good morning Elaine, I take it you slept well?"

Laughing, Elaine telepathically replied;

"Like a newman baby."

Notus chuckled and said;

"Good, now we have to get you back home."

Cautiously Elaine asked;

"Dr Frankenstein, I think you have forgotten something, what about my adaptive DNA? Today I am looking a little green; I will stand out like a sore thumb on earth!"

Notus went straight into his Swiss accent and said;

"My dear Lady, It and you will adapt, you have not yet mastered how to change. On earth, if you wish, you will look human."

Elaine really perked up and said enthusiastically;

"That's fantastic, when can I leave?"

Now, Notus was really on form. In an English butler's voice, Notus said;

"Your carriage awaits you madam."

Notus was of course referring to Notus one. But then, without a warning, Notus dropped a bombshell right in Elaine's lap. In a normal tone Notice said;

"On your way home, you might want to call in on one or two planets and pick up some of your fellow earthlings."

Puzzled, Elaine asked;

"Who from earth would be out here in this vast universe?"

Notus replied;

"Elaine, when you were abducted from the recreational space station (R.S.S), you were not the only one. All of your crew and guests were abducted and another R.S.S's crew and guests were also abducted. In total, the triloraptors abducted four hundred and sixty nine other people! To cover their tracks the triloraptors then blew up all the R.S.S's in orbit around the planet earth. Every abducted human has been now been officially declared dead!

Craftily, at a later stage, the triloraptors were going to use you and the other four hundred and sixty nine other people as either hostages or as a bargaining tool.

Being triloraptors, they anticipated that things could go wrong and if by chance the overlord found that this group of humans existed he would do all in his power to find you. So the triloraptors decided to drop you and these other people off on various planets throughout this universe. Obviously, the overlord evil plans for your people failed but, the overlord is still alive, and these humans are still extremely vulnerable. Elaine, your fellow humans need rescuing and returning home."

For a few moments Elaine was bewildered, then as this information sank in she asked Notus;

"Why didn't you tell me this before?"

Without hesitation Notus said;

"Truthfully, I did not know if we were going to be alive today, and if we were dead, your rescue mission would have been irrelevant."

Elaine could not argue with that logic, so she conceded into rescuing her fellow human beings. She then asked another question;

"Do you know where all of the human are?"

Notus replied confidently;

"Of course, I was able to obtain that information from their black box's data files. There is just one small problem."

Elaine knew that Notus had left that sentence hanging for a reason, and she guessed the answer was not going to be a great hit with her. So talking the bait, she plunged in and asked the million dollar question;

"Ok, Notus, what's the small problem?"

Notus had read Elaine's mind and could feel her anticipation. But, there was no easy way to explain so Notus said;

"The various areas where the humans have been dropped off have been expertly booby trapped by the triloraptors. The only way we can execute a safe retrieval is to enlist the help of the triloraptors!"

When that hit home, it certainly was not a good time for telepathic communication, Elaine yelled out:

"Bloody hell."

She took a few deep breaths and verbally continued;

"These triloraptors have just to kill us all; they also tried to destroy your solar system. In our defence, we retaliated and we have just killed, Oh I don't know, thousands if not millions of them. Why would they now want to help us?"

Calmly Notus said;

"From all over universe hundreds of different species united under one banner, that banner is name you have heard, the Interplanetary Universal Congress. One the requirement to become a member of the Interplanetary Universal Congress you have to accept a simple law, the law of the way. The way recognises that each species has the right to follow its own natural path. The path for the triloraptors is hunting and killing, that is and always will be their way.

They genuinely admired the way we destroyed their battle fleet and mother ship, this earned us their uppermost respect. When Captain Elaine Laurence of the planet Notus and the Newman Empire request them for help, they will willingly provide it.

Elaine knew that Notus had thought this though and from what was said, it would be foolish to try a rescue without knowing how to disarm the triloraptors booby traps. A though popped into her mind and she asked Notus;

"When I was dropped off, why weren't any booby traps set here on Notus? Hey, and come to think of it, why was it just me and not a group of humans?"

Notus had been a little surprised it had taken this long for Elaine to ask why she was the only human on the planet Notus and replied;

"Elaine, when the trilo-craft first came to the planet Notice, the crew were not aware that Notus the planet was going to be the arena for a major battle. It was only as they had landed and were unloading their human's cargo that they were informed by their central command of what the Interplanetary Universal Congress forces had planned for Notus.

They immediately began to reload the human cargo and as their trilo-craft were manned mostly by trilo-bots. I acted on impulse and set of a freak electrical magnetic rainstorm storm that momentarily disabled the trilo-bots. In the moment that they were disabled and the storm was raging, I created a small gravitational whirl wind that rushed in and grabbed one the humans, you!

The trilo-raptor left Notus minus one human being that they presumed had been killed by a whirl wind in the freak storm!

Elaine could for some reason see the funny side to this, laughing she said out loud;

"Wow, I have been killed off twice now, made into a Newman and saved a solar system from destruction. That's not bad for a dead girl!

CHAPTER 21

The Aftermath

After the aftermath of the war, statistics on fatalities, casualty numbers, urban and rural rebuilding programmes and how many battleships and other conscripted ships that were lost are something the Interplanetary Universal Congress would have to provide but, that was not the case for the triloraptors. Yes the war had reduced their numbers drastically but the triloraptors were not in the least bit concerned. The war was over for the Interplanetary Universal Congress, but for the triloraptors that war was just a big battle and now for them a new battle was about to begin, they had a new objective, to hunt down and kill the overlord!

Their new campaign began almost immediately after they were invited to collect their mother ships black box from the outskirts of Notus's solar system. These realised that the overlord had found the R.I.T.S (robomatic inter transdimensional substance) debris useful, so their first job was to scan the entire outer area of Notus's solar system for any usable wreckage and collect it. This wreckage could also be salvageable by the triloraptors and useful for what they had planned.

For this campaign to succeed time was of paramount importance and the triloraptors were apprehensive that the overlord might anticipate some form of retaliation by the Interplanetary Universal Congress into his universe and try to collapse the micro worm holes! They immediately sent out orders for two trilo-craft that was only a few light years away to go to the micro worm holes co-ordinances and secure immediately them.

On route the triloraptors scientists and technicians worked on a micro tunnel made from R.I.T.S that could be installed from one universe to the other. As no exact dimensions for the worm holes were available, they designed the micro R.I.T.S tunnel so that it could expand or detract in length, width and height. Worm holes always have irregular shapes, with numerous twists and turns in them. R.I.T.S was perfect for this as it could also change its shape to fit the twists and bends and different interior contours that would found in the micro worms.

Triloraptors are excellent at analysing potential problems and two became apparent; the first was, when the trilo-crafts arrived at the micro-worm holes, would the overlord have spacial motion, heat and light detectors in the area? And the second was, would he also booby trap the worm holes? Logically these actions would be exactly what the triloraptors would do, so the answer was yes!

For the triloraptors, the spacial detectors would be straightforward to defeat, they had fitted the new cloaking devices to nearly all of their trilo-crafts and with the cloaking system on they could deactivate the spacial detectors without raising any alarms. The booby traps were a serious problem and would have to be deactivated and disarmed when they arrived.

It was deemed that caution should be the key strategy in approaching the wormholes. With that in mind, one of the trilo-craft held back while they carefully approached the wormhole area.

As they had suspected, the area was full of spacial motion, heat and light detectors. With its cloak on the trilo-craft stopped just outside the parameter of the detectors zones. It then sent in a small remote controlled cloaked trilo-craft that was armed with an S.I.C.E gun (Super Iced Compressed Energiser). This gun fired super compressed liquid nitrogen that instantly froze the circuitry of the spacial detectors. Once frozen, all the detectors circuitry was then in a state of suspended animation. This state is then maintained by the liquid nitrogen being constantly re-energised by programmed nano-mites.

With the spacial detectors deactivated both trilo-crafts manoeuvred themselves so they were just one thousand metres from the entrance of each micro worm hole. The entrances were guarded by a highly sophisticated barrier that was made from an intricate web made up of rogue atoms. The rogue atoms were highly unstable and could detonate numerous nuclear explosions if anything collided with them. Atoms are made up of, electrons, proton and neutrons. A quick scan revealed that the atoms instability had been manufactured by introducing twenty five more negatively charged electrons that oscillated into each atom.

To neutralise this atomic barrier, the triloraptors had in their arsenal of weapons some small but powerful electron guns; these guns needed to be radically modified and then mounted on the exterior of the trilo crafts. They were then linked into the trilo crafts on board computers and programmed so they could precisely fire and remove all twenty five electrons at the same time. As there were several hundred rouge atoms, this electron subtraction process was repeated until all the rogue atoms were stabilised and the entrance to the micro worm holes was made safe.

With the micro worm holes safe, the installation of the R.I.T.S tunnels commenced. This was made easier by the overlord who had originally installed R. I.T.S and the entrance and exit of the worm hole to stop them collapsing. Using robotically controlled micro trilo crafts, the trilo-technicians simply slide the R.I.T.S tunnels into place and then connected the all ready constructed front and rear entrances.

With their tasks done, the two trilo crafts sat and guarded the micro worm holes, however they were not idle. Major plans were in the making and it required all of the triloraptors resources for them to win this new battle.

When their mother ship had been destroyed, their super trilo-computer had been also been destroyed. However, on board each trilo-craft was a smaller but highly competent trilo-computer. All the data recovered from the mother ship trilo-super computer was uploaded and each trilo-computer was given an individual assignment. To make these assignments easier, all of the trilo crafts computers were linked into a network that could automatically share data.

Their assignments were from the original schematics, micro engineer all of the triloraptor spacial technology and current weaponry. That also included their fleet of trilo-craft and computers into atom sized components! The trilo-computers than had to design atom sized trilo nano-bots that could carry all of this cargo though the micro worm holes and then when they were in the overlord's universe, re-assemble them!

As the triloraptor were too large to travel to the overlord's micro universe, they also got the trilo-computers to design micro trilo-raptor-bots that they could individually control through their translucent visor fitted around its eyes. They also wanted the micro trilo-raptor-bots to have a trilo-tron that again the triloraptor could control again through his or her visor.

The R.I.T.S wreckage material recovered was invaluable in the manufacturing of some this atom sized micro equipment. As a bonus, if sizable chunks could be found they would be used help re-build the fleet. Working around the clock the triloraptors tested, modified and re-tested each piece of equipment. When each piece of equipment had a one hundred percent pass rate, it was put aside and then another item would be vigorously tested.

One vital piece of equipment that was up and running in a few trilo-hours was micro trilo-recognisance craft. This had been designed and engineered by the two trilo craft at the border of the micro worm hole. It had been sent along the R.I.T.S tunnel in atom sized components and then re-assembled by the trilo nano-bots.

This small crafts mission was enormous, as no information on this universe was available; it had to gather as much information as it could on how many galaxies there are in this universe. Then it had to analyze the galaxies compositions, star and planet formations and detect planets that could sustain life.

Within one trilo-hour, the triloraptors knew that the mission for the micro trilo-recognisance craft was impossible! The proportional relative size of this universe was the same as the trilo-raptors, so even if they had one hundred micro trilo-recognisance craft it would take several trilo-decades to map and find all the planets that could sustain life. This meant the overlord could hide anywhere in this universe and with some luck never be found! The triloraptors needed help and they knew of only one being that might fit that bill, Captain Elaine Laurence of the planet Notus and the Newman Empire!

CHAPTER 22

Delay!

Elaine had decided that it would be sensible to wait for a day or two before charging off on a rescue mission. She wanted to use her spare time in experimenting with her adaptive DNA and getting to master flying Notus one without the guidance of Notus.

With her previous flying skills, taking the control and flying Notus one on her own was quite easy in Notus's atmosphere but leaving and entering a planet atmosphere proved more difficult. She did however persevere and after a few bone shaking exits and entrances she managed to control Notus one reasonably well. She concluded it would take time and practice to hone her astronautical skills.

Mastering her adaptive DNA was proving extremely difficult and exasperating! She knew that when she went on her rescue mission, the other humans they would be freaked out if she were ant nut brown, green or aqua or crystal women! It would be better if she were just plain old earthling Elaine. However the adaptive DNA seemed to adapt and change as soon as she moved from one environment to another and frustratingly, she had no control over it!

Elaine had put Notus one down on a beach in an Elaine called blue coral bay. The reason for this was, as she was landing Notus one she had a fantastic ariel view of the blue coral reef just on the outside of the bay. With the heat of Notus's sun, the sands on the beach had been bleached almost white, while the calm waters in blue coral bay were a beautiful aquatic blue. The views were across the bay and onto the reef were stunning. Looking further out to sea you could see on the horizon the shapes of some small land islands that looked as if they dormant volcanoes on them, this view were breathtaking.

Elaine sat on the beach and watched her skin instantly turn nut brown. Closing her eyes she tried to visualise herself as having her normal, slightly tanned human skin but as she open her eyes, her skin was still nut brown! She decided she needed to try harder, so this time she lay on her back, closed her eyes and kept repeating in her mind; "skin become human, skin become human." She kept this up for a good ten earth minutes. When she opened her eyes she was still nut brown!

Frustrated, she decided to take advantage of where she was and take an inviting swim. The blue waters in coral bay were extremely refreshing. However, within seconds of entering the water Elaine realised aqua women was back but, that allowed her to dive deep in the clear blue waters and enjoy the beautiful coral reef with its highly unusual aquatic life.

Refreshed Elaine returned to the beach for another adaptive DNA session and after trying to for another frustrating few hours she gave up and went back to Notus one. On entering, Elaine skin instantly become reflective and the same colour as Notus one, crystal blue, Elaine thought;

"Crystal women is back!"

Before Elaine could have a grump about her adaptive DNA, she found Notus had installed to the rear of the crystal chamber, a super computer in a clear crystal console and a rather large virtual six metre high virtual reality unit that was displaying millions of galaxies from what Elaine thought was this universe. Elaine slowly walked around the virtual reality display and then she realised she could walk through it! As she walked though it, she could touch and then explore and even expand every galaxy, star and solar system. Excited Elaine said;

"Wow they are fantastic! Where did you get them from?"

Coyly and in a slightly subdued tone, Notus replied;

"From our friends, the triloraptors."

Elaine and Notus then began to have playful discussion about what constitutes theft. Although Elaine had agreed that they were absolutely fantastic pieces of equipment and the virtual reality unit was something she had never seen before. She did however point out that the technology was taken from the triloraptor data base without their consent. Notus presented a plausible defence by saying it came under the universal space salvage law in that it was outside the boundaries of a solar system and therefore it came under the finder keeper bylaw. Their playful discussion came to an abrupt halt when a call came in from the triloraptors! It said;

> "Captain Elaine Laurence of the planet Notus and the Newman Empire, first, we thank you for your past considerations and have acted on them accordingly. We have need of additional help from you. We would ask if you would supply any data and star charts on the overlord's universe that might help us bring this being to triloraptor justice."

At that the message ended. Elaine picked up immediately of the wording;

> "We thank you for your past considerations and have acted on them accordingly."

> "Notus," she said, "What are they talking about, past considerations?"

Notus explained that when they came to retrieve their mother ships black box, they also found information on the micro worm holes and location of the overlord's universe. Notus did not know how Elaine would react to this and was pleasantly surprised when she said very slowly;

> "You sly old fox,"

She paused and then continued;

"For all that that megalomaniac has done to my people, your offspring Olotinium and the Interplanetary Universal Congress; he deserves the wrath of the triloraptor!"

Elaine looked at the virtual reality unit and said;

"Show me a triloraptor."

The virtual reality unit instantly brought up a triloraptor that stood at well over two metres tall with a wingspan of over four metres. Elaine had never seen what she called an intelligent alien before and walked around this imposing and deadly bird of prey. She couldn't help but remark and said out loud;

"It looks look like a big mean eagle."

Notus interrupted her and said;

"If you think that's looks mean, what until you see one in its trilo-combat uniform."

The virtual reality unit artificial intelligence brought up another triloraptor, this time it had its visor on and was in full black metallic R.I.T.S trilo-combat uniform, at its side was its trilo-tron weapon. Elaine found it fascinating and for over a next hour she got Notus one's computer and virtual reality unit to explain and show her as much as they could about the triloraptors past and present history, medical history including their fantastic DNA enhancements, their culture, nomadic existence and more importantly their range of armaments and highly complex R.I.T.S space craft's. At the end of the fact finding session Elaine declared;

"We've done well to defeat them, they are truly awesome."

Notus affirmed what Elaine had said with a big "Yep," and then went on to say;

"You still need to reply to their message; however there have been a few developments while you were researching the triloraptors. I was in contact through telepathic communications with a few of my specie from the overlord's universe, they have supplied me with is a detailed plan of their universe."

At that the virtual reality unit brought up a slightly curved but almost flat balloon shaped universe. Elaine could only speculate but there were millions and millions of small galaxies. Elaine asked Notus to pinpoint exactly where the overlord's planet was. Notus's reply wasn't what Elaine was expecting, Notus explained;

"The overlord does not have a singular planet to live on, he resides in the universe, he is the ruler of this universe and this is his domain."

Elaine asked;

"How will the triloraptors find him, it will be like looking for an atom sized needle in a universal hay stack?"

By now Elaine should have seen this coming as Notus in his best Sherlock Holmes voice replied;

"My dear Mrs Watson, would you believe me if I told you, the great Holmes has a plan."

Playing along with this charade, Elaine inquired;

"Pray tell all Holmes, what plan have you cunningly contrived to capture that dastardly fellow, the overlord?"

Keeping in character, Notus said;

"It's elementary Dear Watson, we send you!"

That comment brought Elaine back to reality, Elaine now slightly bewildered said

"What??? I think you need to explain that plan."

Notus was now serious and said;

> "Elaine, the overlord has decimated several hundreds of planets in his universe. If we help the triloraptors, in their quest to defeat the overlord they will have no qualms in doing exactly the same! My specie is willing to help but, they will do so on one condition, I send a personal emissary, you!"

For the time being Elaine remained quiet, so uninterrupted Notus continued;

> "My plan is to get you to go with the triloraptors to the micro wormhole gateways. Once there, I will use my telepathy to communicate with my specie from that universe. The information I get will then passed onto you and you will direct the triloraptors to the overlord's lair!"

Elaine felt she was being railroaded into another battle and was getting a little annoyed, she interrupted and said;

> "Notus, what's happened to the rescue plan for my people and me getting home?"

Notus knew what she was feeling and continued to explain;

> "That's the part of the plan I was coming to. We need the triloraptors help to rescue your people. That situation has not changed, but now, we can strike a two part deal with the triloraptors.
>
> Part one is we, with the assistance of my specie can help locate the overlord and see it through until the overlord is captured and justice is administered.
>
> Part two, the triloraptors unconditionally help you locate and return all the humans safely back to earth."

Elaine knew that it was the only deal on the table and one for the sake of her stranded humans she would have to take. Calming down she said;

> "Ok, let's contact the triloraptors and strike up an agreement. But before we do, I have a few questions. How will I personally communicate with the triloraptors? The next one is for my personal safety, is my adaptive DNA as robust as their R.I.T.S trilo-combat uniform?"

Notus though for a few moments and then replied;

> "There is something I can do immediately for communications; I can install a triloraptor communications device to your synaptic brain connections and neurological receptors. This will allow you to freely converse with the triloraptors. It will also give you access to their computers and weapon thought controlled weapons like a trilo-tron.

> Your adaptive DNA adapts to environmental changes, it is not an armoured combat suit. I think however, I see where you are coming from; you feel you cannot trust the triloraptors, correct. Can I ask why?"

Elaine immediately replied;

> "Notus underneath this crystal skin I am still human. At this point of time the triloraptors do not know this but if they do find out I am one of the humans they abducted, they are going to be looking at Captain Elaine Laurence of the planet Notus and the Newman Empire in a different light!"

Notus actually gasped and said;

> "Elaine I am so sorry, I completely overlooked that. Please accept my sincere apologies.

Elaine could feel that Notus was genuinely sincere and replied;

"That's Ok, we both have a lot on our plates, please continue."

Notus needed to give Elaine some confidence in this plan and continued;

"How's about we get the triloraptors to manufacture a full metallic R.I.T.S combat uniform for you? And as a secondary backup, I believe I can enhance your adaptive DNA but I have to say that this is optional. Elaine at this point, I don't know how well it will work."

Notus stopped so Elaine could ask questions and after thinking for a few moments Elaine responded;

"The full metallic R.I.T.S combat uniform sounds good. What's the procedure for the installation of the triloraptor communications device and what exactly do you have to do to enhance my adaptive DNA?"

Brimming with confidence, Notus replied;

"The installation of the triloraptor communications device is very simple. Using nano-technology, two microscopic nano-bots' are implanted into either side of the base of your brain. The nano-bots then build the device and actually complete the communications installation and maintenance. Once installed, you will also be able to use a trilo-visor."

As Notus continued, the confidence waned in Notus' voice;

"What I have in mind for the enhancement of your adaptive DNA is to infuse some of Olotinium atoms with yours. It has never been done and could be potentially dangerous to you. But on the positive side, if it works, you will have the edge on the triloraptors.

Without speculating on all the things that could go wrong, Elaine said;

"Doctor Frankenstein power up the generators, you have work to do."

CHAPTER 23

Immortal

Notus asked Elaine to sit in Notus one's command chair, as she did this the chair reclined and a clear crystal foot rest extended out to support Elaine's legs. Notus then asked Elaine to close her eyes, before her eye lids were fully closed she fell into a deep relaxing sleep that Notus had induced by telepathically putting Elaine's brain in sleep mode.

With Elaine asleep, Notus got Notus one to gently lift off and accelerate just below the speed of sound. At a fraction under 338 kph (approximately 750 Mph). Notus one left the planet's atmosphere and headed out into space. At a distance of 384403 kilometres (238857 miles) Notus one stopped and aligned it's self with the planet Notus's North Pole.

Notus then turned off the gyro chamber controls and then slowly began to rotate Notus one until it reached the same rotational speed of the planet Notus 1,670 kph (1,038 MPH). With Notus one and the planet Notus now rotating at exactly the same speed, Notus slowly started to release some of Olotinium's atoms that Notus had stored deep in the ice at Notus's North Pole.

The atoms of Olotinium began to rise from the planet surface at an incredible speed and as each of Olotinium atoms hit the exterior of Notus one, it illuminated an individual facet in Nous ones crystal outer surface. Within a few earth seconds, every facet was illuminated and Notus one began to glow like a small star. Notus checked on Elaine, she and the whole space craft were now spinning at 1.670 kph (1.038 MPH). Notus then introduced a gravitation field around Elaine body that increased the rotational pressure by the power of ten. At this speed and pressure a human body would have began to disintegrate, but Elaine's adaptive DNA was doing its job and she was fine.

Notus slowly began to increase the rotational speed of Notus one; it was only when the space ship rotational speed hit 3.340 kph (2.076 mph) and the gravitational field increased by the power of twenty that Notus began to see a microscopic shift in Elaine's DNA. Elaine's DNA had now reached a critical time and in a nano second, Notus released all of Olotinium's atoms that had gathered individually in the crystal facets in Notus one's exterior.

Elaine's body was bombarded with these pure energy atoms and for a second Elaine's whole body began to glow a brilliant white. Seeing this happen, Notus immediately reacted and in under a nano second, Notus had slowed the rotational speed back down to 1.670 kph (1.038 MPH) and turned off the gravitation field, Olotinium's atoms had now infused Elaine's. Satisfied that everything went well, Notus stopped the space craft from rotating, re-engaged the gyro chamber controls and set a route so Notus one would head back to the planet surface.

Notus now needed to install the triloraptor communication's device. So on the way back the planet Notus, Notus used the triloraptor nano-technology and with the aid of the newly installed super computer, installed the two microscopic nano-bots' implants into either side of the base of Elaine's brain. On instructions from Notus, the super computer had modified the nano-bots and added new security protocols so that the triloraptors could not interfere with them!

Elaine woke from her deep sleep in her crystal command chair, the first thing she looked at was her skin, it was still crystal blue. She gave her forearm a small slap and it felt the same as before, tough and pliable. Mentally she asked Notus;

"How did the DNA infusion go? I feel just the same"

Notus replied;

"From what I can tell, it appears to have gone well. There are a few changes you will notice immediately the first is; as you now have pure energy DNA in with your own you will not require food or sleep."

Standing up, Elaine burst out laughing and said out loud;

"That's really going to scare the triloraptors!"

Notus joined in with the laughter and said;

"Ok, maybe I did not prioritise the list of changes correctly but, there's more to come."

It was just then that the; "you now have pure energy DNA in with your own you will not require food or sleep" hit Elaine.

"Hey," she said to Notus; "I enjoyed eating food and my medical training taught me that if a mere mortal like me does not have my eight hours of sleep, I will go crazy!"

Notus knew that what Elaine was about to hear would come as a shock, so trying to be considerate, Notus said;

"Elaine, I think you need to sit down again."

Elaine could feel her stomach tighten and did as Notus requested. Notus then continued;

"Elaine, you can still eat and as your body still has a stomach and bowels, it will process food in the normal way. As for sleep, you are correct, for mortals, sleep is a necessity, but you are no longer mortal!"

Elaine could only think of one thing opposite to mortal and that was immortal!

"Notus, "she said; "do you mean I am immortal, as in, undying, ageless and never decaying?"

Notus replied instantly;

"Elaine, that is a good description, but I would not push it on the undying. As you are aware, in the right circumstance all things can die, just look at Olotinium."

Notus left Elaine alone for a few minutes while all Elaine tried to rationalise in her mind on never feeling sick, ageing or dying. For anyone being, there are many advantages and also a quite a few disadvantages to having immortality. If you could take a census on the top disadvantage, it would probably be that as time went by, the family you had and the friends you made would have died long ago and you faced spending eternity being alone! Elaine thoughts were lingering on that point and sensing that, Notus thought it was time to step in and said;

"Elaine, you must give yourself time to adjust to being immortal and I can assure you, you will never be alone. You are part of my family now and all of my specie will always be there for you."

Trying to be a positive as possible Elaine said;

"Thank you for that.

Ok, I'm immortal; now let's get down to the triloraptor scaring stuff, what other super powers have your new offspring got?"

Notus knew this was going to sound funny and began to laugh, through the laughter Notus said;

"You can throw rocks!"

Elaine immediately burst out laughing and replied;

"You know, I could do that before Dr Frankenstein."

Replying and still laughing, Notus said;

> "Maybe so, but these rocks will be a bit bigger, come outside and let's see what you can do."

Elaine walked out of Notus one and found that she was now in a hot dry, deep canyon. Her adaptive DNA skin instantly turned to the colour of most of the bedrock; a dull sandy looking light brown. She just laughed to herself. Looking around, she guessed the distant canyon walls were over 2.000 meters high and the area she was standing in must have been close to 20 to 30 kilometres wide. The canyon must have been carved by some great ancient river, but that must have dried up hundreds if not thousands of years ago.

Notus said to Elaine;

You see that large rock in front of you, it weights five metric tonnes, try to pick it up."

Elaine began to laugh and said;

> "If you think I'm going to manhandle that you've got another thing coming".

Still laughing she continued;

> "I'm a medically trained doctor you know and I have seen my fair share of hernias!"

Still keeping the mood light Notus responded;

> "Doctor Elaine, you are wise beyond your years. Please watch the rock."

At that, the rock that Notus had asked Elaine to lift started to shake and then broke free from the dried sediment of the old river bed. As if by magic, the five metric tonne giant rock began to raise upwards. Dust and small bits of rubble cascaded off it as it slowly rose in the air. At five metres above the canyon floor, the giant rock stopped and just floated in the air!

Elaine looked on in wonderment but then was shocked as the giant rock crash back down onto the dusty river bed. Dust filled the air and automatically Elaine covered her mouth. Notus began to laugh again and said;

> Elaine, don't worry about the dust, your immortal, things like that will not hurt you. In fact, you do not need air to breath anymore."

The not needing air didn't surprise Elaine, but eating dust was one thing this immortal wasn't prepared to do. Putting that aside, what was on her mind was how Notus thought she could raise up that five metric tonne rock!

Notus picked up on Elaine's thoughts and said;

> "As you aware my specie has the ability to manipulate gravity, that's all I did with that rock and you can do the same. All you have to do is think of a gravitational field around the rock and then in your mind's eye reduce the gravitation pull the planet has on the rock. It pretty easy, go on, give it a go."

Elaine did as Notus said but adapted the procedure slightly to suit her human side. She closed her eyes and thought about the rock rising up, when she opened her eyes she said out loud;

> "Bloody hell," followed by, "Oh my god, that's amazing."

The five metric tonne rock was floating at least twenty metres above the dried river bed!

Notus sounded as excited as Elaine as Notus said;

> "Now Elaine, concentrate and throw the rock,"

Elaine looked at a point that she thought was a least one kilometre away and in her mind's eye she threw the rock. The five metric tonne rock shot towards that exact spot and crashed with a thunderous roar down onto the dried river bed. The force of the impact shattered the massive rock and rock fragments and dust clouds shot out in all directions.

Excited, Elaine jumped up and down, clapping her hands several times and she was shouting Wahoo, Wahoo, Wahoo. Like a child, Elaine asked Notus;

"Can I do that again, can I do that again?"

At this point of time, it would have been hard to distinguish who was more adolescently excited as Notus replied;

"Of course, buts lets pick a bigger rock and see if you can lift it higher and throw it further!"

After several successful rock throwing escapades in which Elaine could not only lift and throw the rocks, she could also put them back down on the old river bed with a gentle thump.

Elaine decided to push her gravitational skills a little more. Closing her eyes, she imagined a gravity field around herself, then as with the rocks, she imagined that she was lifting off and was high above the canyon. When she opened her eyes, she was hovering almost 3.000 metres above the canyon! The view was spectacular; the canyon seemed to be much bigger than the Grand Canyon back on earth. All the time Elaine was hovering, she had this nagging thought in the back of her head that she might fall. She knew it was stupid and she knew Notus was watching her, but just to be cautious; she gently lowered herself back to the river bed where Notus one had set down.

Notus asked;

"Did you enjoy that?"

Still excited by the whole experience, Elaine replied;

> "I did, if they could install that ride a Disney you would have a best seller"

Notus then reminded Elaine that the triloraptors were waiting for a reply and feeling more confident Elaine said;

> "That's Ok, I am ready but this time I want to send a live message. It's time the triloraptors got to see Captain Elaine Laurence of the planet Notus and the Newman Empire."

Elaine asked Notus one's super computer to contact the triloraptors by a live feed. The super computer instructed Elaine to stand in front of the virtual reality unit and then said go. Elaine felt confident in her crystal blue skin and said;

> "This is Captain Elaine Laurence of the planet Notus and the Newman Empire. We are prepared to help you in your quest to find the overlord but, we have some conditions. First, you will supply me with an R.I.T.S trilo-combat uniform; my measurements are attached in a file. Second, when we find the overlord you will unconditionally help me find and return the humans you abducted from the RSS's in orbit around the planet earth. Thirdly, you will not maliciously destroy any planets, life forms or their eco systems in the search for the overlord!"

At that Elaine ended the message. Within a few earth seconds the triloraptors replied;

> "Captain Elaine Laurence of the planet Notus and the Newman Empire, we accept your terms."

Without wasting any more time, Elaine got Notus one's super computer to send a message to the triloraptors. It simply said that she would meet them at the opening of the wormholes and once there, she would then supply then with a comprehensive star map of the overlords universe.

The message also said that she would be able to provide possible planetary locations as to where he might be located.

It was then time for Elaine to leave the planet Notus and rendezvous with the triloraptors. Elaine gently lifted off in Notus one and accelerated to just below the speed of sound. She was determined this time to depart from Notus's planetary atmosphere smoothly, Elaine manually controlled Notus one into the correct exit trajectory and then eased Notus one smoothly through Notus's atmosphere. Pleased with that, she accelerated and headed out into space and said out loud to Notus;

>   "That's it; you can take my L Plates off now!"

Notus laughed and replied;

>   "Duly noted, Captain Elaine Laurence."

To avoid too much spacial disturbance, Elaine kept Notus one's speed down to one twentieth of a graviton until the space ship had cleared Notus's solar system. Then, slowly Elaine built up Notus one's speed to ten gravitons. Notus had calculated that at ten gravitons, (each graviton is measured by light speed (299,792,458 metres per second) times ten as one graviton) Elaine would reach the rendezvous point in one earth day.

Although Elaine had been is space several times before, the thought of travelling at such astronomical speeds really excited her. However inside Notus one there was no dramatic G Forces as they accelerated, in fact there was no sense of any speed or movement. Even the view outside was a bit of a disappointment, Notus one walls, floor and ceiling were all transparent and when Notus one hit a meagre one twentieth of a graviton all Elaine could see at these speeds were haze of different colours. At ten gravitons, the haze became a dark grey blur.

As Elaine had a few earth hours to kill before her rendezvous with the triloraptors, she decided to use her time constructively. She got Notus one's super computer to show her all the members of the Interplanetary

Universal Congress specie by specie. In all of Elaine's wildest dreams, she could not have imagine the diversity of intelligent life in this universe.

As a medical doctor, Elaine was interested in aspects of medical illnesses, operational procedures, therapeutic treatments and technological and neurological cures and therefore asked the super commuter to highlight them specie by specie. The results were astounding, Elaine found that through medical science and research, the Interplanetary Universal Congress had almost eradicated most of the common planetary illnesses and diseases with global and interplanetary nano-bot vaccinations. The majority of external and internal operations were done by computerised nano surgery and in most cases, internal and external body parts can be replaced within a few hours using cellular re-growth technology! She couldn't wait until the day she would get back to earth to show her finding to the world health authorities.

CHAPTER 24

Planet Zotreg

Zotreg's morning, noon and night were all as one, dark. This once majestic planet had been robbed of its sunlight and seasons by the complex microwave controlled, rarefied plasma force field that surrounds it. The rarefied plasma is normally found in areas stretching between galaxies, this gas however had been atomically modified so no particles or objects can pass through the force field without them being vaporised. As the rarefied plasma is a gas, it has a higher terrestrial temperature (10^5 K to 10^7 K) and this also has an effect on the planet's surface and eco system as it causes massive global warming.

Due to this enforced global warming, Zotreg's ice caps had long since melted; sea levels had risen globally by 6.7056 meters (about 225 feet). This had a massive effect on the low to mid lying areas as they were totally submerged, in fact over one third of Zotreg's land mass had completely disappeared!

The global warming had destroyed Zotreg's oceans, seas and water ways. With the ice caps gone, there was no planetary cold water! Now the oceans and seas had nothing to regulate their temperatures. As a result, water temperatures globally rose; this also made the air temperature rise worldwide by a staggering six degrees! Zotreg's oceans and seas several decades ago had several thousands of aquatic life forms, now with the rise in water and air temperatures, the oceans and seas were barren of life!

On land, the lush dense forests and tall grasslands were gone; in most areas all that was left were the skeletons of ancient trees, fossilised shrubs and hard baked soil. Zotreg's soils were once fertile and rich in life giving nutrients. This paved the way to global crop growing and the Zotreg farming communities thrived. Now, these lands have become vast infertile deserts! Nomadic Zotreg's still desperately till the soil, but without natural sunlight their work is in vain, as nothing can flourish. As one takes a look across the planet's surface, all of the ecological systems have eroded away and the plant life, shrubs, insects, birds and small and large animal life has been decimated!

The Zotreg civilisation can be traced back several thousand of their years. They had a rich culture in art and architecture, loved Zotreg chanting and Zotreg folk law. This all came to an abrupt end when the overlord decided to conquer their planet and make them his personal slaves. Like most who have encountered the overlord, they put up a courageous fight but, all they have left is decaying towns and cities, poverty and never-ending slavery!

Zotreg is just one of hundreds of planets that the overlord had enslaved and then treated them in the same diabolical way. It was his way of total dominance but, he did not stop there. Once the overlord conquered a planet it was fortified with Proton, Neutron, Graviton weapons that sat on the highest mountainous regions. They could deal with any spacial, air, land or sea attacks. Not satisfied with that, each planet had a microwave controlled, rarefied plasma force field around it.

And finally, the overlord was so impressed with his success in blowing up the planet Olotinium, he decided to repeat this operation and installed several hundred thousand atom sized nuclear armed nano-bots to attach themselves to the core each planet he had conquered! Now if he was dissatisfied in any way, he would do as he had done before and blow up the planet!

Zotreg was one of several planets that the overlord would stay on. Long ago, he had built a fortified stronghold at mount silu that went from the top of the mountain and deep into its bowels. From this, and several hundred other strongholds that had been built over hundreds of years, the overlord and his lords could monitor his vast domain.

Each stronghold had in its bowels its own super computer and technological, biological and scientific research facilities. These facilities were manned by the handpicked geniuses who were all the overlords' slaves; they lived to serve him and his lords. Just to ensure their full co-operation, the overlord had every member of their family incarcerated in one of hundreds of vile underground detention centres that he had scattered around the universe!

For the overlord, information was power and the overlord wanted that information at his finger tips. Each stronghold had a link to a universal network and as information was gathered, that information was instantly available to all other super computers. This made it easy for the overlord to monitor and keep on top of any new developments or projects.

One thing the overlord and his species were under no illusions about and that was loyalty. They knew that they were loathed and despised by all their billions of slaves. From conquered intelligent beings that had been brutalised and enslaved what else could you expect? However, a firm line had been drawn; any talk, sign or display of disloyalty was punishable by every family member and then whole community being publically put to death! As one would expect, numerous attempts had been made to assassinate the overlord and his lords. Those who had tried had paid not just with their lives, but for each attempt one million beings were publically tortured and then put to death!

Being cautious and extremely brutal had kept the overlord and his species alive; they understood the desire for disobedience and insurgence and for that reason they could not rely on their slaves to fight their wars or enforce their will. What they had in their place was an army of over one trillion armoured robotic cubed sentinels (A.R.C.S) that were programmed to carry out the overlord's orders without question or hesitation.

Armoured Robotic Cubed Sentinels (A.R.C.S's) are a cube with six equal square faces. Each cube is this universes equivalent of one a metre square and have an anti gravity device fitted that gives them fantastic mobility to travel over all types land terrain. In water, they can skim with great speed across the water's surface or dive to phenomenal depths in the seas and oceans. And if that wasn't enough, A.R.C.S's are highly competent defence and offence mechanisms at low, min range and high altitudes in the air and in the far reaches of outer space!

A.R.C.S's have been ingeniously designed so that each face was split into nine and through a pivot mechanism, each of the nine faces could turn independently. Each of the nine faces represented a different weapon, they are; Proton, Neutron, Graviton, Pulse, Sonic, Light, Laser, Chemical and Biological weapons. At any one time, any nine of these different weapons could be fired in one direction or nine to the front, nine to the rear, nine from the top, nine from either side and if airborne nine from the bottom. That represented an amazing fifty four different weapons that could be fired simultaneously! When you begin to mix up the weapons fired from each face you could end up with a staggering 43,252,003,274,489,856,000 or about 4×10^{19} weapons combination from a single cube!

Another built in feature of an A.R.C.S was its ability to link to each other by a magnetic locking field, this way A.R.C.S's could form into any block type shape that you wished to construct. This feature was particularly handy when the overlord would want to intimidate his enemy or an insurgent group. The A.R.C.S.'s would be linked together to form an immense wall. With its length, height and width unrestricted, you now had a massive weapon that could produce a wall of unparallel fire power!

A.R.C.S's were so successful that they had been modified into armoured spacial spy and communications satellites and now several millions of these were strategically placed in every solar system that the overlord had conquered. They were also employed further afield at what was deemed as strategic points around various galaxies in the overlord's universe.

As a tyrant who has never lost, the overlord had not taken his defeat by Interplanetary Universal Congress and triloraptors calmly. Each time he thought of his meticulous plans crashing in flames around his feet, his blood boiled! Reflecting on what had happened, victory was all but his, and he should have won easily. How could he have known that a new force had been entered into this universal equation, beings from the planet Notus the Newman Empire. He was frustrated and annoyed as he had no information on these beings! What made his mood worse was now his wormholes to the other universe had been captured by the triloraptors! Infuriated, the overlord had ran numerous computer scenarios of what the intentions of the triloraptors were, however he did not really need this, as he ready knew what his super computers were telling him; it would not be long before they entered his universe in force!

Before being able to concentrate fully on this inevitable battle with the triloraptors, the overlord needed to vent some of his anger. He went to the detention centre at the base of mount silu. At base level, the air has hot and dry and the detention centre smelled of Zotreg sweat, urine, waste products and decaying bodies. For most beings, the disgusting odour would have been overpowering, but for the overlord's species, they have no nostrils or any other means of detecting the scent of another being. Therefore, complaints of vile stenches from all of the overlord's detention centres/prisons was something the overlord and his lords would take no notice of. It had to be said; the well being of his slaves was not something the overlord and his lords had never shown. So even if he or they could have smelt the vile odours, they would probably added to them, as opposed to do anything about them!

The overlord ordered the A.R.C.S's guard to select ten of the strongest male Zotreg's. Zotreg's are race of large split head flightless birds. A glance from our universe to theirs would show that each male Zotreg equivalent average weight would be about 145 kilograms (320 lbs) and corresponding universal height is an average three metres tall, that's not including its horns. Each horn faces forward and varies in size depending on the age of the Zotreg; some can grow to our equivalent of up to a metre long.

In battle, they use their pointed horns to lance an opponent and then while skewered, they repeatedly kick the enemy with their two enormously strong legs and stomp with their single toed feet that resemble a hoof until it is dead! Then being carnivores, they would gorge on the fresh flesh from the defeated opponent's body!

Once selected, the overlord had the ten Zotreg's line up for inspection. The overlord made a mental note that the food in all detention centres/prisons needed to be cut back, these ten Zotreg's had been at this facility for some time, they had shed a few kilo's but, they still looked remarkably healthy!

Satisfied with the selection, the overlord got the A.R.C.S's to form a three A.R.C.S's high, sixty metre walled square that surrounded him and the ten Zotreg's.

With his normal arrogance the overlord then announced;

"Today you will have a chance to earn yours and your family's freedoms, all you have to do is fight with me and stay alive!"

Each Zotreg looked at each other in trepidation; the overlords fighting skills were legendary. As he stood in front of them with his knuckles dragging on the ground, each looked at this beast. He, the beast and overlord was our universes equivalent of two metres tall and with his two arms stretched outward, six metres wide! The massive statistics did not end there, the overlord's barrelled chest was a staggering two and a half metres round and each bicep measured one and half metres!

This colossal size and muscle mass is due to the overlord and his species, a large form of primates coming from a planet called Xalinn. Xalinn has four times the gravitational pull then our planets Notus and earth have. It therefore takes four times the normal body strength just to stand up! In the overlords universe most habitable planets have the same gravitational pull as we do, Zotreg is an exception, and it has ten percent less! This gave the overlord an enormous gravitational advantage, and he knew it.

The overlord continued;

"Choose your best Zotreg fighter for the first bout."

In truth, none of the Zotreg's wanted to fight the overlord, win or lose; they knew the treachery of this evil being. Plus, weighing up the simple facts that they were surrounded by a wall A.R.C.S's that were ready to cut them down, gave them no confidence to fight.

Unselfishly, one of the younger Zotreg's agreed he would go first; he had no harem of wife's or offspring's to consider and in past whims of the overlord, the overlord had killed the rest of his family. He had nothing to lose and maybe, just maybe he could kill or injure this bully!

With juvenile arrogance, the young Zotreg pushed out his chest, lowered his horned split head, spread his wings that reached an equivalent in this universes of a span of about 3 metres (9.8425197ft), and then slowly strutted forward. The overlord could see the rage building up in this young Zotreg's eyes, and then all of a sudden the Zotreg charged, Zotreg's can run at a speed in there universe of over 70 km/h (43 mph) and can cover 3 to 5 m (9.8 to 16 ft) in a single stride.

It was a predictable attack; the overlord stood his ground until the last split second and then with lighting speed dodged to his right. At the same time, the overlord thrust his left hand just below the Zotreg's right tarsus (the lowest upright part of the leg) and cupped his left hand under the rear of the Zotreg's body and then thrust upward, this bowled the Zotreg over. With gravity on his side the overlord leap into the air and threw his enormously heavy body onto the fallen Zotreg. The Zotreg gave out a loud shriek as all the air was instantly knocked out of his body. Almost flattened, the Zotreg could not move, but then its life ended as the overlord grasped its neck with one of his massive hands and as easy as pulling up a daisy, tore its head and neck off clean from its shoulders!

The overlord jump back onto his over sized feet and with green blood dripping from his right hand, he swung the young Zotreg's decapitated head around as if it were a medieval morning star. Jeering, he called to the other nine remaining Zotreg's;

"Was that the best you have to offer?"

All nine Zotreg's remained silent. So the overlord continued his taunting;

> "Ok you Zotreg women, I will give you a chance, let's have four of you for the next bout!"

Again, the nine Zotreg's did not respond, so the overlord pointed to an A.R.C.S and said;

> "You have three Zotreg seconds to choose or you will all be killed. I have plenty more Zotreg's to pick from!"

There was no need for a debate; each of the nine Zotreg's knew that if they did not fight, more would be chosen and more would die! Reluctantly four Zotreg's stepped forward, before they had a chance, the overlord bent his knees, thrust his massive arms out and dived forward. In one leap, the overlord had cleared almost thirty metres! Although the Zotreg's were fast, the four Zotreg's could not avoid our universes equivalent of 453.592 kilo's (1000lb) of muscle hurdling towards them! The overlord hit all four of them like an express train; all four Zotreg's hit the floor fast and hard. The overlord immediately bounced back onto his feet and was still holding the decapitated head of the young Zotreg. He swung the horned head at one of the Zotreg, his accuracy was amazing! One horn went straight into the Zotreg's eye the other went into the base of its neck puncturing a main blood vessel. The Zotreg shrieked with pain and began to fall to the ground; before it hit the ground the overlord tugged and retrieved the horned weapon and then swung again at another Zotreg that was trying to recover from the first onslaught. The two pointed horns hit the Zotreg in the middle of its chest with so much force that they were buried up to where the young Zotreg's eyes were! The Zotreg heart and lungs had been pierced and as a result, it dropped dead instantly.

From this bout, the two remaining Zotreg's had fully recovered from the overlord initial attack and had manoeuvred themselves to either side of the overlord. Seeing an opportunity to attack, they both lowered their split head horns and charged at over 70 km/h (43 mph) at the overlord. The overlord has exceptional peripheral vision and from the corner of each eye he could see both Zotreg's charge; he slightly bent his huge knees and waited until the last split second. Just as the Zotreg's were about to crash into him with their sharp pointed horns, the overlord jumped high into the air and back flipped. His timing was perfect and two Zotreg's crashed head on into each other! As the overlord landed, he clenched his enormous fists and using the outside edges of the balled fists; he hammer fisted both Zotreg's heads together! For the overlord, it was just like smashing two freshly laid eggs, the Zotreg's skulls shattered and their brains were splattered everywhere!

Rapidly glancing around the overlord could see that the last remaining five Zotreg's had positioned themselves around him and looked ready to attack. The overlord was now in true fighting mode, he swiftly reached down and with his colossal hands he picked up both of the dead Zotreg's by their tarsus (the lowest upright part of the leg) and like a discus thrower he spun his body around. With precision, the overlord opened his right hand and the carcass of the dead Zotreg's bodied shot through the air and crashed into a Zotreg. In the same circular motion, the overlord opened his left hand and the other dead Zotreg shot out and hit a second Zotreg. The force of the dead carcasses hitting both Zotreg's knocked them almost twenty metres backwards! Their airborne bodied had nowhere to go, both Zotreg's crashed into the A.R.C.S's wall with such force that most of their chest bones shattered and internally their organs were ruptured!

Contemptuously, the overlord called out;

"Two Zotreg's down and three Zotreg's to go."

To the amazement of the Zotreg's, the overlord then sat down on the ground and slowly placed his giant hands on his large hairless head. Then in a taunting manner he said;

"Ok, Zotreg's women, no, no, Children! Give me your best shots!"

This bravado was something the Zotreg's hadn't expected but they wanted to take full advantage of the overlords offer. Without discussion or hesitation, each Zotreg choose a target on the overlords body, they then lowered their split head horns and charged with as much speed as they could muster at the overlord. At just two metres away all three Zotreg's crashed head on into an invisible wall! The overlord had activated his personnel protection device (P.P.D); this is a simple force field that can stop objects with high opposing kinetic force.

Dazed from the impact, the three Zotreg's staggered uneasily on their feet, that was when the overlord struck! He had instantly de-activated his P.P.D, jumped to his feet and in a boxing style, began to pummel each stunned Zotreg with volley of bone breaking punches. One by one the Zotreg's collapsed, within seconds all three lay injured and dying on the ground.

The overlord surveyed his make shift arena, ten Zotreg's bodied lay battered and dead around him and for the first time in over a Xalinn week he felt good. He thought;

"Now it is time to tackle another bird, the triloraptor!"

CHAPTER 25

Copy Cat!

As Elaine approached her meeting point with the triloraptors she asked the virtual reality unit to display all trilo-crafts in the area. She was amazed to find there were over two hundred obsidian-black trilo-crafts! But what was even more amazing was right in the centre of this fleet of trilo-crafts the triloraptors were building a new mother ship and it was the same shape as Notus one! The only difference was its colour and its size. Instead of being crystal blue, it was obsidian-black and proportionately it was at least twenty times as big as Notus one! Elaine thought has stunning it looked and.

Playfully, Notus said to Elaine;

> "Ok, the Right Honourable Elaine Laurence, who's the thief now? That design was exclusive to me! Those thieving triloraptors have copied my Marquise-Cut boat shaped Diamond space ship design!"

Laughing at Notus's protest, Elaine replied in her best high court judges voice;

> "Did the plaintiff take out a patent on this?

In a down trodden tone Notus replied;

> "No your honour, I did not."

Elaine could only come back with one verdict;

"Then Mr Notus, you have no case for grievance. Case dismissed and costs awarded to the defendants!"

Before Notus could ask for an appeal, a call came in from the trilo-raptors central command;

"Captain Elaine Laurence of the planet Notus and the Newman Empire, welcome. As you can see we are in the process of building a new mother ship. The design and shape has been chosen by our new central command in respect to you and your civilisation. We hope this pleases you?

As requested, we have your R.I.T.S trilo-combat uniform; we can transport this across to or you can come and collect it.

Our scientists and technicians have made excellent progress in micro engineering our trilo-crafts, computers and weaponry technology. We have successfully assembled our micro-trilo fleet on the other side of the micro worm holes and are ready to continue our search for the overlord in this micro universe. At your convenience, please supply use with the universal star maps so we can proceed."

Elaine responded immediately;

"Trilo-raptor command, you honour the planet Notus and the Newman Empire by designing your new mother ship to resemble our own space craft."

Elaine could hear Notus whispering "thieves, thieves, thieves," in her head but without faltering she continued;

"Please send over the R.I.T.S trilo-combat uniform, I will then personally come to you and arrange for the universal star maps to be uploaded on to your computers."

Within a few trilo-minutes a trilo-shuttle was sent for Elaine, for Elaine however this was a problem. She asked Notus;

"How are they and we supposed to dock?

With an air of jovial arrogance Notus said;

> "Unlike those copycats, Notus one1 has all of the latest refinements; you can use our patented universal gravitational docking field."

Unconvinced that this universal gravitational docking field was real, Elaine said;

> "Does that mean I have to jump?"

That really made Notus laugh, Notus replied while laughing;

> "No, all you have to do is walk down to the exit and Notus one will extend a gravitational field to the trilo-shuttle."

Without having to do a space jump, Elaine entered the trilo-shuttle through Notus one gravitational docking field, as soon as she entered the trilo-shuttle its bay door closed and it smoothly headed back to the trilo-raptor command vessel. To Elaine's surprise the trilo-shuttle was unmanned and unfurnished. In the centre of the floor was a neat pile that was her obsidian-black R.I.T.S trilo-combat uniform and visor. She immediately tried the uniform on and found it that it was a perfect fit and unexpectedly, it was light weight and comfortable to wear. For some reason she wished she had a mirror to see how she looked but then she thought;

> "I suppose trilo-raptors would find it frivolous to have such things."

Notus jumped in and said;

> "Take it from me, you look stunning. If you were to enter the Miss Trilo-newman contest, you would win it hands downs."

Laughing, Elaine replied;

"A pageant in a one horse race, that's some beauty contest!"

Elaine then picked up her visor and slipped it on. Immediately the visor sensors made contact the implants in Elaine's head and it switched itself on. An array of small symbols appeared in side menus. As she had no idea what any of the symbols meant, she asked Notus to explain.

> "They are the commands for the trilo-combat uniform, trilo-tron weapon and commutations with the triloraptors and their computers. I will run you through each later one but for now you are about to dock and meet with the trilo-raptors."

Within a few seconds the trilo-shuttle docked in the landing bay of the trilo-command ship and its bay door opened. Elaine slowly walked out and was greeted by a formation of about two hundred triloraptors who had formed two lines on either side of a long of a long corridor. Each triloraptor was dressed in full trilo-combat uniform and visors and by their sides were there trilo-trons.

As Elaine began to walk down the corridor every triloraptor began the stamp each foot;

> "Thump, thump, thump, thump, thump, thump, thump, thump, thump, thump, thump, thump, thump, thump, thump, thump, thump, thump."

Elaine was a little unnerved by this, but Notus whispered in her head;

> "Don't worry; they are paying their respects to you. Now walk past them with an air of superiority and pretended that that are not there, they will love that!"

Notus was right, as Elaine neared the end of the corridor the thumping of feet got louder and louder! She then entered a large hall that must have been the triloraptors command centre. In the middle of the room was the same virtual display unit that was now installed in Notus one. Elaine thought "thief" but the criminal Notus chose to remain silent.

A triloraptor dressed in full trilo-combat uniform walked up the Elaine and formally greeted her. Elaine' communication device was working perfectly as in a voice Elaine could understand the triloraptor said;

"Welcome to our command centre."

Elaine thanked the triloraptor and then she was given a tour of the command centre. The command centre had an array of computer terminals with their own virtual display units and various scanners and technological gizmos that Elaine had no idea what they were used for. Each computer terminal was manned by a triloraptor that stood and imputed information in by its head visor. Numerous life sized trilo-bots were on hand and darted back and forth between each computer terminal. With the niceties over it was down to business, the triloraptor asked;

"Could you send the overlords universes star map data over as we feel the longer we delay, the more difficult it will be to apprehend the overlord."

Without delay, Elaine got Notus one to send over the relevant data. Within a few trilo-seconds the triloraptors main virtual display unit light up with the new universes star map data. At the same time, each individual computer terminal received the same data. For the next thirty earth minutes the triloraptors studied the data. Elaine could see them expanded the universes map to reveal each galaxy and then expanded further and further to reveal each star and its own solar system.

Then without warning, the triloraptors shut down there main virtual display unit and all individual computers and their virtual display units. And then, as if they were practicing a fire drill, each triloraptor and trilo-bot quickly exited the command centre. Standing alone, Elaine was confused by what just happened, she telepathically asked for Notus's advice but to her alarm she then realised she could not move her arm or legs!

"Notus," she mentally called out, "What's happening, the triloraptors have gone and I cannot move?"

It was then that an electro-pulse wave smashed into her and knocked her almost ten metres backward. Dazed, she crashed onto the floor of the command centre. Elaine tried to stand up but again her arms and legs would not move!

"Elaine, Elaine, Notus called back. "Are you alright?"

Almost shouting, Notus continued:

"Elaine if you can hear me, Notus one is under attack; the triloraptors have hit it with a powerful electro-pulse wave that has affected its functions."

Before Elaine could reply, she realised she was surrounded by ten triloraptors in trilo-combat uniform with their trilo-tron hovering by their sides! One of the trilo-raptors announced;

"Captain Elaine Laurence of the planet Notus and the Newman Empire you are now our prisoner! You are charged with war crimes against the triloraptors, this charge is automatically punishable by death! Your spaceship is just about to be seized; its technology will be used to bring others like you to trilo-justice!"

At that, the triloraptors virtual display unit light up showing Notus one surrounded by the two hundred strong, triloraptor fleet. Their new mother ship had manoeuvred its self along the side of Notus one. It then did something that took Elaine and Notus by surprise! From its centre; it slowly began to divide in two! The mother ships two sections then manoeuvred themselves so one was above and the other was below Notus one. Then with triloraptor precision, the two sections then manoeuvred themselves so Notus one was completely encapsulated and imprisoned by the two sections. Being made of R.I.T.S the two sections then sealed themselves together and the space craft appeared to be one whole vessel again!

Elaine's head had now cleared and as she lay on the command centre floor she said telepathically to Notus;

"It looks as if we have fallen into a trilo-trap! The triloraptors did not make their mother ship the Marquise-Cut boat shaped Diamond space ship design to look like Notus one out of respect for us; they made it to imprison Notus one! And this trilo-combat uniform I am wearing, this too was made to capture me!"

Replying, Notus said;

"Elaine we have both been fooled! It would seem that the new triloraptor central commanders are all youngsters and twice as treacherous as their predecessor's!"

What Notus said next came as a surprise to Elaine;

"I think it's time we fought back!"

Puzzled, Elaine asked;

"How, I can't move and am going to be killed for war crimes! Notus one has been imprisoned inside a trilo-R.I.T.S prison ship! Oh and one more thing, you are thousands of light years away on the planet Notus and I guess that limits your powers?"

Coolly Notus replied;

"Elaine, the triloraptors and not the only cunnings beings in this universe. First, I have de-activated the triloraptors control of your trilo-combat uniform, you can now stand up."

At that and to the surprise of the triloraptors Elaine jumped to her feet. Un-characteristically the triloraptors warriors began to back away!

Notus continued;

"Elaine, now watch the virtual display unit."

The triloraptors virtual display unit instantly light up and showed a three dimensional image of 'crystal women' Elaine who said;

222

"Triloraptors, I have taken control of all of your computers, weaponry and trilo-crafts! Surrender or I will destroy you!

It was hard to work out who was more surprised, Elaine or the triloraptors. But Elaine knew Notus was up to something so she played along. Looking directly at the ten triloraptors, Elaine said;

"I think you need a lesson in good manners."

Before the triloraptors could take any counter action, Elaine imagined a gravity ball that surrounded the ten triloraptors, she then raised all ten up in the air, glanced to the bottom of the command centre and hurled all ten into the back wall! With their trilo-combat uniforms on, the ten triloraptors were not hurt, but they were stunned at what Elaine had just done! Elaine enquired:

"How do you like to be thrown around?"

Just to show that was simple demonstrations of her powers, Elaine then used several gravitational fields and snatched all ten trilo-tron from the triloraptors! The ten trilo-trons then hovered menacingly as a protection field around Elaine!

While Elaine was having her bit of fun, the triloraptors fleet were desperately trying to gain access to their ships onboard computers and weapons systems. To start with it was a real brainteaser for the trilo-computer technicians, but then though a little more methodical analyses and a bit of luck, they stumbled across the problem. Every computer they had had been contaminated by a rare virus known as a ghost spirit virus. A little more research revealed that they had downloaded this ghost virus when they recovered their mother ships data from outside Notus's solar system!

The ghost spirit virus was complex cycle of spirit worms that had hidden themselves in the root directories of every one of the triloraptors computers. Notus had designed the ghost spirit viruses so once activated, one or more individuals could then ghost themselves in or out any computer programme or network, and at will, control of that computer system.

This clever virus was activated at precisely the same time that Captain Elaine Laurence was shot with the electro-pulse wave. The trilo-computer technicians deduced that Captain Elaine Laurence trilo-visor implants had been modified and was some sort of failsafe trigger device.

But as brilliant as the trilo-computer technicians were, a ghost spirit virus of this nature was a phenomenon that defied the logic of computer science. It was present for one moment and then gone, it could then reappear and disappear at will! The only way the trilo-computer technicians could deactivate the complex cycle of ghost spirit worms was to wipe out all the data from their computers! This was not an option as their trilo-computers controlled everything from their life support systems, food dispensaries, and newly fitted graviton engines, communications and weapons guidance systems!

In all of their history, the triloraptors had never been in such a bad position, but they were realists. This dilemma was brought about by their own foolish actions; they had seriously underestimated Captain Elaine Laurence of the planet Notus and the Newman Empire who they classed as their enemies. And now, to survive, the triloraptors had only one option, to surrender!

The triloraptor commanders re-entered the command centre, this time they were not wearing their trilo-combat uniforms. A single triloraptor then approach Elaine, Elaine guessed it was the same one who gave her the tour of the command centre. The triloraptor said in a loud clear voice;

> "Captain Elaine Laurence of the planet Notus and the Newman Empire, I and my fellow commanders are here on behalf of the triloraptors to formally surrender!
>
> We would ask that you show clemency to our young."

Elaine still did not fully understand what Notus had been up to but without hesitation Elaine replied;

> "Your surrender and terms are accepted. I came here to help you in your quest to capture the overlord, a person who has wronged not just me but this whole universe. You however have betrayed everyone in this universe by attempting to kill the one individual who could have helped you to succeed, me!
>
> I will now return to my space ship and report what has transpired here to the Interplanetary Universal Congress."

Elaine causally walked out of the command centre and down the long corridor to the shuttle bay. It was then that her legs felt weak and her whole body began to tremble, she stood for a moment and took a few deep breaths. As an immortal, Elaine knew that she did not need air anymore, but this was her human side's natural reaction to what had been a highly traumatic situation. Feeling a little more composed, Elaine then telepathically contacted Notus;

> "I need a ride back to Notus one. Can you call a cab for me and on the way back you can you fill me in on what skulduggery you have been up to?"

Now that Notus had control of all of the triloraptors computers, Notus easily accessed the controls of Notus one 1's prison ship but had decided to leave Notus one where it was for the time being. On hearing Elaine's request for a shuttle, Notus promptly had a shuttle waiting for Elaine as she entered the shuttle bay. As Elaine entered the shuttle Notus said;

> "How are you holding up?"

Elaine only reply was;

> "I'll live"

On the way back to Notus one, Notus explained that right from the onset of the triloraptors trying to invade and destroy the planet Notus,

Notus had had misgivings about trusting the triloraptors! Notus also felt that their reaction was to blasé over the destruction of the triloraptor fleet and mother ship. It was at that point that Notus had decided they needed a little extra insurance against any further trilo-reprisals. The opportunity to take out that insurance arose when the triloraptors mother ship was destroyed and Notus commandeered their black box. Notus said;

> "While I had the black box in my possession, I designed and added a ghost virus into the root directory of their entire boot up files and programmes. I knew they would re-install these files in all the surviving trilo-craft and the ghost virus would spread undetected though their whole system. With that done, I then modified your implant so if they tried to hurt you, this would trigger the ghost virus.
>
> And before you say, why I didn't tell you about this, I thought I was being a little paranoid and simply did not want to worry you."

Frankly Elaine did not have any idea what a ghost virus was or how it worked but with affection in her voice, she said to Notus;

> "I am deeply touched and really happy that you were looking out for me, if I could hug you I would! Oh and if it keeps us safe, your paranoia and ghost virus's are fine by me."

Notus remained silent but was genuinely pleased at what Elaine had said.

As Elaine exited the shuttle craft, Elaine was surprised to find herself in a large triloraptor docking bay. Notus said;

> "This is Notus one's new extension, what do you think?"

Elaine burst out laughing and sarcastically said;

"Once a thief always a thief. Your stealing their mother ship, aren't you?"

With a little deviousness in the tone, Notus replied;

"Not exactly, but if you think about it, the triloraptors do not have any other use for it, but I on the other hand have some plans that will save this fine space vessel from going to the scrap yard."

Elaine could not argue with that kind of logic and was now curious, she replied;

"Ok if you keep it, what are you going to do with it?"

Notus replied;

"Isn't it obvious, Notus one is a bit on the small side, so we are going to use the extra space for accommodation when we rescue your fellow human beings. And we now have a lot of new weapons, a shuttle craft and a landing bay which may also help."

Elaine thought most of this was a brilliant idea but, she had her reservations on the weapons. Her thoughts then went back to the other universe and the overlord, she said;

"Notus are we going to walk away from this battle or shall we complete this and then rescue my people?"

Notus already knew what was in Elaine's head and replied;

"Well my warrior princess, if I pleases you, we are going to defeat the overlord but with what has just transpired with the triloraptors, we need a change in our plans."

Elaine had now made it back to Notus one and was eager to hear what changes Notus had thought of, however she had one major reservation, and that was the triloraptors! She inquired;

> "Notus, are we still going to let the triloraptors take part in this new plan?

Notus answered;

> "Directly no, indirectly yes. We are going to requisition their new micro fleet and you are going to be at the helm!"

From what Notus had just said, Elaine cold not see too many changes from the old plan to the new one and asked Notus exactly what was meant by her being at the helm? Notus explained;

> "The triloraptors have ingeniously replicated their whole fleet, weaponry and trilo-bots into a micro form. I now have access to all their micro-technology and I can now, with a few borrowed bits, make a micro Captain Elaine Laurence who will actually go into the overlord universe and capture him.

Elaine thought for a moment and then said excitedly;

> "So on this new mission, Micro-me gets to go through a worm hole into another universe, has a fleet of battle ships at my deposal and gets the chance to personally capture the biggest villain in this universes history?"

Notus replied;

> "In a nut shell, yes, but we have a bit of work to do first. You need to contact the Interplanetary Universal Congress and let them know what the triloraptors have been up to. And while you are doing that, I need to make a micro version of you."

CHAPTER 26

Captain Elaine Laurence

Chair Elect Zissiani was surprised to hear from Captain Elaine Laurence of the planet Notus and the Newman Empire. She was even more surprised to hear that the triloraptors had been defeated again! And through their total incompetence, they were now defenceless and were now prisoners of war to the Captain Elaine Laurence of the planet Notus and the Newman Empire!

It was through her scheming that the new trilo-command had agreed to kill Captain Elaine Laurence of the planet Notus and the Newman Empire. She had wanted her eradicated as she thought she would possibly expose her previous indiscretions with the triloraptors.

Chair Elect Zissiani had to concede that she and the triloraptors had seriously underestimated Captain Elaine Laurence. However being a brilliant military commander and now politician, she thought that the latest events could actually work in her favour. She sent a uni-net holographic communication back to Elaine saying;

> "Captain Elaine Laurence of the planet Notus and the Newman Empire, we at the Interplanetary Universal Congress are appalled at the actions of triloraptors. However to be candid, we are not surprised.
>
> The whole Interplanetary Universal Congress is built upon respecting 'the way' of other being and the way of the triloraptors is killing. Under normal circumstances, the triloraptors contain their natural urges to hunting for prey for

food. The constraints for their natural urges have been thrown into mayhem by recent events.

The overlord must be clearly blamed for this. I will be the first to admit that under pressure; even the Interplanetary Universal Congress has succumbed to uncivilised acts of war against our fellow Interplanetary Universal Congress members and other beings in this universe.

Those circumstances have now past and like any civilised race we must put aside our past grievances. What the triloraptors have done is undisputedly wrong.

Your race has only shown kindness to the Interplanetary Universal Congress. You went with good intentions to help not just the triloraptors but all beings wronged by the overlord, sadly the triloraptors tried to take advantage of this. Under Interplanetary Universal Congress laws they are accountable for their unlawful acts against you. We can send a small fleet to help you detain those responsible and bring them to justice.

Captain Elaine Laurence, the Interplanetary Universal Congress is fully committed in the apprehension of the overlord, with that in mind, the full resources of the Interplanetary Universal Congress at your disposal. You only have to ask and we shall provide our best top military and scientific specialists."

Chair Elect Zissiani was quite pleased with her uni-net holographic communication. She then thought;

"All my recent communications with the triloraptors have been meticulously destroyed and are untraceable. The triloraptors may have failed miserably and that is now their downfall, I as Chair Elect with the full support of the Interplanetary Universal Congress will bring them to justice.

As for Captain Elaine Laurence of the planet Notus and the Newman Empire, at the next Interplanetary Universal Congress meeting, I will propose that they become members of this illustrious body. And Captain Elaine Laurence becomes an emissary for the planet Notus and the Newman Empire.

And then I, the great Zissiani will have triumphed again! The Interplanetary Universal Congress will see that the Chair Elect Zissiani has once again brought some sanity to this universe."

Zissiani then sent copies to all Interplanetary Universal Congress delegates and members and as Chair Elect she called for an emergency meeting, with one item on the agenda, the triloraptors. To help persuade the members of the Interplanetary Universal Congress of how unpopular the triloraptors are and for a little extra publicity, she 'accidentally' leaked a copy of her uni-net holographic communication to Interplanetary Universal Congress press office!

Elaine watched Chair Elect Zissiani uni-net holographic communication and decided that Zissiani was not to be trusted. She did however consult Notus about the triloraptors and while Notus was still annoyed at being lead into a trap by them, Notus said;

"Elaine, we still need the triloraptors micro fleet and possibly some of their other resources and skills if we are to beat the overlord. And once this battle is over, we need then to help locate your fellow human beings and disarm the booby traps they set. I think we need to let the trilo-raptors see the uni-net holographic communication and then have a chat with the triloraptors."

Elaine agreed with Notus and promptly sent the uni-net holographic communication to the triloraptor command vessel. It wasn't long before she had a reply;

"Captain Elaine Laurence of the planet Notus and the Newman Empire, we have watched with interest Chair Elect Zissiani uni-net holographic communication and cannot deny some of its contents. We are what we are, predators and hunters, that is our way.

We also cannot deny luring you into a trilo-trap, we along with Chair Elect Zissiani had planned this. At Chair Elect Zissiani request, it was agreed that all commutations be destroyed, this was then done jointly by a highly sophisticated communications eradication programme. As we have had dealing with Chair Elect Zissiani before we thought it prudent to backup these communications as soon as they come in. These backup files are on our main super computer with the file name 'betrayal'. You have control of our computers, please look at this file.

As too the Interplanetary Universal Congress sending their best top military and scientific specialists, that is not necessary. We give you our word that we will co-operate fully with you in defeating the overlord, and when that is over, as previously agreed, we will help you find the humans. At that point of time, you can decide the triloraptors feat."

After listening to the triloraptors response, Elaine asked Notus to access the triloraptors main computer. Within a few second Notus had found the file 'betrayal and in that file was all the evidence needed to support the triloraptors claims that Chair Elect Zissiani had plotted to kill Elaine. The file also revealed other recorded conversations that Admiral Zissiani had previously had with the triloraptors, proving conclusively that Zissiani had been working with the triloraptors even when both sides were at war! One recorded conversation really got to Elaine; it had Admiral Zissiani alongside the triloraptors plotting to destroy the plantet earth! Elaine couldn't contain herself and half shouting she said;

"That lying bitch, she has been playing all sides! We need to expose her to the Interplanetary Universal Congress!

Notus was in full agreement but had a plan. Notus said;

"Elaine we now have this information, let's use it wisely."

Elaine replied;

"I'm listening"

Continuing Notus explained;

"Using this information at this point of time will gain us very little. However, if we hold onto it and wait for Chair Elect Zissiani to expose the triloraptors as the sole villains, we can then drop this into the lap of the Interplanetary Universal Congress and hopefully this will be her downfall. We can also tell the triloraptors of what we propose and it might redeem them a little as members of the Interplanetary Universal Congress."

After a moment's thought, Elaine said;

"That sounds like a good plan, let's do it, but first, I think it is appropriate to reply to the Chair Elect Zissiani uni-net holographic communication.

Standing with her trilo-combat uniform on, Elaine positioned herself so the virtual display unit could see her; she then began her holographic communication.

"Chair Elect Zissiani, I would like to thank you and the Interplanetary Universal Congress for your concerns over the recent events where the triloraptors tried to kill me, that was indeed a despicable act.

After some negotiations, the triloraptors have agreed to still assist in the incarceration of the overlord and as I have control of all of their computers, weapons and fleet, I do not see any need for any Interplanetary Universal Congress involvement.

Once this is over, the appropriate justice can then be administered to all those concerned."

Elaine then ended her holographic communication.

Speaking to Notus, Elaine said;

"Ok, I think that should give Zissiani something to think about. Now, how's my mini me looking."

Proudly Notus replied;

"I think I have surpassed myself, she has all of you qualities and she's onboard the trilo micro command vessel ready for action."

With a laugh in her voice Elaine replied;

"Its sound like Doctor Frankenstein has done it again. How do I, Queen Frankenstein and mini-stein-me link up?"

Joining in with Elaine's jovial tone, Notus replied;

"I think Doctor Frankenstein would have given his arms, legs and his head for this bit of technology."

Both Elaine and Notus had a little chuckle at what was just said and then Notus continued;

"Elaine, when you put your trilo-visor on a new symbol of you will appear in the left hand corner. All you have to do is think of opening that symbol and you will have activated the micro version of you. When activated, the micro version of you will respond to you by your trilo-visor's interface with direct mind control."

Keen to try this out, Elaine popped on her trilo-visor and followed Notus's instructions. The first thing that surprised her was, she was able to see through her micro versions eyes, it just seemed as if she was their! The next amazing thing was how easy it was to control her micro versions movements. Pleased with this, Elaine said to Notus;

"That's just amazing, but I don't think you should get all the credit, didn't the triloraptors develop this first?"

Notus had to come clean and said;

"They did indeed, but I checked the records and they did not file a patent! Now, the triloraptors command ship is the best place to run operation overlord, I have the shuttle ready and waiting for you and the triloraptors are eager to begin the hunt for the overlord."

CHAPTER 27

Overlords Domain

With only life support and food distribution available, the triloraptors were becoming quite hostile toward each other. It was therefore a relief when Elaine entered the triloraptor command and announced that their command centre would be used as the headquarters for operation overlord.

Elaine got Notus to switch on the triloraptors virtual display unit and then gave the triloraptors limited access to their computers and head visors. The triloraptors got straight to work and brought up their micro fleet on the virtual display unit. Elaine walked over to the virtual display unit and asked Notus telepathically to telepathically communicate with his race for an indication as to where the overlord might be.

Within seconds Notus came back with four distinct possibilities, Zsaraxil, Zotreg, Kzegas 1, and Zaranne. However, Notus was horrified to find that each of these four planets had several hundred thousand atom sized nuclear armed nano-bots on each of their planets cores and what Notus found more upsetting, was, four members of his race had become one with each of these planets!

Notus was then further shocked to find each of these four planet's atmosphere was being choked by a microwave controlled; rarefied plasma force field! And the overlord's dominance and security paranoia got worse. All four planets' were heavily fortified with Proton, Neutron, and Graviton weapons that sat on each planet highest mountainous regions. And if that wasn't enough, to top it all, each planet had a vast army of armoured robotic cubed sentinels (A.R.C.S) that not only guarded the planet's surface but also its solar system and various strategic regions of outer space!

Notus immediately conveyed this information to Elaine and said;

> "This is a lot worse than I thought, the overlord is completely mad! Elaine, let the triloraptors look at this and get them to work on some strategies for operation overlord."

While Elaine was updating the triloraptors, Notus was able to get some holographic footage of each planet, its solar system and some of their planetary security installations as well as details on the armoured robotic cubed sentinels (A.R.C.S). Notus immediately uploaded these onto the triloraptors virtual display unit.

Even with restricted access to their computers and rather sketchy information, the triloraptor command soon came up with some scenarios for operation overlord. One of the triloraptors called Elaine over and said;

> "Captain Elaine Laurence, from what you have said, and from seeing the information on the virtual display unit, we only have a few options for you, if you watch the virtual display unit, we will show our first simulation to you."

The virtual display unit showed the planets Zsaraxil, Zotreg, Kzegas 1, and Zaranne's solar systems being invaded by four separate divisions of the triloraptor fleet. Each small fleet put down a barrage of heavy fire and under that cover, two battle ships from each fleet broke away and each deployed a super G R.I.M. missile. Each super G R.I.M. missiles then locked onto its designated target, the planets north or south poles and within seconds, all four planets and most of the most of their solar system were destroyed!

Bluntly, Elaine said;

> "You have to be joking, that is absolutely barbaric!"

In the triloraptors defence it replied;

"To you Captain Elaine Laurence that may be barbaric, to the triloraptors, that simulation is highly efficient."

Elaine looked straight at the triloraptor and said;

"Ok, what if our information was wrong, and what if the overlord wasn't on one of those that planets? How can you justify killing all of those innocent beings and destroying not just one, but four whole solar systems?

All of what Elaine had just said was inconsequential to the triloraptor, so without entering into a debate, the triloraptor said;

"We are now ready to show you our next simulation."

The virtual display unit showed the planets Zsaraxil, Zotreg, Kzegas 1, and Zaranne's solar systems being invaded by four separate divisions of the triloraptor fleet. Each small fleet put down a barrage of heavy fire and under that cover; two battle ships from each fleet broke away and at top speed crashed into the micro wave transmitters that controlled the planets force field. With the planets force field down, the main fleet then rushed forward and entered the planet's atmosphere, where they immediately came under heavy fire from the mountainous regions defences. Despite their R.I.T.S construction and to Elaine surprise, countless micro-trilo-craft were sustaining heavy damage and then being destroyed! But then without warning, the mountainous regions defences fell silent, they had been mysteriously destroyed! The remaining trilo-fleet then began to man a ground offensive. At that the simulation ended.

Elaine looked at the triloraptor and said;

"That looks a bit better, but I am puzzled, what happened in the simulation to your micro-trilo-craft and then mountainous regions defences?"

Replying the triloraptor said;

> "Some of our micro-trilo-craft have been made by a low-grade R.I.T.S and have been designed to be destroyed. In this simulation they were used to draw fire as part of an offensive distraction. We have constructed another two hundred micro craft and they have been fitted with quzzzuzzz cloaking technology. In the simulation, these cloaked micro-trilo-craft were invisible to the overlord's planetary defences, and while their planetary defences were busy destroying our inferior crafts, our cloaked micro-trilo-crafts we were able to take the planetary defences by surprise and destroy them!"

Elaine began to walk around the virtual display unit pretending to look at it from all angles, but it was just a ploy. Elaine needed a few minutes to telepathically talk to Notus, she said;

> "Notus, what do you think?"

Almost whispering Notus replied;

> "Forget the first simulation, that is a real typical triloraptor kill and destroy everything plan. The second simulation might just work, if the overlord does not blow up all four planets first!

Smiling to the triloraptor, Elaine said;

> "Your second simulation has my approval. Now let's get over to the other side of this micro worm hole and find the overlord."

Elaine put on her trilo-visor to activate her mini me, and speaking telepathically to Notus, she said;

> "What name do you think we should call micro mini me? Oh and don't say Elaine two."

Notus thought for a moment and laughing then said;

"I never thought we would be in a relationship where we would have to discuss naming an offspring!"

Triloraptors do not have a sense of humour and to hear Elaine suddenly burst out laughing certainly ruffled their stuffy feathers. Although they tried to continue with their work, they could not help but give a few strange glances in her direction. Trying to compose herself, Elaine telepathically said;

"Ok Daddy Frankenstein, how does Lainee sound? It's a simple anagram of Elaine."

Pleased, Notus jovially replied;

"You know great minds think alike, that was the name I was going to pick, its perfect.

Now, activate our little Lainee and let's start operation overlord."

Elaine activated little Lainee and found that she was already on the bridge of the micro command trilo-craft. As she looked around, she could see that the triloraptors attention to detail was fantastic. In the middle of the command room was a virtual reality device and around the sides were banks of trilo-computers. Each computer was manned by a micro trilo-raptor-bots that were being control individually by its living counterpart in the other universe.

Through Lainee, Elaine asked if all systems were ready, and if yes, she wanted to begin operation overlord immediately. One of the micro trilo-raptor-bots confirmed all system were fully operational and ready to go. With that, the one thousand strong triloraptors micro fleet split into four teams and moved away from the micro worm holes at maximum speed.

A co-ordinated and well timed assault was essential to the success of this operation. Team one headed towards the planet Zsaraxil, team two's target was the planet Zaranne, team three had the twinned planet Kzegas 1, and finally team four, the one with Lainee on board, headed for the planet Zotreg. All four teams would converge on their designated planet solar system at exactly the same time, and in unison begin their assault.

The triloraptors were convinced that the overlord had already detected their presence in his universe and were expecting high levels of resistance. So for extra security, when the four teams had travelled this universe equivalent of 16093.44 kilometres (10000 mile), each team then sub divided into five small fleets of fifty micro trilo-crafts and took a different route to its designated target planet.

It is normal military procedure to send scouting parties ahead to make sure that there were no ambushes. The triloraptors took this a bit further, each small fleet sent four of their cloaked micro trilo-crafts on forward, side and rear reconnaissance missions. It was the forward reconnaissance micro trilo-crafts that were heading to Kzegas 1 that detected the first line of resistance from the overlord. Using the A.R.C.S, the overlord had set up a forty thousand strong, multi linked laser blockage in the outer regions of Kzegas 1's galaxy.

The A.R.C.S blockade covered a staggering expanse that would be this universes equivalent of 32186.88 Kilometres (20.000 miles) wide and 16093.44 kilometres (10000 mile) in depth! Initial scans showed that the A.R.C.S blockade was dormant and the trigger to activating the A.R.C.S weapon systems was to break the laser beams. Scans also revealed that the area was full of spacial motion, heat and light detectors; it was deduced that these too could act as triggers to the A.R.C.S weapon systems.

The small micro trilo fleet had a couple of options, they could travel the 32186.88 Kilometres around or 16093.44 kilometres (10000 miles) under the A.R.C.S blockade. The only problem they could foresee with this option was they then might possibly find other similar A.R.C.S blockades. This option was further compounded by there being a good possibility that rest of the fleet would also encounter this A.R.C.S blockades problem.

Option two was to find a way through the A.R.C.S blockade. Elaine came to the same conclusion as the triloraptors on this and thought it would be sensible to try to defeat the A.R.C.S blockades in such a way that the overlord would not know the A.R.C.S blockades had been breached. They already knew from previous experience that the small remote controlled cloaked trilo-crafts that were armed with S.I.C.E guns (Super Iced Compressed Energiser) could disable the numerous spacial motion, heat and light detectors, so these were not a problem.

As for the A.R.C.S blockade, it only took a few trilo-seconds for the triloraptors to come up with a solution. In the triloraptors armoury were numerous small micro trilo-drone attack craft that functioned similar to the ones used by the Interplanetary Universal Congress's fleets attack on earth. They too had a mirrored pearlescent outer skin that allows them to blend almost invisibly with their surroundings and would be ideal for stealthily approaching the sleeping A.R.C.S.

A plan was drawn up to create a gap in the A.R.C.S blockade defences just big enough for each fleet vessel to individually pass through. For this, twenty micro trilo-drone attack craft were launched and were using their own mirrored bodied and electrical telemetry to redirect and then to re-connect the lasers beams. Precision and exact timing was the key to this operation, each of the twenty micro trilo-drone attack crafts moved stealthily into position at the exact same time. The triloraptors calculated that the next manoeuvre needed to be done in exactly two nano seconds! To be this fast and accurate, the micro trilo-computer had to take operational control.

With unexplainable speed and with high trilo-precision, all twenty micro trilo-drone attack crafts moved in and redirected and re-connected the A.R.C.S blockades defensive laser beams. Elaine couldn't help it; she gave out a loud sighed with relief as the A.R.C.S blockade was successfully breached, but looking around the trilo-command vessel, the triloraptors showed no emotions! They just told the small micro trilo fleet to continue on its journey towards Kzegas 1's solar system.

Notus quickly jumped in and telepathically said:

"Elaine, hold the micro trilo-fleet back, this has been too easy! I think this is a clever overlord trap! Just send a few micro trilo-drone attack crafts through first!

Devoid of any hesitation, Elaine gave the command that they needed to be cautious and to only send a few micro trilo-drones attack craft through first. The small craft flew through the breached blockage with ease and then the just sat the other side of A.R.C.S blockade. To Elaine's surprise, nothing had happened! The triloraptors looked at Elaine, but Elaine had no answers and asked telepathically asked Notus for advice. On a gut feeling Notus replied;

"Ok Elaine, get the triloraptors to do a microscopic scan of the surface of each micro trilo-drone attack craft."

Within seconds, the triloraptors scan of the surface of each micro trilo-drone attack craft revealed that Elaine and Notus's cautious approach was correct. The overlord had anticipated that they would plan to breach the A.R.C.S blockades and had set an ingenious trap for them! As the micro trilo-drone attack craft passed through the breached area of A.R.C.S blockade, a microscopic atomiser had showered each micro trilo-drone attack craft with several hundred atom sized nuclear armed nano-bots that had now attach themselves to the exterior of each micro trilo-drone attack craft! They could be detonated later at the overlord's pleasure!

One of the triloraptors on the trilo-command centre walked over to Elaine and said;

"Captain Elaine Laurence, that was good work; if we had proceeded the overlord would have been able to destroy the whole fleet and this mission would have ended! Now, what is your next order?"

Elaine first telepathically thanked Notus and then said;

"Notus, I think I know what to do next."

Notus laughed and said;

"I know, remember I can read your mind"

With that, Elaine asked for the attention of all the triloraptors on the trilo-command centre and with the confidence of a leader, she said;

> "The overlord knows we are in his universe. I think the A.R.C.S blockades and all these other traps are overlord games and delaying tactics; let's show him we mean business.
>
> First, pull the micro trilo-drone attack crafts back so they are just inside the A.R.C.S blockade breached area. Second, get the micro fleet to withdraw to a safe distance and thirdly, target each micro trilo-drone attack craft and blow the hell out of that A.R.C.S blockade and any other blockade that gets in our way."

Captain Elaine Laurence orders were immediately carried out by the triloraptors who as Elaine observed, seemed to be satisfied that they could test out their extensive range of micro weapons and actually blow something up! Within the next few trilo-hours every other micro fleet encountered a similar A.R.C.S blockades and promptly the triloraptors took action and destroyed them.

CHAPTER 28

Worthy Opponents

From his fortified mountain stronghold on the planet Zotreg, the overlord had been observing the triloraptors fleets advancing towards the planets Zsaraxil, Zotreg, Kzegas 1, and Zaranne's solar systems. The destruction of his A.R.C.S blockades had not bothered him, these blockades and small traps were simple tests to see if these triloraptors were worthy of his full armed forces attention, and now they had earned his militaries full attention.

Patience was not the overlord's strongpoint, but it this instance, he had indulgently waited until all four micro-fleets to regrouped on the outskirts or their targeted planets solar systems. As each micro trilo-fleet cautiously moved forward, they were suddenly surrounded with was an army of five million A.R.C.S that had just un-cloaked!

In less than a second, all five million A.R.C.S began to unleash their massive fire power. The triloraptors immediately began to return fire and began to destroy several thousand A.R.C.S However this battle soon began to take its toll on the triloraptors micro fleet, and all the micro trilo-crafts that had been constructed with inferior R.I.T.E.S were quickly destroyed. Even the trilo-crafts that were well constructed of R.I.T.E.S were beginning to sustain heavy damage.

It was at this stage that things really got bad for all the triloraptors micro fleets. One hundred of the overlord's elite battle fleet un-cloaked around the outskirts of all four battle zones. At our universes equivalent of 8.04672 kilometres long (5 miles) and 4.828032 kilometres wide (3

Miles), these colossal galactic battle ships were made as a tribute to the magnificence of the overlord.

The exteriors galactic battle ships were plated with material from collapsed dark stars matter, this made the galactic battle ships extremely heavy but in space, an objects weight is not that important. What is important is, because of its extreme density; the dark star matter plated onto the battleships exterior is excellent body armour. This armour can easily withstand most conventional proton, neutron, graviton, pulse, sonic, light, laser and biological space weapons attacks.

To intimidate any opposition, the shape of each battleship had been designed to resemble the overlords overall physical shape. The bodies of these ugly galactic giants resembled ancient robots and had barrelled shaped chests on their fronts, while the back and both sides of their torsos were flat. At the bottom of each torso was two short legs that could independently move in a one hundred and eighty degree angles in a forward and backward motion; these legs housed the two massive graviton engines. The mobility of these legs allowed the battleship to do manoeuvres that would be impossible for other large space craft. Attached at the base of each leg were two rectangular shaped feet that jutted out 1.609344 kilometres (1 mile). The front of these monstrous feet functioned as shuttle bays and the bottoms of the huge feet were the main graviton engines thrusters.

Attached at either side of the battleships bodies were two massive rectangular shaped arms, with what looked like a balled fist at each end. These huge limbs extended the full length of the battleship bodies, legs and feet. Each arm could independently rotate three hundred and sixty degrees clockwise and anti-clockwise, raise up and down a full one hundred and eighty degrees and were the battleships main armaments. And at the top of each battleship's enormous body was a large translucent half globed head; this was the battleships command centre.

In unison and across all four battle zones, every one of the overlord's A.R.C.S began to encircle the triloraptors micro fleets; they then began to move closer and closer. When the circle was tight, the overlord's battleships pointed their giant balled fists directly at the remaining A.R.C.S and fired their F.O.D (Fist of destruction) weapons. For a fraction of an earth second, each balled fist light up like a small sun and then without a sound thousands and thousands of A.R.C.S were sent hurtling directly into the triloraptors micro fleets.

As the A.R.C.S collided with the triloraptors R.I.T.E.S ships a fission process in which the heavy atomic nucleuses are split into two more-or-less equal fragments accompanied by the release of large amounts of energy took place. At the exact same time, the weapons dimentialiser kicked in, and in a nano second, all the atoms from every vessel involved in the collisions were thrown in and out of the fourth dimension. As they stabilised, all that was left of the A.R.C.S and triloraptors R.I.T.E.S ships was numerous tangled and indistinguishable messes of merged matter!

Back at his fortified mountain stronghold on the planet Zotreg, the overlord had been co-ordinating all four battles from his command centre. He slowly scanned the mangled wreckage of the A.R.C.S and trilo-crafts and although he should have been ecstatic at the outcome of these four battles, he thought;

> "This was too easy, the triloraptors came to my universe with the intention of to capturing and killing me, but I defeated them without them hardly landing a single blow! Perhaps this was merely a division and they have forces that are still out there!"

The overlord then increased his universal spacial surveillance, A.R.C.S blockades, elite battleship patrols and also amplified his own personal security.

Luckily, Elaine and the triloraptors had consulted earlier and had agreed that just in case there were any further ambushes, the micro trilo-command ship with Lainee on board and five other cloaked micro trilo-craft from each fleet should hold back 32186.88 kilometres (20.000 miles) from the main fleet. Their cautious approach had paid off, upon seeing all four micro trilo fleets fall into an A.R.C.S ambush and then their ultimate destruction at the hands of the overlord's colossal battleships. For all the remaining trilo-craft, Elaine and the triloraptors agreed that it would be tactically wise to keep their cloaking devices on then re-examine their options.

Because of what had just happened, the planed assaults on the planets Zsaraxil, Zotreg, Kzegas 1, and Zaranne were no longer viable, so Elaine put it to the triloraptors that their first option was to withdraw. Elaine was not surprised to find that the triloraptors hated the word withdraw and that they had already come up with another plan! This plan would entail the micro trilo-command ship and all twenty of the remaining micro trilo-fleet converging on one planet and capturing the overlord. The question was, which out of the four planets was the one that the overlord would most likely to be on? As discussions continued, it was agreed that they would only get one chance at this, but it was a stab in the dark, they had no intelligence to go on. The trilo-raptor command bridge went silent as all the triloraptors looked at Elaine for guidance!

Elaine needed to consult Notus; she closed her eyes for a moment and telepathically said;

> "Notus, I take it you have been following all that has been happening?"

In a formal tone Notus replied;

> Elaine, I have, and I have to say, we just got our backsides kicked by the overlord! That F.O.D weapon he used to destroy the A.R.C.S and micro trilo-fleet battleships is both terrifying and awesome. I have never seen anything like that, and to be quite honest, at this point of time, I have no idea how we can defeat it!

Concerned at Notus's response, Elaine asked;

> "Notus, In view of what you just said, do you think we should carry on?"

Notus was quite for a moment and then said;

"Elaine, turning back is not a realistic option; the overlord's species is slowly dying and if my information is correct, they will be almost extinct within the next few hundred earth years. When the overlord came to your universe before, the overlord saw the human race as his species only chance of salvation! If you cannot capture and defeat the overlord, there is a one hundred percent chance that he will eventually he will come back to our universe, and if he does, he will probably win. The human race will become his physical puppets, and every being in our universe will be taken into slavery!

Elaine, I have telepathically spoken with my species and they feel that out of all four planets, it would be logical for the overlord to be at his command centre at mount silu, this is his fortified mountain stronghold on the planet Zotreg.

I should also warn you again; that the overlord has installed several hundred thousand atom sized nuclear armed nano-bots to the core of Zotreg! He will have no qualms in detonating these if he thinks he is going to be captured!"

Elaine opened her eyes and looked at the assembled triloraptors, with a fighter's passion she said;

"Triloraptors, the micro trilo-command ship and the other five micro trilo-craft will use the remains from the destroyed trilo-craft and A.R.C.S for concealment, hopefully, that should make it hard for the overlord or his battleships to detect them.

Then using your holographic imaging, we will continue to use the wreckage of destroyed trilo-craft and A.R.C.S to obscure detection and get what is left of the micro trilo-fleet to assemble with the micro trilo-command ship.

Once assembled, this small fleet will then proceed cloaked to the planet Zotreg. There, the micro trilo-fleet will first need to neutralise the planets force field and then attack the overlord's fortified stronghold at mount silu. That's where I think the overlord is!"

Without any hesitation, the triloraptors immediately set about plotting new routes for the remains of micro trilo-fleet. The trilo-command estimated that it would a whole trilo-day before all twenty trilo-crafts and the micro trilo-command ship would be able to gather together. That time was spent evaluating what was known of the overlord security, analysing the overlord's battleships F.O.D weapon and running and re-running scenarios for the forthcoming attack on the overlord's fortified stronghold at mount silu.

Under normal circumstances the triloraptors estimated time of arrival for the micro trilo-fleet gathering would have been accurate, but the overlord had set up so many A.R.C.S blockades and spacial detectors that in order to avoid detection, this time had tripled! What made the journey even more hazardous was the overlord's battleships were openly patrolling all key routes to Zotreg solar system!

After three nail biting trilo-days for Elaine, all twenty cloaked trilo-crafts and the micro trilo-command ship had assembled in the debris field on the outskirts of the planet Zotreg solar system. A simple plan had been formed; first, two cloaked micro trilo-craft would disable the planets force field. With the force field down, the other eighteen micro trilo-crafts would give covering fire for the micro trilo-command ship to move in and land. Once landed, the micro trilo-crafts that were left would split into two forces, one giving air support and the others landing and giving ground support to the micro trilo-command ship in a bold land assault. But first, the twenty one strong micro trilo-fleet had to run the overlords security gauntlet. For this, they again split into four teams and with their cloaking devices still on; they all took different routes to the planet Zotreg.

To describe the micro-fleets journey to the planet Zotreg as a cat and mouse game would be a vast understatement. The triloraptors operating this remote controlled micro fleet had to too use all of their cunning and trilo-precision to navigate through the mine field of military obstacles that the overlord had set. As Elaine observed the triloraptors methodically working, she realised that this type of pressure actually made the happy!

This was not the case for Elaine, the tension was making her nerves fraught and for the first time since she was abducted from earth, she craved for a cup of coffee.

Notus could feel Elaine's tension and trying to lighten her mood said;

> "I know that you are craving for a coffee, but did you know that caffeine is a bitter, white crystalline xanthine alkaloid that acts as a stimulant drug and a reversible acetyl cholinesterase inhibitor? Caffeine is found across the universe in varying quantities in the seeds, leaves, and fruit of some plants, where it acts as a natural pesticide that paralyzes and kills certain insects feeding on the plants.
>
> On the planet earth, it is most commonly consumed by humans in infusions extracted from the seed of the coffee plant and the leaves of the tea bush, as well as from various foods and drinks containing products derived from the kola nut. Other sources include yerba maté, guarana berries, guayusa, and the yaupon holly."

Mentally Elaine began to laugh and asked Notus;

> "Being immortal, when my adaptive D.N.A kicks in and I am ant women, will the coffee kill me? Oh and I have another question, where do you get all this useless information from?"

Notus began to laugh and said;

> "Elaine, being immortal means you can drink starbucks coffee with extra caffeine forever and if you must know, I get all this highly useful information from Wikipedia, the free uni-net universal encyclopaedia!"

At that amusing anecdote, Elaine burst out laughing, but her laughter was cut short when the trilo-spokes interrupted her and person said;

> "Captain Elaine Laurence, our micro fleet has arrived at their designated co ordinances around the planet Zotreg. The holographic imaging technology and cloaking technology is working well and everything is in place to begin operation overlord. To avoid discovery, we need to begin the assault immediately!"

Though Lainee, Elaine looked across the micro command bridge, the large viewing port was open and she could see the planet Zotreg straight in front of her. With the overlord rarefied plasma force field around the planet, the planet looked bleak and lifeless. Looking back at the triloraptor that had just spoken to her, she nodded her head and said;

> "Let's do it."

Within a trilo-second of Elaine's order, two trilo-craft targeted the micro wave transmitters that controlled the rarefied plasma force field and fired to micro G.R.I.M missiles at them. The missiles roared towards the rarefied plasma force field and then just bounced off it! Within seconds, two more were fired, but the same thing happened! All four G.R.I.M missiles computer targeting systems were thrown into disarray and they flew off into open space!

Stunned, Elaine said to the triloraptors in the trilo-command ship;

> "What's happening?"

Triloraptors do not have shoulders to shrug but several raised their wings in a gesture of puzzlement. One triloraptor said;

> "Captain Elaine Laurence, we have no idea why the G.R.I.M missiles will not penetrate the rarefied plasma force field; they have been modified with an R.I.T.E.S exterior and should have easily penetrated it!"

Thinking quickly, Elaine said;

> "Ok, get the two trilo-craft to crash though that force field! I want those two micro wave transmitters destroyed now!"

Elaine's orders were carried out instantly, but as the two trilo-craft rushed towards the planet Zotreg north and south poles where the micro wave transmitters were situated, both trilo-craft were destroyed!

Exasperated, Elaine went to say;

> "What the . . . ."

When, several million A.R.C.S and over twenty thousand of the overlord's elite battleships uncloaked. On board these giant elite battleships were the overlord lords. The trilo-micro fleet had lured into a massive trap and were completely surrounded!

For a few moments there was silence, and then suddenly an image appeared on every triloraptor holographic display unit, it was the overlord! The silence was broken as the overlords voice boomed out;

> "Triloraptors this game is over; in a few moments I am going to destroy this pathetic micro fleet. After that, I am coming to your universe and believe me, this time I am going to take great pleasure in destroying you! With you out of the way, I am then going to destroy every planet in the Interplanetary Universal Congress!"

Without hesitation, the triloraptors tried to respond by firing every weapon the micro trilo-fleet had, but the overlord had overridden their computers fire commands! Laughter boom out at the overlord said;

> "Pathetic triloraptors!"

Instantly the triloraptor holographic display unit changed and it now showed the planet Zotreg. Through Lainee, Elaine could see a small gap appear in the planets force field and from that gap another battleship emerged; this one was twice the size of all the others and had the overlord on it! He had come to watch and gloat over the micro fleets inevitable destruction!

Back on the trilo command ship, one of the triloraptors glanced at Elaine and said;

"We will not give in."

In a nano second, the twenty one micro fleet trilo-crafts uncloaked and then set a collision course for the overlord's battleship! The overlords A.R.C.S's and elite battleships instantly opened fire; the micro fleet didn't stand a chance. Within seconds they were pounded by the A.R.C.S's and seemed to be making headway but once the elite battleships fired their F.O.D weapons, the micro trilo-fleet was being reduced to twisted junk!

Observing this, Elaine's eyes began to fill with tears, she felt her heart sinking. Suddenly Notus telepathically said;

"Quickly Elaine, concentrate on Lainee and order her to explode!"

Elaine had to blink her tearful eyes a few times so she could see the side menu in her trilo-visor; she quickly scanned the menu, but could see a self destruction icons. Thinking quickly, Elaine then closed her eyes and concentrated on Lainee, Lainee began to glow and then in one big white flash, exploded! Lainee's explosion produced an enormous pure energy wave that sent the blasts from the F.O.D and A.R.C.S weapons back to their firing source, each battleship shuddered as their own F.O.D hit them! Within moments, the A.R.C.S's and the overlord's elite battleship were reduced to interwoven twisted space wreckage.

Seeing what was happening, the overlord, completely out of character, began to panic! Hysterically screaming, the overlord ordered his massive battleship to do an about turn and return to the safety of the planet's surface. That's when the pure energy wave hit it, and in a dramatic explosion, it the overlords battleship just vaporised!

Back on board the trilo-command ship, all communications with the overlord's universe had now been severed. Elaine could see that the triloraptors were confused by what had just happened, but then when she thought about it, so was she? Telepathically she asked Notus to explain. Notus took several nail biting earth minutes to reply and then said;

> "Elaine, sorry for the delay in getting back to you, I have been busy gathering information. The news I have for you is extremely possitive, the overlord and his battleship with have been destroyed. The same applies to the millions of A.R.C.'s and his elite fleet with the overlord's lords onboard.
>
> The planet Zotreg and all other planet under the overlords rule are just finding out that the overlord and his lords are gone and after several decades in your earth years of slavery and oppression, they are free of the overlord's hideous dictatorship.
>
> The pure energy blast waves from Lainee and all the other spacial explosions would have normally destroyed the planet Zotreg atmosphere. But thanks to the extra security measures implemented by overlord, the power output every rarefied plasma force field had been increased by fifty percent and that essentially saved the planet Zotreg!
>
> As I speak, the Zotreg's are turning of the micro wave transmitters and disarming the rarefied plasma force field. In a short time the planet Zotreg will be able to get natural sunlight and over the next few earth years, life will once again flourish on this planet."

Notus could feel that Elaine wanted to ask a few questions and paused. Elaine then asked;

> "Am I correct in suspecting that you planted a few atoms from Olotinium in her and that's what caused the pure energy blast waves that destroyed the overlord's battle fleet?

Am I also correct in assuming that you never mentioned this to me so that I would believe that it was just me, Captain Elaine Laurence and the triloraptors who would have defeat the overlord?"

Notus could feel that while Elaine was a happy at the outcome, she was also a little angry at not been told that Lainee was potentially a pure energy bomb. Calmly Notus said;

"After seeing the triloraptors fleet reduced to space rubble, I knew that the only way to succeed for the remaining twenty one trilo-craft was to lure the overlord away from the planet Zotreg. Logically the only way that was going to happen is if he thought he could totally destroy the triloraptors micro fleet. The spanner in the works was the F.O.D weapons; I had not seen anything like that before.

Elaine, if you think back to when I was constructing Lainee, I did mention that she was made exactly the same as you. I only installed Olotinium atoms so that yours and her abilities matched.

I had to give some thought to the F.O.D's and came up with the idea of trying to destroy the F.O.D's with the pure energy atoms from Olotinium. Luckily it worked, and as a bonus, it also destroyed the overlord's elite fleet and the overlord, that is not bad when it was only a calculated guess."

Elaine took a moment to absorb what Notus had just said and then asked;

"What shall I tell the triloraptors and the Interplanetary Universal Congress?"

Notus thought for a moment and said;

"Tell the triloraptors that you, Captain Elaine Laurence and the triloraptor have been triumphant and have finally defeated the overlord. They will of cause be curious about the pure energy explosion? Elaine, you will need to be elusive and tell them it is a top secret weapon from the Notus Empire.

As for the Interplanetary Universal Congress, I think it is time for you and the triloraptors new ambassador to address the Interplanetary Universal Congress by the uni-net and explain what has happened. At the same time, you and the triloraptors can expose Chair elect Zissiani for what she is."

Elaine was still a little puzzled at what had happened to the overlord and his battleship and enquired;

"Notus, before the triloraptors command ship lost communications with the overlord's universe, their sensors indicated that the overlord's battleship completely vaporised, surly that wasn't just the pure energy blast from Lainee and the F.O.D's exploding?"

Notus began to laugh quietly and said;

"The triloraptors sensors were correct, as the overlord left the planet Zotreg atmosphere; he opened a small gap in the planets force field. Zotreg the being seized the opportunity and was able to detach the several hundred thousand atom sized nuclear armed nano-bots to the planets core. Zotreg then attached the same nuclear armed nano-bots to the outside of the overlord's battleship. The dark star material that was used to plate and protect the overlord's battleship is so dense that it made it almost impossible for the overlord sensors to detect the attached atoms!

When the pure energy blast from Lainee and the F.O.D's exploded, they also detonated every nuclear armed nano-bot. It was then the combination of all three exploding at the same time that vaporised the overlord's battleship!"

Elaine had one more question;

"Notus, why don't you and Zotreg take some of the credit for all that has happened? Come to think of it, it was really you who has saved billions and billions of being in not one but two universes. You are the true hero in this story."

With a genuine sound of modestly Notus replied;

"Elaine, as advanced as civilisations have become in all universes, we the planet guardians, by the way that's what we like to be called, feel that the beings we helped to create and nurture is not psychologically ready to become aware of our existence. We as the planet guardians have in the past allowed our existence to become known and sadly the consequences have been catastrophically disastrous!"

Elaine knew that Notus and the other planet guardians had good reasons to remain anonymous and respected them for that; she also knew that she had been fully briefed and needed to inform the triloraptors of what had transpired. Without wasting any more time, Elaine asked the triloraptors to gather around and then in a triumphant tone fully briefed the assembled trilo-elders. At the end of her brief she also informed them that full control of their trilo-crafts and computer systems had been restored. For one full earth minute the trilo-elders stood perfectly still and them in unity they began to stamp their feet;

"Thump, thump, thump, thump, thump, thump, thump, thump, thump, thump, thump, thump, thump, thump, thump, thump, thump, thump."

Elaine began to laugh and humorously asked;

"Is this a sign that you are pleased, or are you going to try to kill me?"

Instantly all the triloraptors stopped stamping their feet and their trilo-spokes person said;

"Captain Elaine Laurence of the planet Notus and Newman Empire or should I say, Doctor Elaine Laurence of the planet earth, we the triloraptors have the deepest respect for you! As for your double identity, you do not have worry; your secret is safe with us."

Then the stamping began again;

"Thump, thump, thump, thump, thump, thump, thump, thump, thump, thump, thump, thump, thump, thump, thump, thump, thump, thump."

Elaine was a little shocked by the revelation that the triloraptors knew she was from the planet earth. Her mind raced as she tried to think at what point of time they had discovered who she really was? Then another theory began to emerge; had they known who she was from day one, and why has they played along with her charade? As her mind whirled, a sobering thought popped back into her head;

"Thankfully they were not trying to kill me!

Elaine pondered for a moment and decided that exposing her true identity could actually work to her advantage; she also felt touched that the triloraptors were willing to still play along with her identity charade. So for the time being she said nothing and graciously took a curtsy in recognition of the respect being shown by the triloraptors.

When the triloraptors ceased stamping their feet, Elaine asked them to open a virtual uni-net link at the virtual Interplanetary Universal Congress hall. She insisted that Chair elect Zissiani along with all Interplanetary Universal Congress delegates be present and the triloraptor ambassador for what she was about to tell them.

Within a few earth minutes the triloraptors had set up the meeting and then asked Elaine to stand in the middle of their virtual reality unit so that she could address the Interplanetary Universal Congress.

Elaine walked confidently into the virtual reality unit and said;

"I am Captain Elaine Laurence from the planet Notus and Newman Empire. You may not realise this but I am also Doctor Elaine Laurence from the planet earth and was abducted from an orbiting recreational space station along with four hundred and fifty nine of my fellow earthlings by the triloraptors!"

Elaine paused as gasped and vocal grumblings could be heard through the virtual Interplanetary Universal Congress hall. As the gasped and vocal grumbles continued Elaine raised her hands in a gesture to hush the congress and then realised that her adaptive DNA had changed her back into her human skin! Unconsciously her hands combed through her long auburn hair and she thought how nice it was to be human again. Inwardly smiling she then continued;

"I am not her to complain about this or criticise the Interplanetary Universal Congress or triloraptors for your actions. The war between you and the triloraptors was brought about by one being, the Overlord! I and the triloraptors have stretched our resources and technology beyond this universe into the overlord's micro universe, and I am pleased to report to this esteemed Interplanetary Universal Congress that being known as overlord and his lords that help him preside over his micro universe have now all been destroyed."

In a loud clear and highly confident voice, Elaine pronounced;

"Both our universes are now safe!"

The Interplanetary Universal Congress is a diverse multi species congress and each species within the Interplanetary Universal Congress has its own way of applauding. What was clear to Elaine was the applause was unanimous. As the applause died down Chair elect Zissiani was quick to speak up and said;

"On behalf of all the members of the Interplanetary Universal Congress, I as chair elect would like to congratulate you Doctor or should I say Captain Elaine Laurence and the triloraptors for waging this crusade against this persecutor of both universes."

Playing to her audience, Chair elect Zissiani raised her tone and said with a politician's conviction;

> "As a veteran of the last conflict, I only wish I had been there to help in this noble cause."

Chair elect Zissiani expected the applause to begin again, but a hushed silence filled the virtual Interplanetary Universal Congress hall. Each delegate had now received a file marked **'Betrayal'** and the uni-net translation software had transformed the document into legible reading for all Interplanetary Universal Congress delegate members. The same file had been mysteriously leaked to the Interplanetary Universal Congress press office!

As each Interplanetary Universal Congress delegate read the file, it contained decisive evidence that the triloraptors had been instructed to kill the being known as Captain Elaine Laurence from the planet Notus and Newman Empire by the Chair Elect Zissiani! The file also revealed that even when both sides were at war, Admiral Zissiani had been working with the triloraptors and as a result of this alliance, thousands if not millions of Interplanetary Universal Congress battle fleet and individual members had been killed! The last part of the file revealed a dastardly plot contrived by Admiral Zissiani and in alliance with the triloraptors to destroy the plant known as terra or earth!

Chair elect Zissiani had also received a copy of the **'Betrayal'** file, and as she glanced through it her mind raced with one million and one defensive lies. But even Zissiani knew that she had treachery been exposed, all she could do as six Quzzzuzzz guards arrested her was mumble;

> "I did it all for the good of the Interplanetary Universal Congress."

CHAPTER 29

Finale

The Interplanetary Universal Congress members were in turmoil over their Chair Elects Zissiani terrestrial crimes, a strong debate began over what actions should and could be taken. Elaine decided that this was now their problem, so she stepped out of the virtual reality unit and ended her uni link with the Interplanetary Universal Congress delegates.

Elaine promptly asked the triloraptor command for re-confirmation the terrestrial locations of her fellow abductees. Without hesitation the trilo-spokes person came forward and said that a list of their exact locations had been sent directly to her space ships computer and they had four highly experienced triloraptors standing by to assist her on her rescue mission.

Elaine said her goodbyes and then wished the triloraptors well; she then left the trilo-command centre. As she her trilo-rescue team headed for the shuttle bay, Elaine telepathically asked Notus to set a course in Notus 1 for their first rescue destination. Elaine should have learnt by now that life in space was a little more complicated than that, Notus replied;

> "Hi Elaine, first, I thought you handled the Interplanetary Universal Congress meeting brilliantly. I suspect Chair elect Zissiani will probably incarcerated in a Quzzzuzzz detention facility for the rest of her Quzzzuzzz life.
>
> I have set a course for your first location but we unfortunately we have a problem."

Elaine had heard this before and knew that when Notus said there was a problem it was going to be something spacially horrendous, she looked down at her hand and found her adaptive DNA had kicked in and crystal women was back! Elaine thought sarcastically to herself;

"Oh great, I was only human for a few minutes, now my beautiful hair has gone and the crystal blue ice maiden is back!"

Bracing herself she then asked Notus;

"Ok, what anomalies do I or we have to overcome this time?"

Notus could feel the frustration in Elaine's mind and telepathically said;

"Time is what we have to overcome. Elaine, as you are aware the boundaries of space are endless. The problem is, space mixed with time is not constant. As you travel though space, time varies and is affected by gravitational fields and many other spacial normalities and anomalies. The first destination for your rescue mission has a massive gravitational field close by and time for your people has speeded up! I calculate that for those humans, almost forty earth years has passed for them since they were abducted!"

Elaine was mentally shocked by what Notus had said and she also felt confused. Almost mentally shouting she telepathically asked Notus;

"Why has this not been a factor before? We have travel vast distances and ventured into another universe without any space, time problems?"

To reply, Notus paused for a moment and tried to think of an easy way to explain to Elaine the intricacies that relate space travel, time and gravity. The answer was not easy and then replied;

"Elaine, the answer is up until now we have been and I do put a heavy emphasis on this. We have been extremely lucky! The space travel we have done so far fits neatly into the same time, space continuum.

As I said before, space and time is not constant. The scholars and scientists on your planet earth realised this many years ago in the theory of relativity, it was called time dilation. Elaine when you left your planet's surface to stay on the recreational space station, the time on the space station was a few thousands of an earth second slower than on your actual planet. This miniscule change is due to the planetary gravitation forces at work. Another example is; your own astronauts on space missions have actually aged less than the at mission control crew on earth.

For all sentient beings that travel through this or any other universe, time dilation is a factor that they have to deal with, this is why high speed space craft's with graviton engines were developed. The time, space problem had been a big hindrance for the Interplanetary Universal Congress until the uni-net was developed.

Elaine, even as you have travelled through space, there have been some changes in time but they too have been small. You also have to remember, you are now immortal and the changes in time are irrelevant to you but they are a reality for your human colleges. Now to rescue them we have to face a new spacial area where the time, space continuum works at a completely different pace."

Elaine pondered for a moment on what Notus had said, she knew a little about the theory of relativity and time dilation from her studies at school. Later when she was at college, university and then as a medical student, she had read with interest and then debated some of the theories put forward from Albert Einstein in 1916, Stephen Hawkins theories in 2012 and other great past and present minds on this complex subject. Elaine had even explored quantum mechanics and the quantum gravity theories. But Elaine had to concede that the intricate changes in time and space travel were a complex and somewhat confusing subject.

As a medical doctor Elaine had found that theories are all well and good but there was nothing like good practical hands on experience to solve problems.

The only factors that helped her were, Notus was over twenty two billion years old and had vast experience of space travel! She then recalled that Notus several billion years ago had also travelled from one universe to another, Notus must have encountered similar problems numerous times before! With that realisation fresh in her head a surge of urgency had been injected into her rescue mission and she replied;

> "Ok Notus, let's get there in double quick time and on the way you, the triloraptors and the Interplanetary Universal Congress can work on time travel!"

> The End.

For Captain Elaine Laurence, Notus, the triloraptors and the Interplanetary Universal Congress the story is far from over. As the rescue mission begins they struggle to defeat the intricacies of space and time and encounter some new and old enemies.

This story will be covered in James Moclair's next book, T.I.M.E.

ABOUT THE AUTHOR

James earns his living as a professional martial arts instructor and has been practicing martial arts for over fifty years. In that time he has achieved a tenth Dan in jujutsu and also holds numerous other high grades.

At this point of time, James lives in England and owns his own prestigious dojo and fitness center in Dudley, West Midlands, England.

To date, James has written three martial arts books that have been published. His books are available from most book Internet websites and bookshops for order. James's last book, Jujitsu, A Comprehensive Guide, is classed on Amazon as a best seller.

Since a young boy, James has had a passion for science and in particular science fiction. Over the years he has read many great science fiction books and has been a big fan of Star Trek and other great science fiction series on television and the big screen. Further, James can also boast that he has never missed an episode of the world's longest science fiction program, Dr Who.

The science fiction book written by James is called S.P.A.C.E. (space populations and cosmic enigmas).

It has taken almost three years to write. As always, James has been articulate in his approach and research into this subject, and this reflects in the fantastic storyline and eye for detail.